Time for a Change

Time for a Change

Tanya Anina

authorHOUSE®

AuthorHouse™ UK Ltd.
1663 Liberty Drive
Bloomington, IN 47403 USA
www.authorhouse.co.uk
Phone: 0800.197.4150

© 2013 by Tanya Anina. All rights reserved.

No part of this book may be reproduced, stored in a retrieval system, or transmitted by any means without the written permission of the author.

Published by AuthorHouse   07/08/2013

ISBN: 978-1-4817-6993-8 (sc)
ISBN: 978-1-4817-6994-5 (e)

Any people depicted in stock imagery provided by Thinkstock are models, and such images are being used for illustrative purposes only.
Certain stock imagery © Thinkstock.

This book is printed on acid-free paper.

Because of the dynamic nature of the Internet, any web addresses or links contained in this book may have changed since publication and may no longer be valid. The views expressed in this work are solely those of the author and do not necessarily reflect the views of the publisher, and the publisher hereby disclaims any responsibility for them.

All characters in this book are purely fictional. Any similarities between them and real individuals are purely coincidental.

Acknowledgements

I would like to express my gratitude to everyone who helped me with this book; to all those who provided support, talked things over, read, typed and offered comments.

A special thanks to my translator Anna Shevchenko.

Sincere gratitude to Vivian Roche my editor, for her great help and support.

I'm heartily thankful and fortunate for the constant encouragement, support and guidance from Roger Derham.

I would like to thank April Ross and all the hard working team at AuthoHouse Book Publishing Company for helping me in the process of publishing this book.

Above all I want to thank my family and friends who supported and encouraged me in spite of all the time it took me always from them. Your love, support, fun and kindness means everything to me.

My sincerest thanks to you all!

"No matter how cruel fate is to man. No matter how he was abandoned and alone, there is always a heart. Unknown to him, but open to respond to the call, is his own heart"

Henry Wadsworth Longfellow

Chapter 1

I prefer to travel by airplane. It is a place where I feel free and at ease. I can feel how fast I travel between the countries. During the flight, time is passing by, but, it can seem as if time, stops. This is because, during a flight you are out of reach from others. No one can call, text or e-mail you. No one can disturb you. It gives a feeling of lightness. That's why I love to fly. Flying gives me a sense of ease. I wish everything to be planned as soon as possible. Buy the tickets and go off on a vacation. It is a time of change, joy, surprise and rendezvous. Going off on a vacation is what you dream about. It's something you long for and it's time off that you give to yourself. With such thoughts, I am sitting and waiting for takeoff.

The year is 2004. The flight is Dublin to Budapest. For eight years now I have flown home, preferably via Budapest. There are no direct flights from Ireland to Kiev and there never have been. I have to use flight transfers. A pessimistic person may find this a task. However, an active person, such as myself, it is a welcome opportunity. It extends travel time but it also gives time to enjoy duty-free shops, new collections in boutiques, to buy souvenirs and taste delicious coffee with croissants. I have time to simply "people watch" at my leisure.

My son is sitting on my knee. Today, he is one and a half years old. His name is Henry. It was his first time on the plane and his huge eyes looked with interest all around him. I really hoped he would sleep on the flight, even for a short time. But just in case he doesn't, I have stocked up with toys and other play things that boy his age requires.

Finally, we are in the air. Henry, having tossed and turned on my lap was now asleep. So, I began to reflect on my recent past. Its two and a half years since I was at home in Kiev.

My hometown is Kiev. I love Kiev and I am proud to say "Kiev, mother of Russian cities" A man who visited the city will always remember it's architecture, Kiev-Pechersk Lavra, the slopes of the Dnieper River, dotted with churches, theaters and many other things. The city, which I left when I was twenty years old, is where I happily return to again and again. In Kiev, my mom and sister live, along with our grandmother, friends and of course my dear parents-in-law. I have lived abroad for seven years now. The first three years I had lived in London and then by a twist of fate I found myself in Ireland. I have been living for the last four years now in the Emerald Isle. But my life abroad is another story.

So, with my head full of memories, such as these, I focused on my future during this smooth flight. Focusing to the future, to whatever will happen and of course, to my dreams.

Time for a Change

I reflected on how fast the past two and a half hours have passed. This first flight was coming to an end. During the landing Henry woke up and eagerly has been drinking from his bottle. He had slept well and was now smiling from ear to ear. Finishing his bottle, he began to look around. Thankfully the time passed quickly in the stop-over in Budapest. We had to get another plane then from Budapest to Kiev. This is another two hours flying. It is night when we land in Kiev. Customs was quick and nice. In the half-empty waiting room my mum and my sister, Anya, are waiting and worrying. Anya is holding a huge bouquet of cream-colored roses.

Henry was sitting on top of suitcases. He is a little shocked by all the changes in the last few hours.

"He looks just like Taya, but a boy version!" my mother greeted me happily.

"Henry, Henry, you're so cool" Anya said as she tried to cuddle him.

My sister's name is Anya and she is twenty two years old. She hasn't got her own children yet and Henry is the one and only adored nephew.

We all wept with joy and then rushed to pack the car and start the half hour journey home. Our vacation has begun.

My family will help me to take care of Henry. They have gotten for him a vintage bed. Interestingly, many of the family generation had used this bed too. One of them was Lesha, my sister's husband. The bed was waiting for Henry. But the bed will have to wait for us, as Mary and Pasha, my parents-in-law are waiting for us at their home. As they say, people of the old school have a distinctive and a different outlook on life. God forbid that you do not agree with their views. Then you will get a one hour lecture, with thousands of examples, with a notation at the end and with a migraine for a week. Considering themselves right in all aspects, they never accept common sense or a different point of view. Well, they want to sort out everything and teach everybody. They are over eighty years old and I'm trying to be more lenient towards them. I am their daughter-in-law for ten years.

As soon as we entered the apartment, my parents-in-law happily greeted us and looked at Henry. It didn't matter that it is 1 a.m. They have started to ask about Ireland and the Irish people, not about my son. A few minutes later their old curious minds totally blew up and they started to discuss political and religious conflicts between Great Britain and Ireland that was 20 years ago. They thought that if I just arrived from that place, then by all means, it is urgent to discuss this topic. My patience was at an end. Mum and I looked at each other a few times, trying to find a way out. Poor Henry had fallen asleep in my arms. I had to use my son, as an excuse to politely tell my parents-in-law that we needed to rest after travelling and have a cup of tea then go to sleep. We were exhausted. Finally, after another 10 minutes talking, they left. We live beside them, in the same building, just on a different floor. We had some light food with tea and fell into bed, exhausted.

It is so cool to wake up in the morning and see the sun. No more Irish clouds and rain. The Irish wet weather rules and dominates your daily routine. But here in Kiev we have a bright June sun. The beginning

Time for a Change

of summer and our holiday, there are still two months of good weather and a real rest. What could be better?

In the morning, having slept well, I feel like I've been born again. I'm not even burdened by my situation, I am six months pregnant. This situation was also interesting because my parents-in-law don't know about this yet. Of course, we were giving them hints that we wanted a second child. They were not supportive and only offered opposition and criticism. We understood and respected their opinion but this is a decision of two people and we decided we wanted another child. They had their reservations as to the reasons why we shouldn't have our second child at this time.

First of all they couldn't imagine how it is possible that there would be a small difference in age between both children. But, we feel, this way, the first child will be getting a bit more independent and then you will have more time to take care of the second child. This small age gap is the exact difference between their own children.

Secondly, they question, how is it possible as you live without family support in another country? They continue to point out to me that I have to think about giving birth to my children outside my native country. They worry about who will take care of these children there if anything happens to me? Who will feed them? And so on and on they were commenting on this situation.

Soon this second baby will arrive and our family will be complete. So, I am not paying attention to their old fashioned delusion. Of course inside me there was a storm of protest brewing. They can't actually understand our foreign way of life.

My husband's name is Tim. He is thirty-two years old. He has a University Education. He has two qualifications, one in Technical Studies and the other one in Medicine. He's a Doctor practicing Chiropody. He is very skilled and his client base grows every year. Therefore, this entire parent nonsense we have between us is called "Marcor". We accept it but we didn't pay any attention to it.

I work as an interpreter. I have too much work, because there are lots of foreigners and refugees in Ireland. We rent a standard two-storey house and also we have two cars. For many years we are financially independent and take care of ourselves without any outside help.

This beautiful sunny morning, I had to meet with my parents-in-law and spend time with them.

If they notice my expanding tummy, I shall be ready for their attack. Henry and I were left on our own, my sister had already gone on business and my mother went to work early. After finishing our breakfast we went to the children's playground. After a walk we returned home. Surprise! Mary was at our place, she had keys. So it begins. She always spoke softly through her teeth, chanting like a snake hissing, without emotions, instructive, forcing the listener to listen and not to interrupt.

She starts "You were outside and maybe your child felt hot, acclimatization, we should take him to a doctor and he can give him an allergy vaccine! Pasha and I heard on the radio that everyone is recommended to take an allergy vaccine. Here we have a strong bloom,

Time for a Change

a lot of pollen, he could start to cough and choke. You cannot be so irresponsible to the boy!!!"

My mother in law can't stand to say my son's name "Henry". Even a couple of months ago, when he was issued an Irish passport, she wrote us letters, begging to come round and give my "Boy" a different name. Since then she called him the "Boy". I could only hope for enlightenment in her aged brain. Suddenly she remembered that yesterday she and Pasha haven't asked and learned enough about Ireland. Expecting me to have some time for tea with them and talk about Ireland's history.

Well, I thought if all this goes on, the vacation is going to be hell! Something needs to be done!

After lunch my darling sister has come home. We missed each other so much. There was a feeling that we have not seen each other, not just for the past two and a half years but for an eternity. From our childhood we were as close as lips and teeth. We have five years age difference between us. But we, as a thread with a needle, were always together. Anya for all my life was and is the closest person. So many secrets were told and retold, so much discussed, that often even my mother did not know the half of what we knew about each other.

I brought her a lot of gifts and was expecting her all day. I gave her some food and we began to chat about everything. She was trying on clothes and we chatted excitedly about all the news. Finally, I was happy.

A few days passed in settling in. I had to have tea with my neighbors and my parents-in-law, to fulfill duty to the ancestors. My expanding tummy still wasn't noticed and I didn't focus any attention on my pregnancy.

Everything went on as usual. Henry enjoyed the attention from my mum and step-father. They began a sincere and wonderful relationship. I brought him to my mother. He stayed there for the whole day and sometimes a couple of days. They did not want him to leave. He was at this age of being very amusing and intelligent. And my parents were crazy about him.

Tim regularly called us and asked about our health and our holiday. He was like a buffer between me and my parents-in-law. My husband was very busy at work and had lots of things to do. We were talking for an hour. I adored my husband. I was waiting patiently for our second child and was happy.

Anya, is a stylist, makeup artist and hairdresser. You can't argue with her, Anya always knows what exactly suits you. She knows how to dress and what a woman has to do to be an individual, special and unique. She is so talented, everyone knows that and I gladly gave myself into her hands to arrange my hair and make-up.

I look good at my twenty-seven years old. Either, I was very lucky and I have good genes, or the right way of life. I look at least five years younger. There was a lot of evidence to support this, such as, I'm often wasn't allowed in nightclubs in Ireland without my ID. When I went to buy alcohol or cigarettes at the supermarket again my ID was requested as I looked too young to purchase it. This made me crazy, especially when I didn't have my documents with me. But my husband tried to calm me down "take it as a compliment, many dream about such youthful looks!" he would tell me.

Time for a Change

I accepted this and took it as a compliment as my teenage years were long gone.

I am of average height and athletic build. As they say, there is not a single extra gram on me. In childhood, I went in for sports, swimming and athletics. Now I train at the gym and exercise with Yoga. That`s why I don`t complain about my health and shape. My hair is shoulder-length, dark brown color, blue-grey eyes; lips have correct shape, dimples on my cheeks, oval face. I have no complaints about my appearance. Anya attempted the task, of course in a room without mirrors for me to see it in stages. She has done my hair up in a French style and dyed my hair in light chestnut color. When I saw the reflection of myself, a very interesting and unusual woman looks back at me. It was a new me. I never have had brown hair before. From the age of sixteen, I have been blond. But I enjoyed myself and this is the most important thing.

The summer was hot. Three weeks of our holiday has passed already. During this time I was meeting with friends and acquaintances. Several times, I visited my grandmother; she is eighty-four years old. My Grandmother keeps a stiff upper lip in spite of her illness. She met Henry for the first time and also remarked on how he looks so like me. My pregnancy has rounded and become visible. My grandmother is very happy and was all emotional with my good news. Henry will soon have a brother or sister. I was really hoping that it would be a girl. I dreamed about a daughter for many years. I have a feeling that this is not a boy, but a little girl. I love being pregnant. In this condition, a woman feels her destiny.

One morning, Henry and I decided to visit Mary and Pasha my parents-in-law. We were relaxing together and chatting, when suddenly they said, "Taya, have you gained some weight in Kiev? Is it because you eat better and have more rest here?"

"Yes, yes" agreed my father-in-law "you became prettier and have gained weight that's for sure!"

And here, like a thunder from the sky, I sit and I realize, it`s now or never. I took a deep breath and with all my courage and strength I say:

"Yes, I've gained weight because I'm seven months pregnant".

Silence fell in the room. They were digesting it for a minute. And then, they opened their mouths, with a series of lectures in their heads. Not giving them a chance to reply, Henry and I moved quickly to put our shoes on in the hallway. I was telling Henry that we were leaving and asking him to say goodbye. He waved to them with a happy smile.

Thank God, I thought, it has passed. Right now they will chew it over, discuss it together and boil it over, complaining about their lives. I can meet them in a couple of days to continue the conversation.

Poor Tim, he will call them and will take all the blows onto himself. After all, they are his parents and they adore him and I think he will be able to calm them down.

"What do you mean, you are pregnant?" spat my father-in-law from the doorstep. "What were you thinking about when you were making this child?" he retorted "do you realize that abortion is already too late!"

Time for a Change

I briefly thought that all this week, he was suffering from a migraine and the heat. As this is what was reported by my mother in law. They were about to call an ambulance for him! But now, he feels great and has no headache and is ready for a confrontation.

"Dad" I tried to answer as calmly as I possibly could. "Come in, sit down. Will you have some tea? Yes, I am pregnant and we are happy. We planned this baby. Everything will be ok". Why do they blow up and make a negative atmosphere? They are taking unnecessary stress over this, which is not good at their advanced age or for me in my condition. I tried to calm him down.

He continued "What do you mean? You both planned this second child? We didn't allow you!"

"Mam, Dad, we are adults. And we have a different opinion to you" I answered. They continued with their battle against this "what different opinion can you have? So you are not interested in our opinion?"

I mustered my courage and simply answered "No, we are not interested".

At this very moment the two of them turned silent and defiantly left. In doing this they were showing that they object to everything that was going on.

"Ugh" I gasp. But this rejection hurt me deep down. Why should they be so stubborn, two old donkeys. It is a pity that while I'm pregnant I can't drink. A few drops of brandy in my tea would help me a lot now. I have to drink tea now without brandy.

Henry felt that something has happened to me. He gets onto my lap and begins to hug and babble something "Mama, mama" in his baby language. I calm down and think, they can say what they like, but children are the only real happiness in the world. Especially when they are small and sweet and so carefree. It is worth giving birth to them and to love them.

For a couple of days the weather was cool and then the hot sun reappears and strokes with new strength. My mother took a vacation and went with Henry to her friends to the country for three weeks. I now had absolutely nothing to do. I was lying around, reading and watching TV. On one such evening, Anya came to me. After chatting for a while about our plans we decided to go to the Crimea for vacation, for two weeks. Of course, it was a spontaneous decision and my growing pregnancy did not encourage me. But Crimea is much better than Kiev. It is easier to stand the heat near the seaside. My sister is the best company I could ever wish for. Henry will be in the country for three weeks in total. So, there are no obstacles to our travel plans. We agree that any surprises or stress are not good for me now. I will give birth only in Ireland, but in the meantime, we will relax and swim together in Crimea.

We go to Crimea with only two small suitcases. We managed to drop into a boutique and buy two gorgeous wide-brimmed hats. Our trip was planned to last for two weeks. Where to go? We have not fully decided, we will think about it on the train. When Anya and I are together, we do not care where we are or where we are going. The fact that we are together, makes us the happiest people in the world.

Of course I told my parents-in-law about my departure for two weeks to the Crimea. I thought it is my duty to inform them. They were still in disagreement, and they were even more outraged by my crazy decision to go to the Crimea now that I am seven months pregnant. I phoned them to tell them and used the excuse that my mobile was ringing so I could end the conversation quickly with them.

Tim supported me. He hoped that while I am at seaside, his parents bad mood will pass. Since I am feeling well and healthy in my pregnancy, no one had any worries about this trip.

Chapter 2

It was early morning Crimean Station was blazing, taxi drivers were offering their services, porters were carting luggage, just like in a classic movie. We went on the side and began to think, what to do, where to go? We saw two women in their fifties, standing ten feet away and waiting for something or someone. A taxi driver came up to us and we told him to bring us to Koktebel.

The women, who were standing nearby, heard us and came to us and began to bargain with the taxi driver. He agreed and we all went to Koktebel.

In the car we became acquainted with these women. They are from Kiev and even from our area. One was called Alice and the other Sonia. They were friends. Alice was a lively, cheerful, brisk and humorous woman. I even thought that she is probably a salesperson. Although, as it turned out she is the tax inspector. The second woman, Sonia, was laconic, modest and pensive. She works at the Institute of Chemistry. In short, the two friends are two extreme opposites.

Time for a Change

Alice immediately suggested that we seek accommodation together, like a family: mothers and daughters. They explained that it would be safer for us all to stay together. We might even get a discount. The taxi driver suggested to us a couple of addresses. We choose one and he brought us there.

We were shown a wooden house with two entrances consisting of two rooms, one room for the two women, the other room, for us.

We were happy and felt safe. The place was clean and cozy. If we need anything our two new friends were on the other side of our wall. We had a shared kitchen and shower facilities and this suited us all well.

We settled in, took a rest and then went for a walk. We had to walk for twenty minutes to the sea. We went to a cafe for a snack. Next we went to the local market. Anya bought some wine and fruit, Crimean onion, tomatoes and some other items. Poor Anya was loaded with groceries so we took a cab back to where we were staying and quickly fell to sleep for a nap.

It was awfully hot. That evening, we went for a walk along the promenade, had dinner in a cafe and returned again for a rest. Of course, the evening sea and the music coming from restaurants, was beckoning us, but we needed rest so badly. The most important thing was to get to the beach early around six o`clock the next morning. We were used to going to the beach early in the morning. It was our unwritten rule since childhood. Even when it is hard to get up, we did, knowing that as soon as we could lie down on the sand, we would be fully relaxed.

The alarm clock went off at half past five. We woke up, had some coffee, and went to the beach. In the

Koktebel there is a long, long staircase leading to the beach. I do not know how many steps there are, but it's a lot. We went down to the sea and decided clearly that on our way back we would go around.

We got to the beach, took chairs, lay down and relaxed for a couple of sweet hours. We were woken up by our neighbors` greeting us. They had come to the beach at eight o`clock. They sat down with us and started telling us what they did and saw yesterday, where they have been and all the news from our courtyard. Alice was delighted. It turns out that in our neighborhood, live two old men, they are painters. She said "they are talented and quite famous in their sphere. So, they leave very early to go to the mountains. They draw scenery from all around them. They return very late". Since during the day, they are not at home, we couldn't understand when our neighbors had managed to meet them?

These painters were in their eighties. They promised to show them their works that evening. Our new friends were delighted. They also said they saw the son of our new landlord. He is a young man in his twenties, very handsome and very polite. There are also two more families with children living in the big house. Since they use the other half of the yard, we will not get to meet them. Thus, for half an hour, we learned all about the Crimean yard and its occupants. It was already ten o'clock in the morning. We talked more about this and that with the neighbors and then we started to get ready to go back home.

We looked at the stairs from the beach, with all those steps and decided to go around instead. The heat was rising as noon was coming. Our yard was quiet

Time for a Change

and deserted. We took a shower, dressed in tunics, took our wide-brimmed hats and were going to head out again. Then we saw the landlords' son.

By the description from Alice, he was very nice and polite. He was of average height and in his early twenties, athletic build, broad, fit, tanned, blond with blue eyes. Such a handsome man!

"Hello" he greeted us "did you two go to the sea today?"

"Yes, we just came back. We have been there since six o'clock in the morning" my sister replied.

"And how is the sea today?" he enquired.

"It was just great. It just got too hot for us to stay there" said Anya. We smiled at him and went out of the yard. He smiled back at us. I must say that his smile was charming. He is cool, we decided simultaneously.

We went to a cafe, had lunch and then went to the park. We took a walk in the shades of the cypress and chestnut trees. We were taking pictures changing our hats and gossiping. Then we returned back. Coming closer to the yard we heard a conversation between two women.

"Did you hear?" one was saying to the other "how first she was made drunk with something! Exactly, something was added to her alcohol! And then she was robbed!"

"Robbed?" asked the other lady.

"Yes, yes, robbed. She was found in the bushes on the waterfront. They say her mobile phone was taken, all of her money along with her jewellery. Also they say she was alone. Thank God, she is alive. She doesn`t remember anything" the woman continued.

"Taya! Did you hear that?" Anya asked with fear in her voice.

"Yeah, I heard it, but wish that I hadn't!" I sheepishly replied.

"What shall we do? How will we go for a walk in the evenings? We don`t know how many idiots are around and you are pregnant! We cannot just hang around here staying in this house either" my sister said excitedly.

"Alice and Sonia stay in and read books in the evenings. They talk with these old painters and at the same time save money!" I stated.

"What shall we do?" whispered Anya.

From her childhood Anya was always suspicious and scared. From hearing any noise, her heart would pound like a hare`s heart. She did not get any braver with age or maturity.

"Maybe it`s just gossip? I will go and find out" I stated bravely.

I came out of the house. The landlords wife was still talking to the same woman. I went to the kitchen on the pretense of getting some water. On the way back I ask. "We heard that last night a girl was robbed. Is this true?"

"Oh yes, yes!" they both gasped. "It did happen. The police are corrupt and this bad element comes here in large numbers! They should go back to where they belong! We can`t live like this. So, watch out girls, you are alone here without husbands. Be careful. Anything can happen!"

Alarmed by their response, I went back into the house. Anya heard all of this conversation through the open window.

Time for a Change

"So, what shall we do?!" we said, almost simultaneously.

"Well, this is just not fair! Our vacation has only just begun?" sighed Anya.

"Okay, don't panic, let's think" I suggested.

"Okay" echoed Anya.

"We`d better hide our money, just in case. We might be robbed when we are out and about" advised Anya.

The next problem, where to hide our money?

We began to crawl, on all fours and look through all the corners, to think in which corner to hide our money.

"Under the floor boards? What if the mice eat it!" Anya joked.

All versions of choices such as inside our suitcases, wardrobes and books were considered but decided against as they would immediately be found out. The choice fell to the ceiling. The ceiling was made of plywood and a wooden layer and the top corners were covered by architrave. So we decided to bend the architrave and roll the notes of four hundred dollars into a tube and hide it inside.

This was so and it could be taken out quickly and easily with our fingers. This idea seemed brilliant to us. No one will ever think of the architrave. Our money will be safe and we were happy. Separating out money that we needed for the next five days, we proudly poked all our remaining money into the ceiling.

But that was only one part of the problem! Evening time was coming, it was time to go to a restaurant and we would be two women alone.

"What shall we do?" we thought. We asked our two lady neighbors to join us. They won't be able to come as they plan on staying in. The old men had invited them to see an exhibition of paintings. Where could we find a guard or an escort? We decided to try and get acquainted with the son of the landlord. Maybe he goes out somewhere in the evening and he can accompany us? Or maybe he knows places where it is safe for us to go alone? Anya flatly refused to go to ask, so as her older sister, I did.

"A pregnant woman should not be refused!" joked my sister behind me.

I left the house and went in search of our new found bodyguard. I found him in the wash house. He, sitting on his hunkers repairing something. He was focused and did not notice me.

"Hi" I said.

"Hello!" he smiled in return.

Gosh, he is so handsome, I mused. His smile is so charming and open. I asked him to recommend us a good cafe or restaurant. But also a safe place where nothing could be mixed or added into drinks of tourists. I explained that we have heard plenty of horror stories, so we are scared to go out without advice.

He stood up. He was clearly a little confused and surprised. "Well, I don`t know, I actually don't go out anywhere around here. I work all day and in the evenings I go to swim, to read or to rest. Sorry I can't be more helpful"

Now it's my turn to be surprised. "How can a young handsome man like you just stay in? I didn't understand. Without giving him time to think and

Time for a Change

answer I suggested that he join us for the evening. We will be going for a walk and then having dinner. So why would he stay at home alone? And this way we will not afraid to be out and about.

"What about those ladies? Your mother's?" He blurted out.

I sighed, looked at him and said "they are not our mothers! Every evening they play cards and read books. They don`t go anywhere just sit in the courtyard or in the garden and have tea".

"Well no thanks anyway. Thanks for the offer, but I'm not going anywhere this evening, I have lots of work to do here" he replied.

I thought "what kind of work is more important than taking us two out?" "Listen" I told him "we will pay you. You see, we are afraid to walk here late at night, especially after all of the events we have heard of. You do not want me to go into early labor from a fright, do you?" I decided to try to soften him.

"Ok so" he agreed "at nine o`clock. I won't take a free dinner, but you can buy me a beer. Do we have a deal?"

"Yes I happily agree. That's great, thank you very much. See you then" I smiled at him with a charming appreciative smile.

I returned to my sister and told her the good news. "Anya, everything is done! He agreed and only wants a bottle of beer in return! He was resistant at first, of course, but I managed to persuade him".

We were happy. At five we were ready to go to the beach and swim.

We suddenly realized that we didn't even know his name!

"Never mind that! We`ll get to know each other in the evening better. Let's go to the beach now. We can relax and put all the worries and thoughts out of our heads" Anya reassured me.

We went swimming and on our way home we bought grapes and peaches. Anya took the bottle of wine. Our mood was excellent.

The evening was coming. We were joking, dressing up and looking forward to a fun night out. At nine, we were ready. Our escort, as agreed, was on time and at our door.

"Good evening, my name is Ivan", he introduced himself.

"Anya and Taya", we introduced ourselves.

"Let's go?" he asked.

He was wearing a white T-shirt, which showed off his Crimean tan. He had smart jeans on too.

We were walking along the beach and talking. He was telling us about Koktebel and we were telling him about Kiev. We noticed a nice restaurant and agreed to dine there. We sat down at a table and ordered Ivan his promised beer, I ordered juice and Anya ordered a glass of wine. We were hungry and so we ordered risotto and a plate of vegetables. Ivan declined to eat at first, but we insisted so he also had to join us and eat.

Word for word, he told us that he was born in the region of Ivanovo, near the Sea of Azov. He is twenty years old. He works part-time here in the summer. He lives with our landlords and works for them. In May, he returned from the army. There is no work in Ivanovo. Before going to the Army he had finished the local seminary. He is a trained chef. He came to Koktebel by accident, his neighbor worked here and recommended him. Anya and I look at each other with surprise.

"That's funny! Alice told us you are the owner's son" we informed him. We also told him we thought she liked him also.

He said that she was behaving strangely enough, a couple of times she was buying him beer and joking with him during the day. We answered him that she was like that. She's a divorced woman. We were making jokes to him, he laughed and asked.

"You two are sisters? Which one is your mum? Sonya or Alice?"

"Our mum is at home with her grandson. These women we just met on the way here".

"Oh" he was embarrassed. "How old are you both?"

We started joking "how old do we look?" We had confused him. We told him then that I am twenty-seven and Anya is twenty-two. He was pleasantly surprised by our reply.

"No way, you're kidding! You are so funny, cheerful. I thought you are maximum twenty-three, you look like twins!" he blurted out.

We were laughing and ordered another beer and juice. Anya continued to drink wine. The evening went on very pleasantly. We talked about various things. Ivan was surprised and delighted with all the stories we were telling him and he enjoyed our company.

"Is it possible, that there are simple, friendly and funny girls such as you two?" he asked sincerely.

It was nearly midnight so we went over the promenade for one final time to inhale the scent of the sea. Ivan even took a picture of us and then the three of us went safely home.

At six o'clock in the morning, we were awakened by a knock at the door.

"Who could it be at this early hour?" I asked Anya as I put on a T-short and opened the door.

Ivan was standing there, smiling broadly. "Good morning, beautiful, you said that you get up at six in the morning! So, I have boiled the kettle for you. When you are ready, come to the kitchen for a cup of tea. I will be waiting for you both".

We were slightly surprised. Anya and I got up, got dressed and started to joke.

"This is not bad. At night he is our bodyguard and in the morning he makes us tea! He is all rolled into one!"

He poured us two large cups of tea and we sat at the table. It was in the summer kitchen. An old tall wiry man entered, in denim shorts he had gorgeous gray white hair. Holding his cup out for tea, he said "good morning, Ivan introduce me to these young ladies".

"This is Taya and this is her sister, Anya" he introduced us.

"Nice to meet you both. Where are you from?"

"We are from Kiev" said Anya.

"My name is Sergey. I am a painter and for over twenty years I come to different towns of the Crimea and paint the mountains. My other hobby is photography. If you're interested, I'll be pleased to show you my collection from this season".

"Thank you Sergey, but let's do it another time as we try to spend mornings on the beach" my sister said courteously to him.

"Thank you Ivan, for the tea. Have a nice day" we then hurried to our house to pick up our stuff.

Coming to the beach, we took chairs and settled into relax. At eleven, having bathed and swam, we decided to go for a meal and have a look at what guided tours were available for today. There was a tour, at four o`clock today. It was a boat tour of Koktebel.

The second tour, which we were interested in, was in two days time to St. Paraskeva.

Toplovsky Paraskevsky Holy Trinity Convent is our key location. It has a Saint and a Holy woman as its source. Her name is St. Paraskeva Roman. Here, according to local legends her martyrdom took place. Following this execution, a spring with healing water sprung up. This spring is visited by many pilgrims and tourists. There is a natural swimming pool, where people, by their beliefs dip into the water and recover. The atmosphere of this place is filled with not only worldly but also spiritual beauty. It was interesting and unusual for us and we wished to go there.

After paying the tour, we suddenly realized that our money is running out.

"We should go home and get the money out of the ceiling" I giggled as I suggested it.

We came home. Anya fumbled for the money, but it wasn`t there. It really wasn't. I couldn't believe it. No! We really couldn't find it! Looking at each other, we began to laugh hysterically and then to cry. It seems that the money fell somewhere inside the wall. Examining the perimeter of the wall there was no chance to get the money out without tearing the architrave. We sat on our beds next to each other, laughing and discussing what to do. Well, how did it happen? We thought we had sorted out everything when we choose that place. Apparently, when the entrance door is slammed, the whole house shudders. So the banknotes fell through into the wall deeper and deeper.

Anya went outside and tried to find Ivan, but he wasn't there. Damn, we have our tour soon and we need to book it. What shall we do? We have no money! We are stuck! It was funny and sad. "If we destroy half of the wall, the Crimean people will say this legend to each other for another twenty years!" my sister laughed.

Anya decided to take another chance. She put her hand to the maximum inside the wall and suddenly she felt something with the tips of her nails. I do not know by what miracle, but she managed to catch the tube of banknotes. With her third attempt, it dropped into our hands. Phew! Our joy knew no bounds.

We were short of time, we got ready quickly and went on the tour. At least the motor ship hadn't left without us. The evening was wonderful. We floated along, looking at the bay, the mountains and the landscape, all were beautiful. The tour had passed quickly. We had a lot of fun and relaxation. We were taking pictures from the boat of the background with its beautiful nature and sea.

A week passed, since we were on vacation, we were tanned, rested and looked our best.

Today there was a tour to Toplovsky Convent, where the Holy Great St. Paraskeva site is, glorified with her works and achievements. We woke up early and spent the whole day in the mountains. We visited the Holy Water Well and took water from this spring.

Time for a Change

We were enjoying this unusual, peaceful and calm place.

On the ninth day of our stay, again at six in the morning, Ivan told us that the tea is ready" it's time for you both to get up". We met him in the kitchen. He told us that he hadn't seen us for days and was starting to get worried about us. He asked us where we had been? We explained that during the daytime we are not at home as we were gone to the beach or on guided tours and at night we do not go anywhere but come home early to rest and sleep.

This explanation calmed him down and we invited him to join us for an evening walk.

So that evening, accompanied by Ivan, we went for a nice relaxing walk. Ivan told us that Sergey, the painter, showed him his works. He is talented but perhaps a bit strange as often creative people are. He asked if we had seen his works.

"No, we haven't had a chance yet, but we definitely plan on doing so" we promised.

He was curious as to what we do for our careers.

Anya answered that she is a stylist and a hairdresser and she helps to create or modify peoples' image.

Ivan was surprised he had never met a stylist before. He began to question whether he needs to change his style. It turned out that his appearance completely fits into the Crimean lifestyle.

Next he asked me what I do as a career.

I explained that I am a translator from English into Russian. I am a Doctor by profession and that I live in another country. He was quite shocked he didn't have any friends living outside of the Ukraine.

He looked at me in confusion asking "and what are you actually doing here?"

"I`m on my holidays!" I said laughing. "In two weeks time I have a flight to Dublin. That's where I live".

He tried to ask a couple more questions, but I asked Ivan not to focus on Ireland. I'm tired of this topic and when on vacation I want to relax and not to have to talk about my life there. He understood and the topic was closed.

We ordered coffee and cakes. I tried to turn the conversation in another direction. But Ivan was so surprised that he was not able to comprehend all the information. We started to ask him about his parents and his childhood. Ivan could not settle down and finally blurted out "Well, look at you two? One of you has her own business, she transforms people and is a stylist! I've seen stylists only in magazines! And the other one generally lives abroad and believes that it is normal! I have spent the last four months just thinking how to get a job in Kiev or Yalta!"

"Ivan! Don`t just think about it, do it. There is a huge amount of restaurants and cafes in Kiev, eateries even more, plus pizza places, McDonald's and other fast food restaurants. Anyone can get a job once they want to work. Think about it. There is only seasonal work here, such as painting and repairing toilets. Kiev is the capital and the chances of a good lasting job are much better".

He was interested. Something had changed in his eyes. He was convinced and believed in himself or in luck. The possibility of a different life, filled with his dreams but about which he was afraid to start. We were talking about the prices of houses in Kiev, about wages there and about his future possibilities. We had finished our dinner. We walked along the waterfront, then went home and immediately went to sleep. The next morning, at six o'clock, we get up to go to the beach. This is the routine on our holidays and we like it that way.

There are four days left before our departure. The weather has slightly changed, it's now cold and raining. That day we didn`t go to the beach. About nine in the morning, Ivan knocked on our door, he must have heard that we were not sleeping as were talking and laughing.

"Ladies, the kettle is boiled, it's time to have some tea".

"We`ll come in ten minutes, thanks" we answered, we got dressed and went to have some tea.

In the kitchen there was Ivan, Sergey and his friend, a painter named Matthew. They were having a constructive discussion on photos of Crimea. Their faces lit up when they saw us.

Sipping tea, we were also looking at the photos. There were rare angles of the Crimean Mountains and rocks. One stone looked like a turtle and the other, just like a head in a turban and the third was the subject of this morning constructive discussion.

The old men asked "Girls, be honest, what does this stone look like?" asked Sergey the photographer.

I thought to myself "looks like the male genital organ" but I said aloud "it`s a camel sitting in the desert, with his legs pulled up".

Everyone was speechless. Sergey was shocked. Anya was barely refraining herself from laugh.

"Well" he retorts "maybe Taya in your pregnancy you cannot remember how the male genital organ looks?!"

Anya tried to the rescue me and said "oh, everyone has their own view of this kind of thing. In some way your stone does looks like the male genital organ! But also it could look like a camel!"

"One must appreciate the signs of nature which it gives to us" Sergey replied. Matthew did not say anything during all this conversation. He was obviously deep in thought.

Sergey decided that the dispute is successfully resolved in his favor and solemnly handed me, the photo adding "Taya, this is for you, so you don't forget the great work of nature!"

It was a sharp turning of the dispute. I had nothing else to do but to thank the talented photographer.

Ivan was drinking tea, looking down and also trying not to choke with laughter.

But that was not the end. Sergey invited us into his tiny room and began showing us his works as Matthew quietly left.

Works of Sergey mainly represented landscapes of the Crimea. He was good at drawing, had his own style, like all painters do. Then, he continued with his photography. Photography was his hobby. Mostly he photographed nude women of all ages and body type. For example, one woman is plump and in her fifties, standing naked with her black hair down and was holding a fruit basket on her shoulder. This picture was taken in St. Nicholas botanical garden in September. The photographer especially liked this picture. He talked a lot about it with admiration. There were other

Time for a Change

pictures of naked women, sitting on the rocks in the early morning or in the evening, against the Black Sea. We looked through all his work. Ivan was standing behind us. He humbly looks away from these explicit pictures.

Sergey suddenly suggested to me "Taya, I haven't had a model yet in your condition. Maybe you would pose for me? And I'll give you your pictures to keep".

I replied "you have already given me a photo of the male genital organ stone and this is more than enough for me! No, thank you Sergey, I definitely do not want to be a model in my eighth month of pregnancy!"

He tried to convince me that the pregnancy is an absolutely magical condition and there is no reason to be shy, that I am beautiful and so on.

I peacefully listened to this tirade of compliments and answered "Sergey thank you. But if I say no, it means no".

It was Anya's turn. Sergey switched to her. "Anya, you are so perfect, you are young and beautiful. I could take an excellent picture. You just don`t imagine you're a goddess! Llet us try?" He said snobbishly "any time that suits you. The main thing is to feel it in your body".

Anya looked at him calmly and said "thank you Sergey, but let's do it some other time, in about twenty years! Go to Alice or Sonya, maybe they would pose for you? They love your talent and you made a good impression on both of them" offered Anya.

Holding our laughter, we left. Ivan went with us to our room. "Well" I joked "thank you Ivan, for such an original tea experience!"

"Ivan, it would have been a good idea to caution us about what our neighbors are engaged in!" teased Anya.

A minute later, someone knocked on our door. My sister and I looked at each other with surprise. We said in unison "It`s open, come on in".

"Sorry for bothering you!" Sergey started "Anya, I want to give you a present, a souvenir from your trip" continued Sergey. He held out a photo of the Crimean spring road on the side of which grew yellow flowering shrubs. "This is for you, in memory of our meeting". It was very nice. Anya thanked Sergey, accepted the gift and he left happy.

"We have in the last forty minutes received many gifts and suggestions. Let's sit down and absorb it all" I said.

The three of us sat down and after a few seconds, without a word, began to laugh out loud.

The last day we spent at the seaside, walking in the park and buying souvenirs. That evening we declined Ivan`s offer to go for a walk as were busy packing to go home.

Our train was departing in the morning. We were leaving with the same company: Alice and Sonia, we would travel together. Ivan came to accompany us to the taxi, he kindly carried our luggage. We noticed that he was sad because we're leaving. Anya left him her address and phone number, just in case, in the future he will take a chance to come to Kiev.

I felt that I would not be back to this place again. A new life will swirl and overwhelm me, with all the new events ahead of me. The rest and relaxation here was perfect for me at this time in my life. Alexei was to meet us, but he did not come and we didn't know why. So on our own we went to the house. Henry had missed me very much. His speech had developed since we were gone and was lovely and tanned.

I had missed him too and spent the rest of that day with him.

We had five days left before our flight to Dublin. I invited my grandma to stay with us for a few days.

Chapter 3

Grandma is a very cheerful person. She was not my mother's or my father's mother. She was our Grandma, Anya's and mine! We lived next door to her, she hadn't her own grandchildren. Her heart belonged to us. When I was born, she offered my mum, to nurse me when my mum needed help. That's why, I remember her as long as I remember myself.

When Anya was born, by that time Grandma had minded me for five years, she had become a member of our family. We could not imagine going to bed, without hugging Grandma every night before we slept. In the evening, from ten to eight, she used to come to us. We had tea together, excitedly telling her our news and stories of the day. It was our family tradition. Grandma knew all about us. When we grew up, nothing changed. She is our true friend. Grandma is our mentor and adviser. Most importantly, she is able to keep secrets. If we were asking her not to tell dad or my mum something, she always kept her word. Our own grandmothers were jealous of her. They were saying that we love her more than them. It was true!

Time for a Change

We loved her more than everyone and she was the second person after our mum.

Before my departure, before giving birth, I wanted to spend the last two days with her. The weather was very hot. In the afternoon we stayed in the kitchen or in a room, having tea, relaxing and talking. Beside us Henry was playing, building something out of blocks. These two days I was video recording Grandma and Henry together.

Grandma, over and over again, was looking at Henry and saying "Taya he is such a nice kid! He looks just like you when you were young".

In the evenings, when the heat was less strong, we went out for walks. I was talking to Grandma about everything. About all the years that have passed by. All eight years of living abroad, Grandma was writing me letters and sending cards. She always supported me with her wisdom, she knew my every important step, my anxiety and pain and of course my joys too.

Sitting in the kitchen, as Henry was sleeping in the living room, we talked quietly and had tea. "Tomorrow I leave" I update her. "Well, we have to go, everything is ready. The heat is unbearable! It`s mid-August already. Hopefully I don't give birth on the plane" I was joking. "You know what, Grandma? If a woman gives birth on a plane, then over the country where the plane passes, during the birth of the child, the newborn gets the citizenship of that country!" I laughed.

"Ah, Taya, give birth here or else he will be Irish! It is safer to give birth on land. Here you are on your own home ground" answered Grandma wisely.

"Ssh" I say "Grandma, do you hear? There is someone walking around in the corridor" I began to listen.

"Are you expecting someone?" she whispered.

"No, I'll go and have a look to see who it is". I was wearing only a T-shirt as it was so hot. I went out to the hallway of my own apartment. I can see a man standing there, in the middle of the hall! "Hello" I say enquiringly. I don't know what to do with myself as no other clothes are nearby for me to grab. I cannot scream as Henry would wake up frightened. Grandma had remained in the kitchen.

He looked at me, with a strange look, obviously confused where I had come from. I am actually half-naked. He stands silently, looking at me as I look back at him.

Suddenly, my father-in-law comes out of the bathroom, looks through me and says to the man. "Please do come in". The man enters, through the bathroom.

At this moment Grandma shouts "Taya, who's there? Did you see anyone?"

I go back to my Grandma. On my way back, I put on a bathrobe in the shower room. I take a bath towel for my Grandma to cover herself because she is wearing only a long vest. I say to her "don't worry, its father-in-law, Pasha, with some guy. Stay here. Please".

I go back to the hall and say as calmly as I possibly can "Pasha, haven't you learned to ring the doorbell before coming into our apartment? Or at least to give me a call and inform me that you are coming in. Who is this man?"

Time for a Change

"That man is a plumber" he began to shout "your toilet does not work!"

"Excuse me" I retort "I am constantly at home, everything works here. Do you think I would not have noticed if the toilet didn't work?" I am showing my anger now.

"F* * * off" he shouts back at me. "Who do you think you are?"

Without saying a word, I turned and went to the kitchen, in passing I heard the plumber say I do not know what you're talking about? Everything works!"

But it is not my business now. I walked through the kitchen and went out to the balcony. Grandma remained sitting in a chair in the kitchen, without understanding anything. A lump came in my throat and I couldn't breathe. I sat on my hunkers and began to cry. How long can I suffer from them, old goats? After ten years, I am still no one to them! So, what else do I have to do, so that they will respect me and take me into the family?

I came closer to Grandma. Crying, I embraced her like in childhood and said "Grandma, you know me well. Am I not good enough for them? I love and live with their son. Really, am I still no one? How can I continue to live like this? What do I do?" I was sobbing.

"Taya, my little girl, you are young. You have to live with and learn to love them. Respect them. Pasha is a kind man. He will never hurt you or your children" she was calming me patting me on the back. As you know, when somebody calms you, you want to cry even more. I was crying, setting my head on her shoulder. I remembered my childhood and loneliness in Ireland, the feelings rolled over one another, tears flowed like water.

After a while, with her comforting me I felt a bit better. Later, Henry woke up, we had a snack together and went to accompany Grandma to her taxi.

"Grandma, my dear, cheer up. As soon as I give birth, I'll write to you. Everything will be fine! I know, I feel it. I`ll have a daughter! I love you very much, I'll call you! Take care of yourself. I will miss you! God bless! Please look after yourself" I said my goodbyes to her.

My heart was broken. I was very, very sad. I felt pain and sadness. I hate this feeling of sadness and loneliness.

Anya came in the evening. Of course, I told her everything, complaining about my life. We were talking for almost half the night.

Mum came in the morning to see us off. We called a taxi. Anya was going to go with me to the airport.

Mary, my mother-in-law, phoned. She did not understand why we hadn't visited her on our last evening, as she had been waiting for us. She was annoyed.

I calmly replied, "Mary, please, ask Pasha about that" aand I hung up.

My impression was that she was pretending that she didn't know what had happened between Pasha and I with the arrival of the plumber!

She called back a few minutes later. She reported that Pasha had said how yesterday, for some reason I had acted flaky and without saying goodbye, went out crying. She continued "Taya, it's not nice to leave without saying goodbye and in the evening, not to

Time for a Change

come at all to see us" she continued her tirade. "Pasha had booked a plumber as our toilet didn`t work. We decided, since he came to us, he should review your toilet too. We thought that your toilet didn`t work well either" she was muttering.

My eyebrows went up and up and with them my feelings of resentment. I suppose I should be grateful to have such caring parents in law! I simply replied, "Come out, at eleven fifty to the main entrance. A taxi will be waiting for me. We can say goodbye to each other then" and I hung up.

I had no need to be nervous or to worry. I expected such a trip, the flight, in a word, is a long way and the separation from my family and people I love is so difficult. This demands strength and power from me.

We walked out of the main entrance and the taxi arrived on time. We hugged and kissed my mum and as always we burst into tears. Mum was kissing Henry but he couldn't wait to get into the taxi. He was excited for the plane and he missed his Dad. He pointed a finger at the sky and said

"Bye, bye, puff puff. Henry puff puff".

My parents in law came out to us. I gave them a cold hug. Thanked them for everything. There was nothing to thank them for, really. But the rules of decorum are to be valued. On their faces there was no trace of sorrow or sadness. "They are small, wizened mummies!" I thought as I smiled at them.

"I`ll phone you when we arrive. Thank you all" I said, getting into the taxi.

At the airport check-in, everything went without a hitch.

Tanya Anina

"Would you like to be Godmother?" I asked my sister. "Oh yes," she replied enthuastically. "Eeverything will be ok" I reassured her. "I'll call you. I love you very much, take care of yourself". My heart was breaking.

"I love you too" she sobs "take care of you and Henry. Will you miss your Aunty?" she addresses Henry teasingly.

Henry clearly did not understand what was happening, everyone crying and kissing each other. Then they are laughing before crying and again kissing. We say one final goodbye and then cross the Ukrainian border.

We are again on the plane. Henry had a lot of running around at the airport, so now he is tired and will sleep for most of the journey back. He had some water and without waiting for take-off, fell asleep. It`s cool to travel when the baby is asleep, I was thinking. But the second child was kicking inside me, reminding me that he/she did not like the fact that the older brother rests on him. And what can a mum do? Change position or move Henry off my belly?

Time kept moving on, just three hours to Berlin. We were flying with German Airlines.

That's how it is, I thought, it seems that children are a joy. Of course I know people who live happily and self-sufficiently without them. They build a career, their lives and feel themselves well without children. I could not imagine my life now without Henry.

But not so with my parents in law. These are their own grandchildren! (Henry and my unborn child). They seem not to love and not able to express their feelings. Like two stale pieces of bread. They are seventy years old and already finished with giving love

Time for a Change

to their grandchildren. If love is in the human heart, it is forever. Where do they get so much sarcasm, criticism and complaining from? Life runs so fast. As an Irish saying goes "The days are long, but life is short". I felt sad again, I was sad for them and for us.

I try to tell my nostalgic mood to go away. I should take a duty-free magazine to look through it and distract myself and enhance my mood. No one was sitting next to us, the chair was free. Henry slept soundly, a drop of sweat rolled down his forehead, his lips were bowed. He is so sweet. I slowly handled him to a free seat; he rolled over and continued to sleep.

The lunch was brought. I ate, had coffee, there was still an hour of flight left. I did not notice that I had fallen asleep. The stewardess woke me up and asked me to fasten my seat belt.

Berlin met us with languid primness. The airport, as always takes on a life of its own. I went to look at the shops with Henry. Before departure my mum had given him a new toy car and Henry was playing with it in all available surfaces. He was busy and happy. The time flew by.

Another flight and in a couple of hours we would be in Dublin. We arrived in the evening. Tim was waiting for us at the airport. He brought us our jackets. The temperature difference was considerable, thirty degrees there and ten degrees here. The rain was drizzling down. Ah, cool damp Ireland.

We got into the car. We put Henry in his car seat. Tim took with him his favorite biscuits. He crunched biscuits and mumbled something in his own baby language. The roads were half empty. I had missed

Ireland with its green fields and white sheep peacefully grazing.

Tim was filling me in on all the local news. All updates about our neighbors, about his work, about his life and what he did without us during these weeks. I listened with only half interest. Not because I was not interested, but because I was thinking how to start a conversation about his parents? I patiently waited for the end of his news so I could start my story.

We continued to travel to the outskirts of Dublin. The road was empty and he was calm driving the car. I started the conversation. I told him all that had happened to me in the last few days.

"Tim, you know how good I treat all of your family. We are already ten years together and I have not done anything wrong. Why don't they love me? I was sixteen years old when I met you. I always treated them like my mum and dad. I do not know what else to do? How can I get them to like me?"

I couldn't stop the anger and the hurt that is seething through all of my cells in my body. I do not want to accept the fact, that, so far, I am no one in their family.

Tim was silent.

"Tim, why should I patiently suffer from their dirty comments? I think they are not capable of loving and that feeling is strange to them" I started to cry.

Tim continued to drive in silence. We were silent together. I said everything that I had wanted to. I was very angry and annoyed by this whole situation.

He started to talk calmly, without emotions,

"Taya, you know, they are like that all their life and they cannot be changed now. They are different, they

Time for a Change

live in their own world, have their own point of view" he continued.

"Tim" I interrupted him "I've heard this a thousand times. At least can you protect me now? If they do not accept me by now, explain to them strongly to respect me at least. I'm your wife and the mother of your children. I have the same rights as everyone else in your family. Your father has to understand that it is offensive and rude to say foul things to me and expect me to accept his comments. I am pregnant, it's so upsetting. He is such an old fool" I stated again.

"Taya, ok! What do you want from me?" he asked, as always calm and without emotions.

I hated his calmness. Tim and I, in this way, are two opposites.

I worry about everything. My thinking about my life is that everything is an eternal duty. But this duty does not burden me. I plan everything, organize everything, think several moves ahead and worry for everyone. I am emotional and as alive as mountain water. It's not boring to me, I am able to live and appreciate this time in my life.

Tim is like a cat. He is calm, relaxed, smart and intelligent. He never appears to worry about anything. I know all that his parents and grandmother did for him before I met him. Now for the last ten years, I have done everything for him. I've made a relaxed atmosphere in his life. He is comfortable in it.

I realize this and I don't complain. I am an optimist and Tim is a pessimist! He takes all meekly and believes that it should be like this. And his parents are our cross, mine especially. I was thinking and analyzing all this and finally, formulated, what it is that I want from Tim. So I explain it all to him "Tim, I'm asking you, tell them that I'm your wife and they have to respect me. Support me in this, please! I want to feel that I am your woman and your beloved wife. Secondly, from now on, make them communicate only with you. I can't and do not want to see or hear from them. If they want to talk to me, they should apologize first. At least Pasha should apologize" I sighed.

"I`ll do my best" he said quietly.

We were driving in silence, the evening was spoiled. I wanted to get home quickly. I wanted to have a shower and to wash away all this negativity. My wish was to start a new life tomorrow, wwith my family, in my house, in Ireland, away from everyone else.

Chapter 4

A month back home passed quickly with daily worries and duties. I packed up to the hospital and was about to give birth.

My pregnancy dragged on. A full forty two weeks. It was about four in the afternoon, Tim was at work. Henry and I were going to have tea. I boiled water and when pouring a cup of tea, I realized that I don't feel the temperature of the cup with my hands. The cup seemed to be cold. Steam was coming from the cup, so, it's hot. I started to pinch and prick myself. It was a classic syndrome, like wearing gloves and socks, when the sensitivity disappears in the arms and legs. I felt like I have a numb neck and suddenly I felt a strong headache. I was scared, so in a panic I called Tim.

"I'm delivering the baby" I said "but there are no labor pains!"

I calmly opened the front door lock (just in case if I lose consciousness and Henry is locked alone inside with me before Tim gets home). I dressed Henry and sat in the hallway waiting for Tim. During this time I partially lose my voice. Tim arrives and understands everything. He takes Henry to the neighbors.

We rushed to the hospital. We were driving on the opposite side of the road, overtaking cars. The maternity hospital was about fifty miles away from our house. I was looking through the window and silently was crying. I want to live I don't want to leave Henry and Tim, my mum and Anya. I prayed not to die from a stroke or something else. I understand how scary it is to be in a wheelchair. I did not know whether I could recover my voice or whether my child is alive? Panic and fear gripped me. Realizing my helplessness, looking at this world in my vulnerable condition, I prayed.

This is my third labor and now problems again. What have I done wrong in God`s eyes?

My first pregnancy and labor, I was only nineteen years old. I was a private patient in a good clinic. I went into labor on my due date. Everything that fateful day went like clockwork. There were no signs of trouble. I sighed I can never forget the doctor's verdict "the child is dead". Needless to say now my heart was broken with these sad memories and I felt sick with anxiety.

My second child, Henry, was born here in Ireland. I was advised to have him in the main hospital for the best maternal management. This hospital was one hundred and eighty kilometers away from us and in Dublin. At that time we were also driving on the opposite side of the road and in the bus lane, racing at all speeds. Henry was born by emergency caesarean section. I was eight-months pregnant then. Thank God, Henry was born alive and without any complications.

Time for a Change

Memories and hope have taken me for a moment from the reality. We were close to the hospital. I was shivering and shaking like a leaf. It's because of the stress, I thought, I need to calm down.

In the hospital, I was immediately prepared for a cesarean section. The doctor on duty that day was originally from Ethiopia. But she studied, in Kiev at the Medical University. She was telling us about it to help calm me down. She noticed my Ukrainian surname, considering my condition, seeing my panic, my eyes filled with horror and prayer and my muteness, she took my hand and said in Russian.

"I know that you're afraid to die. I will not let you die. Do you hear me? We qualified in the same medical school. You know how advanced our department is. We were taught by the same teachers, in the same school. Everything will be fine. You're going to live. I promise you. Do you trust me? Do not cry. Conserve your strength. You will need it".

I nodded and tried to smile. I closed my eyes, tears fell like water. I was taken to the operating room. Tim stayed with me. He was sitting at my bedside, encouraging me.

A few minutes later I saw my daughter and thought "what a wonderful girl". She didn't look like Henry did when he was born.

She was a beautiful little girl. Above all she was alive and healthy. After the theatre, she was put to my breast to suckle. Then she was taken to the children's room and to an incubator for the night.

I was taken to the ward to rest. A delighted and relieved Tim went home to Henry.

I do not remember how or when I fell asleep. In the morning when I woke up, my mind was racing. My speech had come back. I've been speaking slowly, mixing up letters and syllables. I still couldn't feel my arms and my legs and I had a terrible headache. This went on for several days.

They were bringing me my daughter so I could feed her. We had chosen her name a long time ago, Yana.

Yana, she is my sweet little girl. I was telling her, kissing and hugging her. I thank God for the fact that we are both alive and well.

A week later, we were discharged from hospital. It was over, all my anxiety went away. My speech was restored as was the sensitivity to the feet and hands. I still had a headache, but it was only slight now.

Henry, wasn't jealous towards his new little sister at all. He cared for her in his own way. He tried to feed her with bread then tried to get her to drink juice. Of course, it was hard for me as I was still sore. Neighbors said in a couple of months I will be fully healed and well again. I am the happiest mother ever. I have the best and long-desired for children. I want all the joys of motherhood and my happiness has no limits.

Four months has passed since Yana's birth. She has started to gain weight and is a calm child. Henry goes to the childminder. He was in his own world, where he is very happy. Life did not bring us any surprises. As I promised, I wrote a letter to Grandma and sent my daughter's pictures. I called Grandma several times, but no one answered the phone. I thought she must be gone out to the village.

One evening, I called mum and asked.

Time for a Change

"Where is Grandma? Wwhy doesn`t she write to me?"

My mum sighed, "Grandma has died, the day before you gave birth" mum answered dispiritedly. "We were afraid to tell you at that sensitive time for you, in case something went wrong because of stress. "That`s why we were silent all this time" mum cried.

We talked about the children for a while and then I said goodbye.

I was very sad. I lost not only my beloved Grandma; I had lost a dear friend too. A few days passed like in a dream. I appeared to be doing everything normal, but inside I was empty and lonely.

Two weeks later was the New Year. It was the first New Year for Yana, she was now four months. She was such a lovely baby. Henry received a lot of gifts from Santa Claus. Every day after the Christmas, he used to come to the Christmas tree and check whether there were more gifts. Our New Year celebrations were fun too.

The pain abated. When I remembered my Grandma, I wanted to cry. She would never, ever have wanted to see me cry. I believed that she was in heaven and would be praying for me and protecting me all my life.

On the eleventh of January, early in the morning, the phone rang. Tim and I were in bed. The children were still sleeping.

"Taya. Happy New Year! And congratulations on the birth of your new daughter" a joyful and strange voice greeted me.

"Thank you and Happy New Year to you too" I replied not recognizing who it was on the other end of the phone.

"Don`t you recognize me?"

"No, I'm sorry but I don't. Who is this?" I asked in confusion.

"Guess" I couldn't calm this guy down.

"Honestly, I don't know!" I didn`t even try to guess.

"Well, think harder" insisted the stranger.

I started to get angry. Tim was looking at me questioningly. "Who is this? If you do not identify yourself I will hang up on you".

"This is Ivan, Taya. Ivan from Koktebel. Do you remember me?" he asked worriedly.

Now it was my turn to be surprised. "Ivan who?" I couldn`t believe my ears.

At this moment, Tim was trying to find out who it was. He was making expressive gestures and grimaces.

"What Ivan? Who is this?" he pressed to know.

"Of course, I remember. Where did you get my number? Where are you? How are you doing?" my questions tumbled out one after another.

He replied excitedly "I`m fine, I work in Kiev now. Anya gave me your phone number. I am at her place at this moment. We are having tea together"

"Congratulations. That means you have found a job?"

"Yes, in a restaurant in the city center. I live outside the city. I came with a friend and we rented a house" he reported.

"Taya, hello", my sister laughs into the phone "have I sprung a surprise on you?" she was having fun I could hear it in her voice.

I don`t know why, but I was pleased to hear from Ivan and to know that he is ok. His dream had come

Time for a Change

true and that he now works in Kiev. I talked for a few minutes with my sister. Then I hung up.

Probably I had a fat smile on my face, as Tim said "Taya, who was that?"

"That was Ivan. Our summer bodyguard, from Koktebel" I joked.

Tim's never been interested in the details of my life. So this time he didn't ask any more information and seemed pleased just to know who it was and where I knew him from.

Meanwhile, the kids woke up and again the everyday life has begun with nappies, feeding, bathing, stories, walking and playing. Without the end, you can recite the duties of parents with their young children. Winter has passed and the weather hadn't been too cold. A beautiful spring was in the air.

Chapter 5

Spring in Ireland is always early and beautiful. Young leaves on the trees, the fields covered with fresh grass, small newborn lambs. All that pleases the eye and inspires the heart. Trees and shrubs are blooming. We all wish for a warm summer and plan our holidays.

On the eighth of March, Tim was working. My friend dropped in to visit me. I just was going to go with my children to the hospital and he offered his help to me.

His name is Arthur. He is from Moscow. I knew him for about three years now. It was a sunny, warm day. Henry walked and Yana was asleep in her baby buggy.

We entered the clinic. In the reception room, there were a few Irish with their children and a group of Chechens. Chechens were living in our town. They were easily recognizable by their appearance. Men were wearing leather jackets, sweatpants and flat caps. The women always wear long skirts and headscarves. They were kept in groups of five to six people. At the reception five of them were in a line to see the doctor.

They recognized me because of my translation work. I knew many of them by name. I nodded to them. The crowd approached me with greetings for the eighth of March. They asked me "Have you come with your husband to the doctor?"

I laughed and said "This is my friend Arthur. My husband is at work".

They were clearly shocked by the fact that I was walking around the city, not with my husband, but with another man.

After the clinic, Arthur and I went into a cafe. We have been joking and talking about different customs and nationalities and we enjoyed tea and a couple of cakes.

Tim came to join us in the café after his work. We told him about Arthur that he was mistaken for my husband.

I stayed in close relationship with Arthur for about three years. I was not only his friend with a shoulder to cry on, but also his muse. He was writing poems and songs, I was the first person who listened to all. He accepted my criticism or praise.

He no longer had a private life. He had the ruins of fifteen years of marriage behind him. His child, now with his wife, had left him broken hearted and lonely. His wife`s cheating had caused him a lot of pain. His soul is deeply wounded and covered with a thick layer of grey grief.

All these experiences and his long-suffering soul, he poured out onto paper in the form of his poems and songs. In me he saw a good listener and someone who he got comfort and understanding from. Our friendship has lasted already for three years.

From time to time, he had relationships which quickly faded away. He had an imaginative nature, ambitious, vulnerable, impulsive and emotional but is kind and trusting.

Some of the songs he dedicated to me. Claiming that after our conversation, he lights up and lives from meeting to meeting. Tim at first, was jealous of him and his attention me. Then he got used to it, or put up with the situation. Arthur became a friend of our family.

As a man, he was not interesting to me at all. He was not my type. However, many women were crazy about him.

He was thirty-seven years old. Tall, athletic, handsome, ggallant, fashionably dressed and with a good sense of humor. He felt superior to other men. By this I mean immigrant men mainly. Among these men, he was followed by reputation, a Moscow dandy!

Our friendship did not strain me. If I needed any help, he was always ready. I shared with him my thoughts and secrets. Some people have seen in our relationship not only a friendship. But it did not bother me at all. Since people will tend to gossip and tell lies anyway.

I loved Tim, I thought he was the best husband and father in the world. My world was just for him. Arthur knew it and has been always saying with a sigh "Tim, you're so lucky, you have such a wife! She's gold, she is a real person. You're the luckiest! And she loves only you".

Tim got used to his statements, songs and sighs. He was like a member of our family.

Time for a Change

The first word, Henry said, was, "Un-cle!" Because he saw Arthur, very often, he was walking with him and playing. Sometimes he took care of him when we were at work.

This year Easter was in April. We had a lot of days off. Tim took personal time off and I also didn't have too much translation work to do. We went to visit our children's godparents in Dublin. We had a fun time with them.

Our children's godparents are Russians. We knew them for three years now. They also had a boy and a girl, the same age as our children. I loved especially to visit their godmother as we had become good friends. The kids were playing with each other, husbands had bottle of beer. We spent our time together rushing to the shops, drinking coffee in small cafes. Never stopping our talking during the visit. We went to sleep late and got up early. We had such a fun time together, our two families we felt very comfortable.

We still had a week off. Everything was fine and we were enjoying our time off. However, I had a feeling that something was wrong. Had something happened between Tim and me? It was more of an intuition feeling than a fact. Something silent and strange had crept in between us.

One night, after putting the children to bed, we lit the fire and the candles and turned on the TV. We talked about friends, work, parents and problems. Having this time off to relax from our usual routine, I then realized in the past six months, we hadn't made love. Of course we were having sex, but we hadn't made love. Our frequency was at an average rate for a young couple with 2 small children and demanding lives. On the whole it was adequate, but I wanted more. I wanted romance, deep passion and an intimate connection that lasts.

There was a concert on the TV. I snuggled closer to my husband, like a cat, looked into his eyes, trying to kiss him. I was trying to get that spark of passion going, as only a woman knows how.

He was sitting like a statue, without resistance, but not expressing any interest to my advances towards him.

"Tim, I want you" I whispered, sitting on his lap.

He kept ignoring me. I took this to be a game. I continued to try to provoke him, to inflame his desire. I continued to sit on his lap and to touch him seductively.

He suddenly stood up and quietly, even indignantly said, "Taya, I don`t want to have sex with you. I do not know what is happening to me, but I don`t feel attracted sexually to you anymore".

Deeply hurt and offended, I swallowed a lump in my throat aand asked, "And what shall we do with this problem?"

He said calmly, "I don't know, we'll just have to wait and see". He stood up and went to our bedroom to sleep.

So I was left alone, sitting there like a fool. The fire and candles glowed but the romantic moment was gone completely. I was too numb to even cry, I just sat there trying to cope with the flood of feelings sweeping over me and trying to stay positive. Tomorrow is a new day. May be he is having a midlife crisis? I had to find an excuse for him.

Time for a Change

In the afternoon I went to the newly opened boutique and I bought stunningly seductive silky lingerie. I cooked Tim's favourite dinner. Put the children to bed. Unfortunately, it was another night of failure. He showed no sign of any interest or passion towards me. I cuddled and caressed him, dressed in my beautiful lingerie, trying to seduce him. My efforts were in vain.

I sometimes think that underwear was invented by women for women to enjoy. A man doesn't need us women either in seductive or ordinary underweare. If they want us, they want us, regardless of what we are, or are not, wearing.

Days are passing by and his attitude towards me has not changed. We share the same bed, but we have no sex, at all. He avoided the subject. I tried to analyze what had happened and what to do. I hadn't changed after giving birth. I was fifty kilograms and had a petite shapely figure, as before. My shape and size used to drive Tim wild with desire. I have not a single stretch mark on my body. My breasts are fully recovered and more plump after childbirth. I fed Yana for a couple of months but that phase is complete now so my breasts are mine once again. What could be wrong with my body that he no longer desires it comforts?

I asked Arthur. He came to us for tea. Tim was sitting at the computer.

"Arthur" I began, "tell me honestly, have I changed since the birth of my two children?"

"I do not understand!?" He joked, "of course, you have changed, Once there were two inside you, now you are alone again!"

"No, seriously, Arthur, have I changed?" I was trying to calm down.

"In what sense?" he couldn't understand my questioning.

"With my appearance. Is it the same as it was before having the children?"

"Hmm" he ponders "actually, you're the same as before. Just more tired and with more stresses. Your physical appearance, as far as I can see is as before, but you glow more now as you are a happy mother. "What has brought about all this questioning?" he adds. What's happened?"

"Nothing" I sigh. "Everything is fine, never mind. Thank you for your reassurance".

A couple of weeks later, Tim returned to work. I still couldn't understand what is eating away at him. Hiding resentment and anger at him, I tried to seduce him again. He was again, as cold as ice! No, I can't take this anymore! I got angry at him and blurted out "if you don't want me and don't pay any attention to me for the past two months. What am I to do with my needs? Should I go to the neighbors?"

In our neighborhood, lived thirty-year old guys who often had parties and who whistle at me as I pass them by.

"Who needs you with two kids? Go to them if you want" he said seriously, without any emotion.

It was quite a shock. Like a slap to me. I had expected any answer. Right down to his tiredness or a depression. Not this cynical suggestion for me to "play" away. Yes, who needs me with two children? I did not answer his rudeness. I just went out. My anger had no limits. "What an idiot! What a meathead!" I was saying

Time for a Change

to myself. Now, he will big pardon in front of me for this insult.

I was doing the usual routine with child care. We never returned to the topic of our lack of intimacy again. Why should I expose myself to that stress again, I decided Tim too has to put up with everything.

I bought tickets to Kievv until the end of May. It has been ten months since I was home last. I was going to fly away for the whole summer, to get away from it all and relax. Mum and Anya were delighted, they promised to help with the children.

My relationship with Tim didn`t improve before my departure.

I told all my troubles to Oxana, my best friend.

She listened and said "What do you want from your life from now on? He is certainly being selfish and rude to you".

Chapter 6

The year is 2005. We have another flight booked to Budapest. We fly in the morning.

The children are sleeping in the car until we come to the airport. I have a lightweight baby stroller for Yana. She chews on a biscuit and is satisfied with her life. Henry, spinning like a top, was pointing his finger at everything, bursting with energy for action.

On the plane, we have three seats. The children sit down. Then they get up again and they are driving me crazy. I was hoping that they will fall asleep. Yana tries everything that comes into her hands and slips it into her mouth. Henry talks non-stop and turns in his chair constantly. I have to have patience, I remind myself. But they were not going to sleep. I give them juice and cookies. Then I gave them toys, all two hours I was entertaining them and they were entertaining me.

Transfer in Budapest was just one hour. We rush to the nursery, swept like a whirlwind through duty-free. Then we rush to the other plane. It is stuffy in that second plane. The entire cabin is full of children, of

Time for a Change

all ages. Many people flying from Italy. It is noisy, the parents of the entire flight were trying to calm their children down. I occasionally heard children crying from different places in the cabin. My children, at last tired, fell asleep. So we had a relaxing flight.

During the two-hour flight, I managed to rest. I had two small bottles of wine and I ate two dinners, mine and Henry's. For me it was a piece of paradise. I would spend two months at home. Then Tim was planning to join us and we would go to Turkey, for two weeks. We would take Henry with us and leave Yana at home with his parents. In August, we would return to Ireland.

I loved Tim very much, in my soul, despite all the difficulties recently. I forgave him and the anger had gone. Where it went I didn't know and didn't question. I decided to freshen myself up. Like all married women, I've read about the decline of sexual activity. Usually in eight, ten, thirteen years of marriage. I was hoping that he would miss me, sort out his situation and all would be fine. When the plane came in to land, I woke up the children. I dressed them up in summer clothes and began to wait to get off the plane. Some children were upset and were crying. It was so very stuffy and hot.

In Borispol, as usual one bus arrived for three hundred passengers! People stood sweating in the crowded bus, swearing, calling on a cell phone to their families. They happily reported their arrival. Passport control and customs done and we passed quickly through.

In Kiev sunny summer greets us.

Anya, with her friend, met us at the airport. My sister has her hair cut and has changed the style. She looked sexy, cheerful and happy.

Anya friend's name is Michael. He is younger then she by a couple of years. A tall, smart and interesting guy. We got in the car and went home. In the car Anya patiently tried to become friends with my new daughter. Her neice. Yana, sat on my lap. No matter how I try, even with Anya beckoning Yana, she continues to cling to me with her hands, wearily looking around.

Henry sat between us and said "Yana, this is Anya, do not worry" and she was smiling then. He gleefully became the owner of a new red colored truck. He held this truck close to him and talked to his beloved Aunty.

Mum was waiting for us at home. Everyone was in a good mood. Michael took out our bags and helped us to bring them in. He said his goodbyes to everyone and left quickly.

Mum and Anya tried to draw Yana`s attention. She carefully looked at them. Yana still didn`t walk, so she sat on my lap and didn`t want to get off. We switched on cartoons, give them a box of toys and sat together on the floor and finally Yana got interested in the toys.

"How was your flight and how are you?" asked my mum. "I am very glad that we are together again" she added.

"Yes, this is so cool! We decided that I should move to you for the summer. Iwill be helping you with the kids" Anya said. "But what shall I do with my dog Fanny?"

"Take Fanny with you" I offered.

"What about your children? And you parents in law?"

"What about the children? They'll get used to Fanny. She is a kind, funny dog! Spaniels generally are a friendly breed. We will live together!" I answered. "Well! My parents-in-law, in any way, wouldn't be pleased! I'll tell them that Fanny lives with us and that's that!"

They hadn't said sorry to me during the past year! We were not talking. Why should I think about what they may or may not say to me now? Forget it!

The doorbell rang. The dreaded parents-in-law had arrived.

Henry keeps an unsure, watchful eye on them.

"Where's the girl? Show us the new baby then!" Pasha demanded. "Yes, she is pretty. Looks like her mum, Taya" he added.

"No she does not. She looks like my Tim" thwarted Mary. She continued "look, Pasha, don't you see that she has only Taya's eyes". "Otherwise she is a copy of Tim! I brought a picture of Tim when he was little, so we can compare" she triumphantly added.

"Mary, what are you saying? His face is different!" Pasha protested.

Henry got up from the dispute, approached me and got on my lap. With fear, he furrowed his brows, watching two crazy people, standing in the doorway of a large room, moving their hands and arguing. We silently watched the show. The dispute lasted between them for several minutes more. We remained silent.

Then suddenly they stopped speaking, went into the sitting room and sat down on the sofa.

"Pasha" asked my mum "Galina, do you have the day off? How are you?"

They completely ignored Henry. No joyful embraces, no greetings or presents. He left his aunt's lap and went to the bedroom. Behind him was Anya.

"What shall we do? They'll be stuck here for the whole day?" she stated sadly.

"I'll be busy putting my children to bed now. Then, I will go to join the others again in the living room. I will then be back to you here in a few minutes". Placing my two dear children on the bed, I said to Henry. "I'll be right back. Please, play a minute with Yana and then I'll read you a fairytale on my return".

I returned to the living room. They were talking about my mother's work. I asked them to speak more quietly, turned off the TV and I informed them that my children were preparing to sleep.

My two were sitting on the bed. We lay down comfortably and read a fairytale. Anya brought them to drink and stayed with us in the room. After another ten minutes or so, my parents-in-law then left for a walk with my mom. Yana fell asleep. We surrounded her, for safety, with pillows and then left her in the bedroom. For Henry's enjoyment, we switched on the cartoons. We were going to have dinner in the kitchen and leave him to his cartoons. He regularly came and checked in on us and what we were doing. Anya washed him some strawberries, and Henry ate them gladly.

Mum returned from her walk and helped us prepare our late dinner. She was pouring us soup and we got the rest of the meal from the fridge.

"Do you have a beer, Mum?" I asked.

Time for a Change

"Yes, we do" Anya said as she got it out of the fridge.

"It`s so hot, let's all have a beer" I said. "Mum, will you have a beer too?"

She agreed and we sat down at the table. We toasted each other for this reunion and for our holiday together. We raised and clinked our glasses together and saluted each other's health and happiness.

"When are you going to tell your parents in-law about Fanny?" asked Anya.

"Anya, what does their opinion matter to you? Who cares what they will say" I answered sharply.

"Tell me, Taya, what are your plans for tomorrow?"

"You should ask Anya, she has it all planned for us. This evening, we`ll have a walk with the children. Then we`ll bathe them and put them to sleep early. Tomorrow, after we have had a good sleep, we`ll go to the shops. Maybe Anya will dye and cut my hair?" I said questioningly.

"Do you work tomorrow?" I asked mum.

"Yes, the whole day" mum said disappointingly. "I have two days off then. I`ll cook you some food in the morning".

Anya poured the remains of the beer into glasses. "We have planned that our neighbors will call to see you" She joked.

"To say hello and to argue" I added and laughed.

"Taya, don't worry. You know them for a long number of years. Many are old now and a bit peculiar! But they are still good company and fun too" my mother said.

We finished our food and began to unpack the suitcases.

Henry had finished eating his strawberries and then climbed on my mums lap. She rocked him in her arms and he fell asleep. Mum stayed for a little while longer and then she went home. Yana woke up. I fed her and she was crawling all around, holding in one hand a piece of dry toast and in the other, a cracknel.

Finally, Anya and I were left alone. I got my chance to ask her "Who is Michael?"

"Well, he is just a friend. I asked him to help me collect you. He`s kind of my admirer. That`s why he happily agreed" she added with a sly smirk on her face.

"Where is Alexei, will he come to us in the evening?" I asked teasingly.

"Taya, darling, I did not want tell you on the phone. He now lives with his parents. We had a big fight and we broke up" she said as a matter of fact.

"Was that a long time ago?" I ask feigning calmness. Inside I was shocked.

"It`s been two months already. You see, with his work in the bank he has to attend eternal corporate parties. He was always coming home drunk. He was always causing me all kinds of stress because of this. When he was so drunk he would lose his keys or his wallet or could not remember how he got home. In short, I suffered for over six months. Then I couldn't take anymore and I threw him out. He went to live with his parents. Maybe there he will control his drinking as they will not tolerate this behavior from him" she was trying not to get upset as she told me this tale.

I could see the stress and tiredness in her because of this life experience. She could hardly hold back her tears. Her face showed all the emotions of pain, bitterness, resentment and frustration.

"I am so very sorry for you. Why didn't you tell me on the phone?" I asked.

"I didn't want to upset you" she tearfully sighed. "What could you do to help me? You live miles and miles away. At that time you just had your baby Yana and got the sad news of our dear grandma dying. I didn't want to add to your sadness. Your children constantly demand to be taken care of by you, so you have enough on your plate. I'll move in here with you and Fanny can join us. I've let out my apartment for two months. I have a friend she asked me to let her apartment for a couple of months. She'll just have time to find an apartment by September".

"I will be very happy if we live together. Fanny is not any trouble" I hugged sister. We clung to each other and we felt easier and cheered up.

Henry woke up and we got ready for our walk.

"Taya, are you going to call your parents-in-law?" asked Anya.

"If only you knew how much I don't want to, but I have to. I dialed the number, it was eight o'clock in the evening.

"Good evening" I said to my in-laws on the phone. "Are you free to go for a walk with me now?"

"Oh no, it's so late. Are you crazy to go for a walk and with the children too at 8 o'clock?" I moved the phone away from my ear as my father in-law continued to roar insults into the phone.

"There he goes again" I whisper and wink at Anya. I reassure him that it will only be a brief walk. It's such a pleasant evening and the fresh air will help the children to sleep better. Adding, that if they want to join us, they are both welcome too.

"We are busy with our plans. In the evening we watch the news then we have tea and settle for the night. We are old you know" he said indignantly.

"Ok so, just trying to be friendly by inviting you both. Good night, sleep well. Maybe we will see you tomorrow?" with that I hung up.

Anya and I, with the children stroll through the streets. Henry swings on the swings. Yana played in the sandbox. They both had a fun time and we got to relax in the lovely balmy evening.

We bought some beer and fish then returned home. We bathed the children and put them down for sleep. Then we sat down in the kitchen to talk. Though we were tired, we weren`t sleepy. We stayed up talking and supporting each other over life's problems until just after midnight.

Early in the morning, Anya went to work. All day I was doing the usual housekeeping routine. I went with children to the market and then for a walk. In the afternoon, we all had a nap. Everything was relaxed. Tim phoned early the next morning. He wanted to know how we were doing. He was hurrying out to work. I had been without the Ukrainian Sim-card. I promised that I will buy a Sim-card and text him updates on our activities.

Anya arrived in the evening. She had all her belongings and Fanny, her dog, with her. Michael had brought her. Henry was delighted by Anya`s appearance and he was even more excited when he saw Fanny.

Time for a Change

Fanny was a Spaniel dog. Completely black and she is three years old. She was a wonderful, playful dog. Fanny was sniffing everything and running around the apartment. Jumping up and down she knocked Henry onto the floor. This frightened Henry and he began to cry. We pretended to be angry with Fanny. But having a restless, cheerful dog rushing through the apartment was fun. Henry said "bad Fanny, bad dog". This made him feel better and less afraid.

Yana wasn't scared at all. The dog licked her small palms and she laughed. Henry will get used to the dog too, I reassured myself.

Anya went to have a rest after her busy day in work. Then we ate dinner together and she helped me put the children to bed.

My sister got the palette of hair-dye colors. I had lightened up my hair color in Ireland a couple of months ago. Anya focused and spent two hours on my hair. Then out of the mirror was my reflection, now a super blonde. This image always suited me. I was very pleased with myself. I had a long, graded haircut, elongated plait fringe, which effectively emphasized my cheekbones.

"Mum will take your children tomorrow" Anya said. "What are you planning to do with your free time?"

"I do not know yet, I don't have any plans" I answered honestly.

"Let me treat you to a manicure and a massage. You will spend half a day and you will get all done and be relaxed too" she suggested.

"Sounds bliss, thanks. Book me in for eleven o'clock. I`ll take the children at ten to Mum's and I will be free after that" I reply happily to her.

So that's tomorrow sorted for me. This evening was quiet and warm. We had bought a bottle of "Khvanchkara" and with the cold cuts of meat I bought that morning, we sat on the balcony. We poured the wine and started our meal.

"Taya, are you all right?" asked my sister, looking at me worriedly.

"Whatever do you mean?" I replied puzzled.

"You know! Is there something wrong with you? You are distracted and distant. This is not like you, especially when you are with me. I noticed it since you arrived. I thought you were tired after the journey. But something is wrong with you. I know you, you are in contemplative mood. You talk reluctantly about Tim? What has happened between you two?" she asked again expressing real concern.

"Anya you know, everything seems to be fine, but we do not sleep together. I mean we don`t have sex. Already three months, nothing at all" I shamefully confide in her.

I told her the whole conversation with Tim. About the purchase and the failure of the seductive underwear and about his total lack of mood for me in that way. Anya knew that I wasn`t a prude about sex.

"All my attempts and efforts have brought me nothing but refusal. I am so hurt at his rejection. That`s how the things are" I tell her all as we sip wine together. I continue my tale of woe "I don`t know what to do or what think. He definitely doesn`t have another woman as far as I am aware. He is at work or

Time for a Change

at home, he doesn`t hang out. In the evenings he sits at home playing on the computer or reading or sleeping. Ignoring me. I do not know what to do? I think I might go to see a sex therapist?"

"What, for three months, nothing at all?!!" my sister couldn`t believe it. "That isn't normal for a young couple"

"I know, I feel the same way. I do not know what to do? I do love him, I do not want to look for a lover. I don't have time for one as I am too busy with my life and the children. We have to re-establish our relationship, somehow. Hopefully, living apart now for a while, we will miss each other. Then everything will work out. I'm only twenty-seven, and he is only thirty-two. It is abnormal" I repeated.

We have finished our wine. Anya tells me about her new job. Also about how Alexei has sent her a message, inviting her to a restaurant so they can talk about if they have a future together or not. She`s still thinking and will take her time in replying to his request.

"Where did you meet Michael?" I ask teasingly.

"I met him in a restaurant. He's cool and kind. He cares for me but for now I don't have any attraction or feelings towards him. But maybe something will happen, someday. For now he's just a friend and it's nice for me to have a caring man around" Anya replied.

It was late by now and we needed to sleep as we both had a busy day planned for tomorrow. Anya stayed in the same room with Henry and me with Yana. We wished each other good night and went to sleep.

In the morning Anya cooked breakfast and had fun playing with Fanny. I fed and dressed the children. Called a taxi and went to my mother`s place.

On our way we brought Anya to work at her new salon.

Mom was glad when we arrived. I had tea with her, then I left my children there, they were excited with this. We agreed that I would buy a sim card and call her immediately to check that I have a good phone connection.

"If my children don't give you trouble, then I will see you in the evening" I said kissing my mother on the cheek.

Chapter 7

I'm free! The first step is to buy a sim card. At the news stand I buy one. Next I go into a cafe and order a piece of "Viennese" cake and an Espresso. There are a lot of free tables. I sit by the window. Ever since London I had a habit to sit in a café by the window and look at the passers-by. One of my favorite pass times. In London, I used to order a cappuccino and a croissant. Fixing my new sim card into my phone, I think "should I text Tim?" A sense of duty tells me that I should. However my heart resists this call of duty. So I decided to call my mother and Anya instead. When and if to text Tim, I will think about that later, while I am in the beauty salon.

Anya was glad I called. She told me to finish my coffee and come then immediately to her work. She has arranged my manicure with one of their best manicure technicians.

I found the salon quickly, Anya introduced me to the girls she now works with. Firstly, I had my acrylic nails done. Next, my nails were covered with daisies, each painted on. After that I had my eyebrows shaped.

Anya, meanwhile, finished her work and called someone a couple of times. And then she told me that she had to go on business for the salon.

This all sounded a bit mysterious to me, but I knew when she will be ready she will tell me what she is really up to.

When all the beauty treatments were over, I brushed my hair, refreshed my makeup and looked at myself in the mirror. I was wearing a blue silk dress. I was fresh, bright with a sexy glint in my eyes. I was ready for the world. However, sadly, I thought, I have no plans for the rest of the day.

Coming out of the salon, I had literally only walked three meters, when from the bench at the main entrance, a guy headed towards me. There was something familiar about him, I did not have time to think, what it was?

As he came up to me he addressed me with a surprised tone "Taya, is it you? I didn't recognize you at first!? Your hair is so different now".

I was in total shock. It was Ivan standing in front of me from our holidays last year. He was our summer bodyguard. "Hi Ivan" I just about managed to say in my shock. "What are you doing here?"

"I`m waiting for you Taya, for almost two hours. Anya told me you are coming, a week ago. I wanted to surprise you. Anya told me she had organized a salon treat for you. And with me, she arranged this meeting.

I had no words to express my shock "Ivan, I am very glad to see you" and I hugged him.

He was slightly embarrassed with this and said "you are so beautiful and this time without your baby tummy".

Time for a Change

"Well, I'm not an elephant, to be pregnant for two years!" I laughed in reply.

"Taya, I can`t believe my eyes. You're completely different. You are like a heroine in a fairytale".

"Ah thanks, you are too kind" I reply shyly and add "so where is Anya? Did she really go to the shop?"

"Probably yes, but I'm not fully sure" Ivan says doubtfully.

"I'm really hungry. Let's have a meal together, so that I don`t faint from hunger" I suggested.

"There is a very nice cafe of national Ukrainian cuisine near here. We can go there if you like" he offers gently.

Ivan took my hand as we strolled together. I accepted his hand and tried to relax with this unplanned but very pleasant encounter.

On our way, we talked easily. He enquired about my life in Ireland and my new baby daughter. I enjoyed answering his questions and replied with a light heart.

We entered the cafe. The interior is in the national Ukrainian style. It was known mainly to locals, so only a few tourists were present. We sat down at the table we were shown too.

"Taya, here they specialize in a delicious green soup and meat in pots. Does that sound like something you would enjoy to eat" he asks politely.

We ordered what Ivan recommended and also fruit-drink and beer. We were having cold beer as we waited for the soup. Ivan was talking and sharing with me about his life since we last met. He was telling about how he arrived in Kiev. He had arrived during winter and it was so cold. He had to search a lot to find suitable accommodation that was near to his job.

Our soup arrived. The green soup was really delicious. While waiting for the main course, I called Anya.

"How are you?" she answered cheerfully.

"I'm fine now, once I got over my shock! We are eating in the cafe, at Artema Street" I replied to her, pretending to be angry.

"Well, did I surprise you?" she asked excitedly.

"Yes, you did. It was a real surprise for sure. Ivan says "Hello" to you. Come here if you are free and join us for a coffee" I offered her.

"Ah thanks, but I can't. I still have things to do. See you in the evening time when you get home" answered my sister.

The food in this cafe is delicious. We ate and enjoyed the meat dishes. Finishing off the fruit-drink, I called my mum to find out how she was coping with the children.

Mum said that the children are asleep for their nap at this time. When they wake up later, she will feed them a snack and then they're going to go to the playground. Everything is going great and no need for me to worry or rush back for them. In fact, let them stay the night with her and I can pick them up tomorrow evening. That way I can spend a night out with Anya enjoying myself. She is just the best mum ever.

"I have a great mum" I say to Ivan. "She has offered to keep my children overnight so Anya and I can go out tonight and have some fun".

"I have cool mum too. I know that if you meet her, you will like her very much and she will like you also" Ivan replies with suggestion in his voice.

Blushing, I ask "And where does she work?"

Time for a Change

"She is a childminder in a creche" he answered proudly.

"Well, shall we go now?" I suggested.

"If you are ready to" agreed Ivan. He paid the bill and we left the cafe. We didn't yet set plans to spend any more time together that day so I headed towards the subway.

"Where are you going?" asked Ivan puzzled.

"I'm going home. I have to feed Fanny, that is Anya`s dog. My sister lives with me at the moment and her dog does too. On the way I will go to get the groceries. I have to prepare dinner for Anya. Then, now that my mum has kept my children overnight, we may decide to go out for the night" I answer factually.

"Can I come with you?" he pleaded, adding "You can relax, while I make dinner for you both? Have you forgotten that I`m a chef?"

It was a tempting offer. I didn't want to leave Ivan. He was friendly, open, funny and attractive. A nice guy you can talk too easily about everything and feel good about yourself in his company.

"Ok so. Come with me now. You can cook dinner for us" I agree. "Anya will be pleased too. We can enjoy catching up this evening".

On the way home we stopped at a supermarket. He bought food products which he was going to cook. We also took a bottle of brandy and delicious cake for desert.

"The house is in a mess" I apologized as we enter the apartment. "This morning I was rushing to pack up the children so everything is upside down now".

Fanny gladly greets us. I feed her and I went to walk the dog. I left Ivan to do the cooking.

Outside, I was suddenly met by my mother-in-law. She explains that since the heat had calmed down in the evening, she decided to go out shopping.

"Taya, why are you with a dog? And where are your children?"

"This is Anya's dog, Fanny. Don't you remember, she has a Spaniel? This summer she and Fanny have moved in to live with us" I respond to her queries.

"Taya, the dog will spoil all the carpets and furniture. It will also bark and you have to walk a dog. That's a lot of extra work on you. What about the children with the dog? What if it bites or scares them?" she chattered on and on making obstacles out of everything.

"We will be careful and she is a gentle dog. Today my children stay at my Mum's place. My mum offered to take them to give me a break and for her to spend time with them" I replied, losing patience.

"Taya, you also changed your hair color to blonde and changed your haircut?" she looked suspiciously at me.

"Yes, Mary. I like my new look very much".

"What is this blue dress? It's transparent! You're a married woman and should have respect for yourself!" she said in disgust.

"Mary" I laughed, "it should be like that. It's silk, it is not transparent, it's slinky and figure hugging. That's the design of it".

She sighed and said her goodbyes. She had stated her views clearly. She does not approve of anything I do. Not my hair, neither its color nor shape. Nor my dress either. She never has a good thing to say to me or about me.

Time for a Change

"Say "Hello" to Pasha from me" I say through gritted teeth as she departs.

Relieved and at home once again, I could smell delicious aromas from the kitchen. Fanny, with excitement rushed to the kitchen, hoping to get something delicious. Ivan gave her a couple of slices of cheese. She stayed in the kitchen. Faithfully looking into his eyes, hoping to get something else using her special technique.

"What are you cooking?" I asked as I was now hungry again.

"Meat, cooked in Mexican style, with salad. It's called "Caprice". For garnish we will have grilled vegetables. For our dessert we will have that delicious cake that you bought" he said smiling at me.

"Mmm, sounds great Ivan, keep cooking! I'll take a shower now".

I even didn`t have any thought to help him in the kitchen. He is a chef after all, so he knows a kitchen better than I.

After taking a shower, I made myself up. I put on a turquoise racer-back tank top, which effectively emphasized my bust. A gray-blue corduroy pants, with a low waist completed my outfit. I looked excellent.

Looking at myself in the mirror, I smiled and said, "Taya you are so lovely, I love you". I have learned to say this to myself a long time ago. I believe that if you do not love yourself, how can others.

In a good mood I returned to the kitchen. Dinner was almost ready. We`ve been waiting for Anya. I turned on the music, a collection of summer hits. Ivan continued cooking while I set the table. By seven o`clock in the evening my sister had come home.

"Oh", hi there Ivan. Wow, you cooked dinner for us?" joked Anya.

"I did. It is such a pleasure and an honor for me to cook for two such beautiful girls" smirked Ivan.

I suddenly realized, I do really like him. He is an honest, good person. He has pride but is not full of himself and has talents.

"Taya, you also bought drink? Well done" praised my sister. "I'm so hungry, for all day I only had coffee and cookies. I have been running around the city. Then I can finally come home to relax".

Ivan laid out the meat and salad on plates. He cooked wonderful grilled vegetables. He also has prepared some sauces. Although Ivan and I had eaten only a couple of hours ago, I was now eating his delicious dinner with a good appetite.

"So, how was my surprise?" asked Anya, invitingly.

"Well, I almost fainted with the shock when I saw him" I replied, slightly embarrassed.

"I had told him not to come over until the afternoon. It's not my fault he was so interested that he arrived hours too early!" teasingly she said.

"Oh I didn't mind waiting for such a beautiful lady. I was hoping you might finish early and I would be there for you then. I spent the time relaxing and smoking a couple of cigarettes. I was just sitting and reading a newspaper. Then you came out, a vision for my eyes" said Ivan seriously.

"The meal was delicious" I interrupted, to change the conversation as my cheeks were burning with his admiration.

"Maybe you'll cook us from time to time? We are so lazy" joked Anya.

Time for a Change

We raised a few toasts for this meeting and for future meetings too. We toasted the summer, for love and for life. Ivan drank this toast standing up, saluting us.

Our conversation next turned to our horoscopes.

"Taya is the Lion and the Snake. I'm Sagittarius and the Pig. Which birth sign are you Ivan?" asked Anya.

"I`m Cancer and the Dog" answered Ivan.

"Oh, so you have your birthday this month?" I asked.

Ivan hesitated, then said, "Yes, actually. It's today".

"Today?" we both asked simultaneously and surprised.

"Why aren`t you celebrating with your friends?" We asked him, staring at each other.

"I am celebrating it with my friends. Both of you! My best friend and other friends are all working. I have no other close friends in Kiev" answered Ivan.

"Well, at least we have a cake! Now we`ll find candles and you`ll make a wish! Get ready!" I smiled.

"We don't have a birthday gift for you" added Anya.

We sang to Ivan, "Happy Birthday". He closed his eyes and blew out his candles. I wondered what he had wished for?

At about nine o'clock, I called my mum. I was anxious to find out about how my children are. She tells me that they are already asleep. Mum is so pleased that she has my children in her company to take care of them. We agreed that, tomorrow evening, I`ll come to pick them up.

"Ivan, will you come and see us again? Anya, my children and I will stay together all summer. That`s why we need a cook and a friend, all in one" I said joking with him.

"Ivan, I know! We`ll give you the present of a nightclub! By the way, how old are you?" exclaimed Anya.

With this he got embarrassed and replied, "I`m twenty-one today".

I nearly choked on my tea. Twenty-one, he's still a kid! His adult life is only starting. In my heart I was hoping that he would be at least twenty-five.

"Come on! Let you two go to the club and dance the night away! I will call a taxi for you" Anya said with glee.

I tried to say something, but she cut me short saying, "don't argue, Taya. I haven`t been to a club for such a longtime. This will be our gift to Ivan. You take charge of him. You're the grown-up, so you mind him! I wish you both a good time!"

"And what about you?" asked Ivan.

"I`m very tired as I worked hard today. And tomorrow I work again from early morning. Ivan you don't start work until the evening tomorrow and Taya doesn't have the children until late afternoon. So you and Taya have all day long to sleep tomorrow".

Ivan did not expect such a turn of events. He was happy, but seemed confused. I put on a short denim skirt from Mexx and a silk top. The style is glamorous sporty. My sister refreshed my hairdo. I put on night time make-up and we finished our brandy.

Chapter 8

Coming out of the taxi, we plunged into the night life of Kiev. The evening was amazing. A cool wind soothed upon us. We walked along the Khreschatyk. There were lots of young people. Everyone moving from somewhere to go somewhere else. There were flower sellers who were offering bouquets to young people in love. The night atmosphere of the city was exciting and charged. We walked slowly. Ivan was smoking. I linked my arm, in his arm. We got to the Arena. Here there were many night clubs newly opened in the last few years.

For five years, I haven`t been in any night club in Kiev. It was now an interesting and unusual experience for me. Of course, I'm not an old granny, but inside I felt I didn't fit in to this type of place anymore. I mentioned this to Ivan. He confided that he too felt out of place here. This helped us both to relax as we had that in common.

There were many people in the club, but there were still free seats at the bar and tables too. We sat down at the bar, ordered a beer, and looked around. I noticed that most people had an age group of around twenty-three years old and above. Also there were a lot of foreigners, mostly Europeans. They smoked a hookah while they were entertained by young ladies. They were going to have a very pleasant night. We sat for a while, then we went to dance. Ivan was telling me something, but because of the loud music, I didn't hear him. But I was smiling and nodding.

We went out to take a breath of air and rest. It was hot inside. I was in great mood. A couple kissing were not far from us. We returned to the club to hang out for a while more. I did not want to sleep. But I had enough of dancing. I wanted to walk around the city by night to enjoy the balmy air and the lights.

"Ivan, let`s go for a walk around Kiev" I shouted over the music.

"Ok, let's go" he nodded.

So we left the noisy, hot night club. Where to go? I knew that I missed Kiev. But in my joy, I did not know where to go.

"Let's go to the Podol" Ivan suggested.

We passed Khreschatyk, European Square and walked down to the bank of the Dnieper. Near the water it was colder, even slightly too chilly. In Ireland, it can be colder, I thought and walked faster.

"Taya, are you cold?" asked Ivan concerned.

"Yes, just a little" I answered "let's have coffee somewhere and I`ll get warm".

But it`s not so easy to find coffee at three o'clock in the morning. It`s good that we saw and remembered McDonald's on our way. It turned out that we were also by now hungry again. Ivan ordered a coffee and a meal deal. We were then refreshed and warmed up. After this we went for a walk down the promenade.

"Ivan, do you miss your home place?"

"No, not too much. I call my mother often. My brother Alexii works away from home too. He lives in Yalta with his girlfriend for three years. My mother and stepfather both work, so that keeps them busy and happy. So I don't think too much about home. My friends have all left and gone in different directions. Here, my friend Alexander, stays with me. He has recently become acquainted with a girl. I don't have time to miss home as I work a lot.

"And do you miss your brother?"

"Yes, I miss Alexii. We haven`t seen each other for three years, since he left home. I'll tell you about him later" he said with a reluctant tone in his voice.

"You know, Ivan, my first dawn experience, I saw here, with my school class on the banks of the Dnieper. It was after our prom dance. In the mornings, dozens of buses filled with graduates come here to experience the dawn. It is a memorial to Lybid. Do you know the story of the legend of Kiev?"

"No, I don't" he confessed.

"Well, I will tell you so. In the fifth century, the three brothers Kyi, Schek, Khorom and their sister Lybid, floated down the Dnieper and saw the hills and forests. They stopped here and liked this place. And they decided to build a city here. They decided to name it "Kiev" in honor of Kyi. The river that flows through Kiev, was given the name "Lybid" in honor of their sister. Khreschatyk, the center of the city was named in honor of the middle brother Schek. The highest hill was called Horalova Mount, in honor of the youngest. That's the story of the foundation of Kiev. The story has a great history. Kiev is a great city" I finished my tale smugly.

I began to remember lots of other city tales and to share them with Ivan. I was having fun. I wanted to run and jump, to talk about everything. I was myself again. I was simply Taya!

With the first subway train we got home. Fanny heard our noise, and growled with displeasure as we had disturbed her at the door.

"Ivan, go and sleep on the sofa in the living room. Cover yourself with a blanket" I pointed to the door of the living room.

"I'll go to sleep next to Anya. She has to get up in two hours".

I heard Anya get up and get ready to walk Fanny. I put on my silk robe and went into the kitchen to say "good morning" to her.

She was just finishing her coffee and getting ready to leave. "How was your evening?" she asked me with interest.

"It was great. We even dropped into McDonald's at three in the morning! We also walked from the Postal Square to Osokorky!

"Where is the Ivan now, sleeping in your bed?" she asked, wanting gossip.

"No", I protested. "Be quiet, he`s sleeping in the living room".

"And why he did not go home?" she continued to tease.

"Well, I thought, as it was so late when we got in that I should let him sleep here. In the afternoon, I'll send him home".

"Taya, do not seduce the youngster!" joked Anya.

"Don't talk such nonsense, Anya. I'm going to sleep now once you've gone".

"Lucky you. All I have to look forward to is a day in work" and with that she was gone.

I poured some water for myself and then one for Ivan. I went into the living room. He was sleeping on his side, without his shirt, but still in jeans. I feasted my eyes on him for a moment. I put the glass of water down quietly and left. Tim is an idiot, just a jerk, I thought. You can't turn down sex with your wife. Especially when she is young and beautiful. And most important of all, turn it down for no apparent reason, and to advise me to go seek it elsewhere. What an insult.

A wave of resentment rolled on me again. Frustration, resentment, anger were all bursting inside of me. Why? When I did everything for my husband does he not appreciate and respect me. Why? When you give the whole of you, down to the last piece, that it is not appreciated. I was so upset and angry then that I didn't want to sleep.

I called Fanny, "How are you today my dear pet" I say to her as I pat her. I begin to share my troubled heart and thoughts with her as she gazes up at me with big understanding eyes. "Fanny, I feel abandoned. I was faithful and loving towards my husband and what for? All I get is alienation and rejection. He has lost his desire for me! Asshole! Do you agree, Fanny?" she was looking into my eyes. "You are such a good pet, come with me to take a nap".

Lucky Ivan, he can sleep and isn't sad about family relationships. I hugged Fanny and fell asleep.

I was awakened by knocking at my bedroom door. Looking at the clock, it is already twelve! With a fright Fanny ran away from me.

"Come in Ivan" I said, lying under my bed sheets in my dressing-gown.

"Hi, Taya, how are you today? Do you have a headache?" he asked smiling at me.

"I`m fine. I will take a shower and will be like a new penny" I replied jokingly and added "and how are you? Are you ok?"

"Yes, thanks, I am good. Can I take a shower here?" he asked with hesitance.

"Yes, of course. I will give you towels. I stood up from the bed allowing my naked leg to lead first from under the bed clothes. Naughtily I was thinking, at least I can let Ivan appreciate and admire me.

Blushing he went to the shower. I prepared tea and sandwiches for both of us then. I quickly went to the bathroom to freshen up. I didn`t change from my silky dressing-gown.

"Ivan, while you were taking your shower I prepared breakfast for us" I said to him playfully.

I knew I was starting to have an attraction and feelings for him. But I also knew that I don`t know much about him. My inner thoughts were doing battle against each other. "Taya, all in its own time! And now you're not in great shape after a sleepless night to "Seduce a boy!" This was my internal dialogue. I've always lived in peace within myself. I usually don`t argue with my inner voice. My inner voice is wise and has never lets me down.

Ivan came out from the shower, all fresh, even though he is still in yesterday's T-shirt. "Taya thank

Time for a Change

you, I feel so much better now" he said, looking straight into my eyes and trying not to look below my neck line.

I sat so that the robe slightly fell baring my upper chest and shoulder. I saw his embarrassment and not making anything of it, I asked "Do you first go home and then go to work?"

"Yes, I have to shave and change clothes".

"Good and I'll take a shower, then go to buy berries for my children. After that I'll go to my mum's to pick them up" I said it as careless as I could.

"Taya, may I have your cell phone number and home phone number please. I'll call you. Maybe sometime soon, if you have some free time we can meet to have some coffee? Or I can come here and cook for you and your children and spend an evening together? Ivan asked hopefully.

I agreed with his suggestions and gave him my numbers. Ivan left then and he seemed happy with himself.

I spent the evening at my mum`s place. The children were delighted to see me again and had lots of stories to tell me of the time they had. Henry was showing his new toys, cuddling me and playing the fool. Anya called us and asked that we wait for her to arrive before we start dinner so she can join us.

"Taya, what do you think about Anya`s Alex? I am distressed for them. I can feel my blood pressure rising and my heart aches when I think about their expected divorce" said my mum with a worried look on her face.

"I know mum, it is awful. But what can you or I do to change it? We can do nothing except to support Anya. Since he continues to drink and won't try to stop and get help. He even borrowed money from my grandmother! He put items into a pawnshop too! How can she continue to live with him? God has not sent them children for three years, maybe now that's a blessing. I do not know. Anya has suffered a lot. He does not listen to his parents, he listens to no one. Good friends have left him too. It`s hard of course. But I do not see any other way" I replied sadly. "Mum, try not to think about them too much. You can`t change anything. We just have to accept any changes for them and stay united for her".

"We shall see. He may still come to his senses" sighed mum.

Anya rang the doorbell. Henry joyfully ran to see who was there? "Mom, its Anya!" he gleefully exclaimed. Anya came in. Henry was so excited to see her. Anya looks tired and distracted with worry about something.

"Hi, darling, we`re waiting for you, mum has fried yummy pancakes, your favorite especially for you" I said looking at her with concern.

We ate our dinner leisurely. Telling each other the latest news in our lives. It was always like this, from our childhood days. Mum is and has always been our friend. We always like to sit in the kitchen and tell her everything that is happening to us. We share all our dreams and all our worries.

"Mum, Anya, I miss you both so much when I am in Ireland. These evenings in particular I miss. When we sit quietly, have tea and chat with no hurry. I listen to you and you both listen to me. I feel so lonely now a lot of the time as Tim stays at his computer. I`m fed up with him. He plays for the whole evening" I confide in them.

Time for a Change

They are listening to my monologue, so I continue "Mum, you know. I thought that after having children, couples become closer together? We have just the opposite! We only talk to each other as needed. We don't share our deepest thoughts and feelings anymore. Mum, I'm scared. To realize in ten years that instead of unity, we`re on different paths" I begin to feel tears well up in my eyes as my hear breaks to hear the raw truth spill from my mouth.

"Oh, my girl it is because of tiredness and because of the routine of existence of everyday life. He`s tired, you're tired! He is a good man, he is quiet, does everything for you and your children. He works really hard. Be patient, get some rest. I'll help you during your holiday with your children so you will have renewed energy. Anya will live with you and you both can support each other. Tim will come here and everything will work out in time" mum was trying to calm me.

"Yes" I tried to agree and wanted to believe her. "Mum, don't worry, everything will be fine. Perhaps, it is really because of the routine of life and the children" I sighed.

Mum called a taxi for us and we went home. On our way my children fell asleep in the car. Fanny woke them up, with her barking as soon as Anya put the key in the door. Henry started to cry as he was frightened with the barking. Yana opened her eyes and scolded the dog with her finger. Anya went with Fanny for a walk and quiet was restored to all again. I put the children to bed. Only then did I realize how damn tired I was. By the time Anya returned from her walk we were both too tired to talk anymore and we were happy to go to bed.

The children woke up early the next morning. I turned on cartoons for them and continued to have a light nap. Anya had a day off so she too continued to rest.

By mid-day we were both up and about and feeling more alive again. "After we have a snack now, let's bring the children to the lake or the beach. What do you think Taya?" suggested Anya.

I agreed whole heartedly. A day out together would be good for all of us. I prepared the snack and we ate quickly. Then I prepared the children for the day out. We collected our things like toys and little shovels. We took playing cards for ourselves so that we too had something to do to pass the time. To be completely happy, we even decided to take Fanny. She loved to swim and we can let her run around too. We called a taxi and all together we entered the lift. Suddenly, it stops not on the ground floor, but on the fourth floor. The door opens and my father-in-law, Pasha, gets in.

"Good morning" he greets us. "And where are you all going?"

"Good morning" I reply. "We are off to the beach for the day".

He stood still for a second. I was waiting for his negative comments and sure enough he didn't disappoint. "To the beach, yeah! Have you forgotten that there is only mud and dirty water there! You can't swim and you are at risk of catching a disease too". He would have continued to speak further, but we were saved as our taxi was waiting for us as we stepped off the lift.

"Bye Pasha!" I wave and give the sweetest smile, just to annoy him even more.

Time for a Change

"Anya, he doesn't know about the existence of clear lakes and private beaches" I whisper to my sister.

"And don't explain it to him either or else he will want to join us next time" she responds under her breath and laughs.

The children are messing around. They are having such fun playing in the sand and splashing in water puddles. Their happiness has no limits. We sunbathed as we looked after the children. Fanny was happily running around but staying near us and not causing any trouble.

Out of the blue my sister asked me "So, what's between you and Ivan?"

Surprised by her question I reassure her that we are just friends. I enjoy his company as he is a sincere funny person and is easy to talk too.

"And do you like him?" she teases me.

"He reminds me of our Artem" I reply factually.

"Mmm, I often wonder where is Artem and what happened to him?" she says thinking, "Our only cousin and he vanished without a trace!"

"It would be cool to see him" I said dreamily. "He's already twenty-four years old. He's probably tall and handsome" I continue.

"Yes I agree, Taya. Ivan does have the look of Artem".

After some more rest, we decide to play cards. We just dealt the cards and I receive a message.

"Is it from Tim?" inquired Anya.

"No, it's from Ivan" I laugh. "I have not yet texted to my foolish husband. He hasn't called me either! Let's not talk about him, it puts me in bad form". I read Ivan's text aloud "Taya, good morning. How are you and your children? What plans have you for today? From Ivan".

"That's how it all starts" explained Anya.

"What shall I reply?"

"Text that you`re sunbathing, warming your ass!" she laughs. "Or, Ivan my sweet kitty, hurry fast to me. I`m waiting and missing you" joked Anya.

Not following this foolishness I texted, "Hi, we are fine. We are on the beach sunbathing, swimming and relaxing. Taya".

When the children got tired, we then had our snack and later on we went home. Once at home, we put the children to bed. I then went to the store to buy yummy food for our dinner. I also took also a bottle of wine for the evening. I was tired after our day out in the hot sun.

"I'm exhausted from the sun and heat" I grumbled to Anya on my return.

"Me too" nodded Anya in agreement.

We went to our separate rooms so we could have a rest, while the children were asleep.

That evening Tim phoned, "Hello, how are you?" he asked cheerfully.

"Yes we are all well. We went to the beach today" I continued to update him on all of our activities.

"Taya" he interrupted, "You've already been there for a week and you still haven`t visited my parents? You live at the same apartment block, just on different floors" he scolded. "Is it so hard to drop by them in the evening with the children?"

I offered an answer "we see each other from time to time. Last night I meet Mary when I was outside at the shops. This morning we meet Pasha. What do

Time for a Change

you want from me?" I was losing my patience. "They are not in a hurry to see their grandchildren either. Ask them why?" I demanded. "They brought no toys, neither candies during this week. You know what they are like. They argued about who Yana looks like when we arrived. They are like Tatar-Mongols and not like loving devoted grandparents!" I protested.

"Taya, calm down. Ask them to stay with the children in the mornings or to go for a walk with them to the playground, when it`s not too hot. Do try to do this" he pleaded.

"If you want this, then you call and tell them. I`m fed up with their negative comments to me always!" I stopped speaking.

"Taya, try to be soft with them, they are elderly" he continued.

Oh, I was burning with anger. He can see no wrong when it comes to his parents. I can barely hold myself from shouting back at him. "Well, Tim, I have no more to say to you on this matter. I'm glad that you are fine. Kiss you, goodbye!" and with that I hang up.

In about half an hour, Mary called with an offer "It`s already eight o`clock. We can go to the playground with children now if you like?" she suggested strongly leaving me no option but to agree.

"Don't you usually watch the News at this time, or the soaps?" I taunted.

"Well, yes that's true. But Tim called and he was angry that we don't spend time with you and your children while you are here on holidays. We promised him we would help you and that we could go with them to the playground in the evening" she admitted.

I thought to myself "what a sacrifice for you! You would do this because your son asks, but not when I ask!" But I said aloud "Ok so, call by at eight. We will be ready".

"Anya" I implore her "open a bottle of wine, I have to distress after talking on the phone to Mary!" We have a glass of wine and leave the bottle on the table.

At eight, my parents-in-law arrive to collect the children. I went to the kitchen to get a feeding bottle for Yana. Mary followed me. No doubt to see how clean the kitchen is and to make some comment on it.

In our absence she loved to fumble through our drawers or the fridge. She is so nosy. Then she will criticize the contents of your fridge or the groceries in your press. I've gotten used to her behavior a long time ago and the best I can do is to ignore it.

With her beady eye, Mary saw the opened bottle of wine on the table. Then she noticed the two half-full glasses of wine. She was shocked and made no attempt to hide it. She scolded, "Taya, you drink too much. Do you drink wine on your own? And without any guests? Tim has entrusted his children to you!"

"Mary" I answer strongly, "people all over the world drink wine from wine glasses. Only rednecks, drink from shot glasses! I am not drinking alone, my sister and I are enjoying the bottle together" I could not hold back. She was shocked by my curtness.

"You have come to collect the children? Here you go! In one and a half hours I will be waiting for you to return home with them". I handed her a baby bottle with milk in it for Yana. Pointed to the door and waved goodbye to the children. She left confused.

Time for a Change

When she had left I said to my sister "That`s it Anya, we are alcoholics in her eyes! So pour some more wine! We had our delicious dinner. Anya joked and I laughed all during our meal.

"Let's remove the bottle. She`ll have a heart attack if she finds out we've finished it!" Anya continued.

"No such luck that she will have a heart attack. She is more likely to give me one with all her negative attitude to me" I add.

We went to walk Fanny and plan on meeting the children at the playground. On our way back we can pick them up, thus not letting Mary back into our house.

Ivan texted a couple messages during the next couple of days with various contents and requests. I had replied a few of times, now I decided to call him. He had offered to help with the children or to meet up for a meal or a coffee. I had refused.

Chapter 9

These days, I was busy with meeting my friends and keeping the children busy and happy. After two days, my best friend Oksana came from Ireland. She has a stopover in Kiev. She could not cope alone with her children. I promised to meet her in Boryspil and help her to get to the train station.

I decide to call Ivan to ask for his help. I explained to him, that if he is available, I will need him to accompany me to the airport to meet my best friend. This will be in two days time. I will need him to help me take her and her children, with their luggage, to the train station.

He agrees as he is off work then and is keen to please me.

Now that he has me on the phone he asks eagerly "what are you going to do in the evening today?"

"The usual routine" I reply, "I will go for a walk with children, then to the playground, or maybe to the park, if the evening is nice and cool".

"Can I join you, about six? I have a day off, I switched places at work. I work the whole day tomorrow. I would enjoy time with your children in the playground and you can introduce me to them".

"Ok so" I agree. "By the way, buy two liters of milk, a cake cheese and butter on the way" I make a request, knowing he won't refuse.

"Great, I`ll be with you at six. See you, Snow White" (his pet name for me since he saw me last time at our apartment) he hung up, before I could reply.

I cleaned the apartment. First, I brought the children to Mary, so they don`t get in my way. I washed the floors and aired the rooms. I sat to drink a glass of cold water and admire my hard work. Good! I love cleanliness. I smiled to myself.

I phone Anya to arrange the evening plans. "Anya hi. I plan on going for a walk in the evening with the children. I've cleaned everywhere. I won't cook this evening. Is that OK? What time will you be home?"

"About eight" she replies. "Don't worry about the cooking. I'll eat somewhere in town. Thanks for the cleaning. Kisses. See you later" and she's gone.

Wonderful, I thought. I took out a green light chiffon tunic, with small white polka dots. It suits perfectly this kind of weather. I changed my clothes and put on make-up. I went to pick up the children. My father-in-law is resting as he had a headache from the heat. My mother-in-law is silent. I was relieved as that saved me from wasting time on idle chat with them. I thanked them for their help and left quickly.

Henry and Yana loved to go out with buckets and shovels. Henry was romping with his toy car. Ivan joined us in the playground then.

"Children, this is Ivan" I said introducing him to my children. They turned their heads in his direction.

"This is Henry, my favorite boy, he`s three years old. This is Yana, my sweetest girl. She`s ten months old. Isn`t she pretty?" I introduced my children to Ivan.

"I can`t believe she was in your tummy. Such a lovely baby! So cute!" he said delighted. "Look, Henry, drags something in his mouth" jumped Ivan.

"It's probably a cigarette butt! They are idiots, those who throw away cigarette butts! And the children find them in their sandbox". I went over quickly to Henry and removed the butt from his hand saying "Henry that's dirty, Ugh, drop it! A bad guy was smoking that".

On our walk time had flown by easily. Having come home, it was time to prepare the children for bed. Ivan went to the shower to wash Henry, and I was busy with Yana. The evening was glorious we were sitting on the couch, talking and eating ice cream. The mood was excellent. "It is good that he came" I thought.

By nine o'clock, the children fell asleep. We went out onto the balcony. Ivan was smoking he held a cigarette differently, in his own way. We watched the passers-by.

"Get down!" I suddenly pushed him to the couch as he had been standing on the balcony.

"What?" he was dumb struck and confused.

I kept watching the street. It was my parents-in-law, out walking for the evening. Mary as usual raised her head and looked up at our balcony. I waved to her. Then, the father-in-law looked, I waved to him. They ceremoniously turned the corner arm-in-arm.

"Phew. Thank God! They have passed by. You can get up now!" I instructed Ivan.

Time for a Change

"What was the problem? Would they be angry if they saw me standing and smoking?" Ivan wondered.

"Ivan, you have never met my parents-in-law! Believe me, the less they know, the better they sleep!" I said pointedly. "Give me a cigarette" with the shock I wanted to smoke.

"Taya, you don't smoke, do you?"

"What's the difference? I smoke or I do not smoke? Today I will smoke!" I replied.

He pulled out a cigarette and lit it for me.

"I love the evening time. The children are asleep. Summer evenings are long and warm. Many things can be done" I say dreamily, smoking a cigarette. Strange, when I smoke, I get a sense of confidence and freedom. Cigarettes have a strange effect on me! This is probably because I smoke once in five years!

Ivan was looking at the dog that was trying to jump up on all passers-by and people were rushing away from her.

"Do you have a girlfriend?" I asked suddenly. I didn't understand, why I asked him.

"No I don't" he replied indifferently.

"Did you ever have a girlfriend?" I asked filled with curiosity.

"Yes, I had, when I was in school, in my graduation class. We were together for about a year. I was studying in college by then".

"And what happened then? Did you love her?" I pressed on.

"I guess not. I liked her a lot and we used to go out to nightclubs. Nothing serious really" He was saying this without showing signs of any emotions.

It was clear to me that it was nothing serious.

"You`ve been for six months in Kiev and still haven`t met a beautiful girl? There's a lot of waitresses' working with you. You work in a big restaurant with plenty of possibilities" I was interested to know why he remained unattached.

"Everyone I work with is either married or has a boyfriend. Anyway, I'm not interested in any of them" he protested.

"You`re only twenty-one! It`s summer outside and this is the time in your life for fun with the ladies!" I said teasing him.

He said nothing and lit another cigarette. My cigarette had extinguished a long time ago. I no longer wanted to smoke.

"Finish your cigarette and then let us eat cold strawberries" I said to lighten the atmosphere and went back inside the apartment.

Ivan remained on the balcony alone, with his cigarette and his thoughts.

It was late and Anya still hadn't arrived home after working late. I switched the TV to watch a comedy "Love-joy". We were watching this and eating strawberries and laughing so much that we didn't hear Anya come in.

"Hi" she greeted. I noticed she looked tired. "Oh, we have a guest!" she smiled and went into the bathroom.

"Ivan is just leaving" I shouted into the bathroom to her. "He just came over so I wouldn`t be bored and to help me with the children". Following him to the door, I thanked him for the evening and his company.

I then quickly reminded him, "See you the day after tomorrow. At eight in the morning. Don't be late!" I goaded him.

Time for a Change

"I'll be there" he said cheerfully. "Good night, sisters" and he left.

"How was your day?" I asked my sister when she came out of the bathroom.

"Can you imagine, I am coming out of the salon to go home, when suddenly Alex appears? Unannounced, unexpected and sober! He has a suit on too. He had sent me several text messages, but I didn't reply to any of them. So he decided to visit me as he wanted to talk about our future. We went for a pizza. He talked, I listened. He says the same sort of things over and over again. How much he loves me. That he hasn't been drinking for over two weeks now. Let's start everything from the beginning again. Let's try to live together as a married happy couple" she draws a deep breath.

With a wavering voice she continues her tale of the encounter. "As he is speaking I am looking at him and thinking. Here he sits in front of me (because it suits him now) complaining, depending on my pity. Pulling memories from our past, using them to beg me to come back to him. He's pathetic, this man I loved, for whom I lived. The man was my future and filled my dreams. What is he now? I hate when somebody uses pity to get what they want from you" continued Anne. "In summary, we had dinner together. He told me that his friend is getting married soon. He asked me to go with him the wedding ceremony. I promised him I would think about it. He updated me then about his parents. He was also asking about you and your children. The evening was such a failure" she added sadly. "We said goodbye. I called a taxi and came home to you. I`m so utterly exhausted" she finished up. "I'm off to bed. Good night, Taya. Thanks for listening to me as always".

I cleared up after the dinner I had eaten with Ivan and went to bed with a heavy lonely heart.

The weather is hot every day now. I can feel the heat even first thing in the morning. The next morning I wake up early as I couldn't sleep. My mind and emotions all over the place. Anya also couldn't sleep well. The children are awake and keen to start their day with playing. I go into my sister's bedroom. "I'll stay with you for a while. I'm too lazy to start my day just yet. I want to share with you my cool dream" I tell her excitedly.

"What dream?" Anya asks lazily.

"In my dream, I saw a stranger about thirty years old. A man I don't recognize. He is average height with blond hair and muscular. He takes my hand tightly and leads me to the mountains. It seems that it is happening on an island in the sea. Around, the water is clear, azure, the bottom is visible. Even though I do not know him, I go with confidence even joy, with him. We climb to the top. Once there he asks me "Will you marry me?" His eyes are adoring and gentle. He is filled with kindness, love and passion for me. In this glimpse is my future. A future filled with so much love, that, my head is spinning with happiness. I answered "Yes, I will marry you". He gently embraced me, we start to kiss. He holds me so closely that I can hear his heart beating. I can taste his mouth on mine. His lips are driving me crazy. A light breeze blew on us and the smell of the mountains and the sea bewitched us . . .

I woke up then and the feeling of happiness and joy remained with me on waking. I can still feel the pressure of his kiss on my lips. It all felt so real" I finished up and my cheeks were ablaze with the memories.

Time for a Change

"Yeah, that`s a good one" Anya was now sitting up in bed with both eyes now fully open. She stretched herself, with pleasure, like a cat. "If you stay horny for any longer, you`ll see not only strangers in the mountains in your dreams!" she scoffed. "This time, tell me, what is it between you and Ivan?" She just won't let this one go, I acknowledge in my head.

"Well, nothing, really. He hasn`t got a girlfriend. When he was seventeen years old, there was someone. A casual girlfriend from his school days to early college years" I repeat what he told me last night.

"Ah, that's sad and he is such a nice attractive young man" Anya commented.

"Tomorrow Oxana arrives. Ivan has agreed to help me fetch her from the airport with her children and luggage. I will bring my children to our mother. She has a day off" I explained.

"Ok, let's get up. Who will walk Fanny?" inquired my sister.

"You do it and I'll cook breakfast" I offered.

I checked my phone. There were two messages. The first was from Ivan and the second was from my friend. Ivan had texted me "Taya, thank you for the evening. I'm very happy with you and your children. Good night, Snow White".

The second text was from my friend. She was requesting to meet at noon, for a coffee. I couldn`t have coffee with her as my children are with me all day. So I sent her a message and invited to my place for coffee instead.

I decided to surprise and delight Ivan so I called him. "Good morning, how did you sleep? This is Snow White" I said, smiling with my very soft voice.

"Good morning" he was dumb struck a little. "I had a good sleep. I am in work now. We are not too busy now but it will be much busier at lunchtime. Now I am on my coffee break. Thanks for calling, such a nice surprise! How are your children today?" he asked.

"They are good, thanks. "They are playing now. We will stay at home today. In the evening I will take them to visit their grandparents.

"You don't visit them much, do you?" he questioned.

"Yes I do, when I can" I answered more sharply than I had intended too. "All right, have a nice coffee break" I wanted to say goodbye now as I was irritated.

"Before you go, are we still meeting tomorrow morning?" he asked softly.

"Oh yes! My friend is depending on us. I will be ready for you at eight in the morning. Bye!" I was gone off the phone in a flash.

"So, how's Ivan doing?" asked Anya as she came back from her walk with Fanny. "What did he have to say to you?" she enquired suggestively as she made sandwiches.

"Well, nothing at all really. We just talked in general" I updated her as I made the tea.

"Yeah, you and he have a strange relationship" reflected my sister aloud.

"The question is, do I need him or not in my life? I know I am starting to have strong feelings for him. But he is so much younger than me!" I confess to her.

"Ah, come on. Six years, is not such a big age difference! You'll tell him what to do, how to love a woman! You'll have to role-play with him as "teacher and student"! Such scope of fun you could have with him!" she is joking of course, isn't she?

"It's an attractive offer" I smile in reply. Could I handle such an interesting possibility? "I'd have to read books on this matter" I joke further "you never know what young people are interested in now days!" Breakfast passed in such adult talk and much laughter.

Chapter 10

The children were busy with puzzles. They had new pictures, which they pieced together, Yana had maxi puzzles and Henry had Thomas and Friends. I had some free minute so I decided to call Tim. We hadn't spoken to each other for five days now. Tim was glad I phoned. We spoke briefly, about our children, about me but nothing personal. During this conversation I realized that nothing has improved between us and spend ten more minutes on nonsense talking then finish up the call.

"Be calm! Just be calm" I thought. "Do not let yourself wither!" I remembered the inscription on the postcard. It showed a cactus in the shape of penis. I smiled, this card, Tim had sent me to London many years ago. Yes, at that time his mood was clearly different from his present one. What happens to a person? We date a person, think we get to know them. Fall in love and marry them, only to discover we don't know them at all or maybe even like them. Then we move on and have an affair to fill the void. Such thoughts were running one after another through my head, like a short film.

I was standing by the phone, looking in silence at the handset and felt completely lost. This is the state where my brain works in ultrafast mode. When I'm in a daze, staring into space, I deal with the situation. Usually, it brings clarity and relief. The situation is solved in my favor. I was afraid of this state, I did not like to make problems and then to solve them. But I obviously can't escape and hid from such real and true problems in my life.

Yana interrupts my thoughts. She is sitting on the floor and playing with Fanny. The dog is licking her palms and Yana is laughing. She has a very infectious laugh.

I smile and come out of that brain freeze. My decision is made. My desire to live has returned. I go to the children`s room. I have bailed on the phone and on Tim.

At noon my friend Lily arrives as planned. We have not seen each other in about a year. She had lots of news to tell me. I cook our lunch. She brought a bottle of "Pinot Grigio" and we sat down to talk.

She is twenty-five. We have known each other for about eight years now, from my time in London. We could always speak free and easy to each other, we are good company together. We don't waste time on stupid questions such as. "How is life in Ireland?" Lily, has been living in England for five years now. She knows that life in Ireland is similar to life in England. She looks great and is been in good spirits.

"Taya, listen" she rubbed her hands. "I have a boyfriend! He is six years younger than me too!"

I nearly fell off my chair. I smiled, encouraging her to continue.

"We met at the gym. He even thought I was younger! He has been going there for a year now and before this but we never even saw each other!" She is telling me all excited as we sip our wine and eat salmon. "We meet in Jacuzzi. After that he invites me to the bar in the evening, a couple of times. That`s how it all started. You know, he is something! At first sight he does seem so young for me. But no, he is kind, from a well-educated family. He studies foreign languages, in his third year now. He is caring and we are head over heels in love" she glows.

"Wow, Lily, that's so cool!" was all I could say in my surprise.

"Can you imagine, we are together now for six months. He lives with his mother. I do not know how much she knows about me! For sure he didn't tell her my age!" Lily was laughing.

"Lily, so what about your age? Twenty-five years old is still so young and he is nineteen so it's no big deal" I add reassuringly "Don`t think about his mother".

"Well, it's not only about his mother I have to worry about. There are his work colleagues too!" said Lily.

"Why, where does he work?"

"He works for women's magazine!" she explodes.

"Ah now I can understand. Yeah, that's funny" I laugh.

"Well, imagine! He's surrounded by mature women all day. His "Aunties" said Lily trying to keep a straight face.

Time for a Change

"Look at you. You`re a young, sexy woman! You look awesome. You don`t even look your age. You have already been married and now you tempt an employee of women's magazine and he is six year's your junior!" I praise her in a jesting manner.

"What's his name?" I asked next.

"Robert. For me it's an unusual name. His mother is Jewish and his father is Italian" Lily said proudly.

"Now I understand how he can be so macho, this handsome man of yours! He has such a great mixture! You will have a passionate time with him but he could be moody too with that level of hot blood!" I said with envy.

Lily looked like a girl from Nekrasov novels. She was pale-skinned, blue eyed, with gorgeous blond long hair. She had full lips and a mysterious expression. She is tall, slim, but with large breasts, which were the envy of her many friends. She didn`t have any lack of attention from men of any age. She is good mannered too. She is the only daughter to intelligent loving parents. She almost resisted her feelings for Robert. She lives with her mother. Even with all of her beauty, she is a modest and intelligent girl. She has completed her Degree and then her Masters in Economics. She is working for a European company as an Economic Consultant. She speaks German and English fluently.

I know that the relationship with Robert has shaken her world. I know this as I can tell by her appearance and her burning eyes when she speaks of him. We have coffee and she fills me in on our common friends.

Then she asks, with concern in her voice, "What`s wrong with you? I know you for a long time now so I can read you. You seem to be listening to me but you are distracted by something else? What has happened?"

Wearily I reply "It all depends on what you mean. Nothing has really happened yet. Tim is probably having a mid-life crisis. Our relationship, in my opinion, has hit a wall. Basically, nothing like this has ever happened to us before. It seems that we live together, do everything together, we share interests and friends but we have nothing to talk about. I am very sad and I don't know how long more I can put up with this situation. My mother tries to calm me telling me that "everything will be fine in time". That he will join us here and we will get to relax together. We have a holiday, for just the two of us, booked to Turkey" I was pouring my heart out to her and trying to convince myself that mum is right "everything will be fine".

"Taya you both have been together for ten years now. You're both just tired with work and the children" my friend tried to calm me.

"Lily, I know, maybe that's true. But am I not still sexy at twenty seven years old!? I can't stand it. Tim rejects all my advances, it's destroying my very soul.

She looks at me puzzled "I don't understand, in what sense does he reject you?"

"We have had no sex for three months. None at all! We have had no sex with feelings for a long time now. It crushes me inside. I feel old and useless. You know, he insulted me also and now I don't even want to see his face or hear his voice. He arrives in three weeks. I am in a confusion. I don't know what he will do. Do I forgive him or do I try to continue to live with him?" I am in anguish and despair.

Time for a Change

"Taya, what about the children?" Lily asked frantically. "Maybe he is gay or has another woman?" she assumed thoughtfully.

"Let's stop talking about him. There is no other woman, although I`m not sure about anything anymore". I wanted to change the topic.

"I still think you two will stay together. All things like this must pass. You have loved him all your life. You are doing everything for him. You have to think about yourself, there is no escaping him" said Lily.

"Do you remember? I was telling you about our journey to the sea with Anya last year at Koktebel".

"Yes" replied Lily.

"Well, there was a guy I meet there! By the way, he and I have the same age difference as you and Robert! In short, now he is working here in Kiev. We meet each other as friends. He visited me and Anya on a few occasions. On the one hand there is nothing serious. On the other, I like him and he seems to like me too. He does not have a girlfriend. We`ve been to a night club together. Tomorrow, he is helping me with my friend. He promised me he would accompany me to the airport and help with her children and their luggage. I do not know how it will end, but I have feelings for him. He's so cool and he looks at me with dreamily with love in his eyes. I know that look" I sigh.

"So, try your luck. Live it up with him. What do you have to lose? Look at you, a woman in the prime of your life. Make love and don`t get out of bed! Your husband is a Fool! Who is to blame? If I were you I would live it up with him. And then see what happens" advised Lily.

"What about the six years difference in age? How do you manage that?" I was saying.

"Believe me, my experience, it means they have a lot of "get-up-and-go", all night, if you get my meaning!" she winked at me.

I sighed and said that I would have to think about it.

By now my children have woken up. Lily enjoyed playing with them. She cuddled them, stayed a little longer than planned and then started to get ready to go home. She had a couple calls from her "darling Robert" during these hours. I could see she is very happy. I was pleased for her. I always knew how to be happy for other people. I loved that quality in myself. I will use that quality now to give me my strength back to face my uncertain future.

"Thank you for coming. It was so great to see you and to hear all your news! Thank you too for the gifts for my children. I'll call you in a couple of days" I promised as I closed the door behind her.

The children had yogurts and we began to get ready to go my mother`s place. I called a cab. The children were happy they loved to travel by car.

We arrived at my mother's about six. She was waiting for us outside.

"Hi, my two bunnies" she happily greeted us. Henry immediately climbed onto her lap. "How are you little man? Did you have enough sleep?"

"Yes, they both slept well" I replied. "We also came by car to you so they won't be too cranky" He was cuddling into my mum and smiling.

Yana stayed on my lap and looked all around.

Time for a Change

"Let's go out for a short walk with them" offered mum.

Not far from her, just a five minute walk is a park. In the park there is a nice, new playground for children. They loved to go there. There were always a lot of children, but there is enough space for everyone. We came to the playground and Yana immediately pointed her finger to the swings. Surprisingly, she is not yet a year old and she can stay on a swing for 15 minutes. I put her on the swing, my mother was pushing Henry on a merry-go-round. Everyone was busy and happy.

"I've cooked you dinner. I've made chicken cutlets for the children with boiled potatoes. When would you like to eat?" mum asked.

"Oh, Lily came to me this afternoon. We had a meal together so now I'm not hungry. The children have had a yogurt before we left" I replied.

"And are you, hungry mum?" I asked.

"No, I'm fine, thanks. As soon as you called and said you were coming to me, I had a snack" mum said.

I was very comfortable with my mother and I was glad that I'm now with her, in Kiev. Mum is my true friend. I thought about it and smiled.

The kids were playing in the sandbox. We sat on the bench, in the shade, talking about lots of different things. I appreciated all the hours spent with mum. As I now live in Ireland most of these hours are spent talking with my mum on the phone. I love her very much. When I get sad, I try replace that feeling with ones of happy memories of mum and I together and it always helps me. Knowing that mum is alive, healthy and loves me is my sole source of comfort in dark times.

Mum still had some years until her retirement age. She still works in a pharmacy. Mum is fanatically devoted to her work for all of her thirty years working. There are some jokes about it. To her, like to Lenin, farmers used to come for help. Different people used to come to my mother her advice as a pharmacist. She is known even in the central pharmacy department. She is the headwoman and smart in one word! She has contacts and profitable connections in a wide range of industries. The whole family lived with her pharmacy life and stories. We did stock taking together, helping mum to count. Really, I`m not surprised that I went into medicine and became a doctor. After all I grew up in a pharmacy.

My mum didn't spoil me. I always felt her love and support. I cherished our relationship and friendship. Mum always compared me to Anya`s which drove her to desperation.

Anya is a completely fulfilled person and an individual. She did not need examples on how to live. But mum had her own opinion. And we did not argue with her. I never argued with mum, I just always appreciated our time together.

The children had enough of playing now and are happily going back to my mother's. I left children with my mother and I went home. Mum had a day off tomorrow. I plan on meeting Oksana. I`ll pick up my children in the evening, on my way home.

I received a message from Ivan while I was in the tube. He texted, "hi, I miss you. Say hello to Anya. See

Time for a Change

you tomorrow. I`ll be there at eight. Good night, Snow White".

Good night, I thought, coming out of the tube. Well, he is attracted to me. He does not call Anya "Snow White". Only me!

My sister is waiting for me at home and has already walked Fanny. She has had her dinner and is now resting, browsing the Internet.

"How was your day?" I asked her, sitting down on her bed beside her.

"Yea I'm good. I`ve managed to finish work early today. I came and you were not here. Then I remembered you were going to mother`s. So I took a shower, had my dinner and while I was waiting for you I was looking through my e-mails" she explained.

"Today Lily visited me. She stayed here a couple of hours. Can you imagine, she`s met a guy a couple of months ago. Robert, he`s younger than her by six years. They are so in love. She`s in pink, she`s floating on air" I said.

We looked at each other "Well done to her!" we said simultaneously and laughed.

"How`s mom?" asked Anya.

"Great. We walked in the park. The children played there. It was nice and relaxing" I said.

"Let`s go to the cinema. We have no young children to hold us back. I'll look on the internet to see what is on new release?" suggested my sister.

"Ok so, let`s go" I agreed.

"There's an American comedy or an Horror movie" Anya reported having found the website advert. "Let's watch the comedy. I could do with a good laugh". We agreed and started to get ready for the cinema.

Tanya Anina

The cinema was not far from our house. The evening was beautiful. We watched the movie and had lots of laughs. We also had beer and popcorn. I was very surprised that in cinemas in Kiev they sell beer before movie begins? Popcorn, I can understand, but beer? We returned home after midnight and went to sleep.

Chapter 11

An alarm-clock woke me up at seven-thirty. I`ve spent about fifteen minutes in the bathroom and was ready to go.

Ivan came at eight. "Hi" he happily greeted me.

"Good morning, can you speak quietly, Anya is still asleep" I said in a whisper. "Will you have tea or coffee? Did you have a breakfast?" He shrugged his shoulders and I realized that he hadn't eaten.

I made coffee and toast for us. We ate in silence and then left quietly. Anya was still sleeping.

Once outside Ivan asked with a tone of irritation "What did you do yesterday? I sent you a message and you did not answer it?"

"We went to the cinema. It was late when we returned and I was tired. I thought you would already be sleeping at that late hour and I didn't want to disturb you" I answered honestly.

He accepted this answer and his tone softened saying "No, I was still awake then. I didn't sleep until very late as I was watching a movie"

About ten o`clock we arrived at the airport. He had never been to an airport before. He followed me, curiously. I looked at the arrival schedule for her flight number. I was aware that Ivan didn't look comfortable here so I asked him "Ivan, have you ever travelled by an airplane?"

"No, I haven't" he said embarrassedly.

"And would you like to?" I asked.

"Yes, I guess I would" he replied sheepishly.

"You will fly sometime. Dreams do come true" I said optimistically. "Look, it's my friend!" Oksana came out with two children and two suitcases.

"Hi, how was your trip?" I was kissing her children and hugging her at the same time. It was so nice to see her again.

"It was good and we`ve passed through customs quickly" Oksana said joyful.

I introduced her to Ivan "This is Oxana. She is Henry's godmother. And this is Ivan, my friend. Let's go to the taxi". Ivan grabbed the suitcase and the bag. I took the second suitcase. And we went to the parking area.

"Who's he?" Oksana was moving her lips silently.

"Just a friend" I smiled.

"Yeah he's just a friend. I can see how he looks at you. He has to be more than "just a friend" she is dying for more information.

"For now he is just a friend! Then we'll see in time!" I said quietly to her.

Ivan and the taxi driver packed the luggage. He sat down on the passenger seat and we sat down behind him.

"It is a pity that I go straight to the train station" Oksana was saying "I don't have time to see you

Time for a Change

properly or Kiev! This is a terrible life. I'm always rushing!" complained Oksana.

"It's true It would be cool if you could stay. Taya knows Kiev like a book! She recently arranged for me such an interesting tour at night" said Ivan proudly.

"Yes, I see you do not waste your time!" Oksana was joking.

"Stay longer and you also won`t waste your time!" I was joking too.

"I would love too, but parents are already waiting to meet me back home"

We reached the train station. We still had time before the train departures. We bought some water and some other small foodstuff. Ivan put their heavy suitcases in the luggage compartment of the train. The children were looking forward to the train journey.

"Thank you" Oxana thanked us "What would I do without you?"

It was time to say goodbye "Have a good onward journey, see you in Ireland" We kissed each other. Ivan stepped off the train first. I stopped for a second "What do you think of him?" I asked her.

"He`s ok, seems to be nice" Oksana shrugged her shoulders "Why?"

I laughed "Nothing, I'll text you. Send me your mobile number, from home". I came out of the stuffy train carriage and enjoyed the cool breeze on the platform and the pleasurable sight of Ivan standing next to me.

"Why do you keep thanking me for my help?" blushed Ivan. "You know I am always happy to help you in anything you need. This was just a small favour carrying suitcases".

"Are you going home now or you have some free time?" said Ivan taking out a cigarette. Finally he had an opportunity to smoke.

"Yes, now it's only twelve. I'm actually free for the whole day. My children are staying with my mum until the evening. Let's go to the Botanic gardens? I have not been there for a many years" I suggested.

"I have never been there" Ivan said as he exhaled on his cigarette. "Let's go so".

Chapter 12

On entering the tube station, we stepped on the escalator. We were facing each other. His face is a happy and joyful one. He took my hands in his and looked deeply into my eyes, saying "Taya, I'm glad you are free all day. I`ve been dreaming about time alone with you for a long time now".

I was speechless, so said nothing. I was looking at him and thinking "you're so open and free".

He continued "I have been so distracted by my thoughts of you and us that in work I put too much salt in the food I was preparing. I will lose my job if I continue like this".

Just then the tube train arrived and we walked into the carriage. I smiled at him and saying nothing, shrugged my shoulders.

The carriage rumbled, interrupting his speech, but I heard and understood all that he said to me. My heart translated its meaning to me "I'm in love with you!"

At this moment, the train was approaching the station it became quieter in the carriage. He said this phrase aloud to me and the whole carriage heard it! Passengers turned their heads in our direction. I smiled, without saying anything. He put his protective seductive arm around my waist. I felt a wave of happiness rolling over me and my heart-beat quickened. I knew I had to say something but I took a deep breath and waited.

I needed to leave the tube station before I could gather my thoughts. I tried to understand myself and at the same time to extend these seconds of uncertainty. We, at last came out of the tube station. Ivan was a little surprised with my silence. We bought ice cream. It was just what we needed, to cool down. We went to the park and in silence sat down eating the ice cream.

Once the ice cream was eaten I joked "Ivan, be careful with your words and your salt!"

"Seriously, in the last three days, I over salted all of the salads and the customers complained" he exclaimed. "You have a husband, you never speak about him, but I think that you love him! I understand that you are here just for a vacation that you have a great relationship with your husband. I fell in love with you a year ago, in the Crimea. When you left, and I was thinking about you all the time. Recalling your face, with your laughter and your stories. I realized that between us are not only the borders but also a huge abyss. The main obstacle is your family. And if I tell you all this, you'll think I'm crazy! I kept fighting my thoughts and feelings for you. I was forbidding myself to think about you. But the heart knows what it knows. Then I came to Kiev, found Anya and asked for your number to wish you a Happy New Year. You can't imagine my disappointment when you even did not recognize my voice! After speaking to you then I felt that my feelings for you were only on my side. You have your own life, a world where there is no place for me. But something could not let me let you go from my life. Anya told me that you were planning on coming here in the summer. So I was waiting, I knew that if I saw you once again I would understand my feelings more clearly"

He lit up a cigarette, he was flustered, his voice became muffled. He continued with blind intent, "When she told me that you had arrived, I could feel restlessness within myself. I had to see you again. The day before our meeting, I couldn't sleep and I smoked too much as my anxiety mounted. I didn't expect you to become blonde, because I remember you different. After our walk that night, I knew I had finally lost my head and my heart to you! I never felt so good with anyone else in my whole life. I will do anything and whatever you wish. And if now you'll ask me not to meet you anymore, then I'll go. I don't want to disturb your world or upset you in anyway. But I had to tell you my true feelings for you. I love you, Taya!" the cigarette burned his fingers and he threw it away.

I sighed. I tried to answer as gently as possible. "Ivan, I can't answer you right now, I have to think. Love is a serious feeling! Because of love there is lot of joy in our lives, bbut also because of love a lot of sadness could come to others in our lives too. Yes, I have a family to consider in all of this. But I know I would have their support too if I made a big decision in my life. I am just an ordinary woman, nothing special. We don't need to do anything sudden or rash now. What will be, will be. There is no need to go away from me either. We have a good friendship and I enjoy your company and having you around in my life"

He took my hand and we went wandering through the beautiful scented garden. I wanted to grab and caress him, but I held back my desires.

We sat down on the grass and in silence, holding each other hand, were admiring the landscape. Anyone looking at us would think that we are a young couple in the first flush of love.

Our day was passing pleasantly. Now we were hungry, so in Pechersk there is a small café. We stopped there to have a snack. After our open sharing conversation, something changed inside us and between us. The sun began to shine on us in a new way.

Ivan then suggested "If you're free tomorrow, come to my restaurant for lunch. If you want you can bring Anya or a friend. You`ll see where I work, I'll introduce you to my colleagues?"

"I'm not sure of my plans for tomorrow yet. I'll text you tonight. Promise you won't posion me with salt!" I teased and he laughted at that.

I decided to tease him some more. "Ivan, do you believe in fortune telling?" I asked, finishing my espresso.

"I think its complete nonsense" Ivan said dismissing my comment.

I persisted "finish your coffee and I'll tell your fortune". I examined the stains at the bottom of my cup.

"So, what have you got there?" Ivan was now interested.

"Oh, love is on the way to me from a young handsome man" I was joking.

Time for a Change

He gave me his cup.

"Ivan, what waits for you in your future? I can see an image like a tree and fire! What could this mean? Something is burning like fire? Maybe it's your passion?" I was talking nonsense. Poor Ivan peered into the cup to see if he could see what I was pretending to see! Then he looked tensely at me. Our eyes met and he saw me narrowing my lids slyly and trying to keep my laughter in.

He grabbed my hands "Taya, you are a witch! You have me completely under your spell. You are a dangerous woman for me! He was kissing my hands, we were laughing.

"And you thought we went to this garden for nothing! I was picking out a love potion to hold onto you forever!" I whispered closely to his ear, with an ominous witch voice.

We had fun, we were laughing. Some people even looked at us, but we were happy. After paying the bill, we went out of the cafe. I had to go to pick up children, I didn't want to leave, I asked him to go with me to my mother's. He happily agreed.

I asked him to wait for me outside.

"Hello Mum, how are you doing?" I greeted her as I went inside.

"I'm OK, did you meet Oksana?" she enquired.

"Yes, we've met and saw her off, Ivan helped with the luggage. He is waiting outside. I have a few minutes, to get the children ready and he will help me to bring them home" I answered as factually.

"Oh and who's this Ivan?" mum asked curiously.

Dressing up my children, I was telling her, "remember we told you about Ivan, from Koktebel.

He's the one who was accompanying us to our lodgings last summer. He worked for these landlords, where we were staying. Do you remember we told you?"

"Yeah, I remember something, but what is he doing here?" mum looked at me surprised.

"He works as a chef in a restaurant, here in Kiev. Anya and I are friends with him. I asked him to help me to meet Oksana. Or should I say lift her heavy suitcases. Okay, we're ready to go. Children say goodbye to my mum. Mum, you call me and tell about your plans for the weekend" I said, kissing mum.

"What plans can I have? I plan my life around you and your children. Keep in touch too" she kissed the children and we left.

"I hope we didn't stay too long?" I addressed Ivan when we were outside again.

The children looked at Ivan with interest. He took Yana in his arms. Henry was walking along with no help. We went to the tube, it wasn't too late, there was no sense to call a taxi. On our way, I sent a message to Anya. "We're going home now by tube. Ivan is with us. We are hungry. Text me, if you want us to buy something special for dinner." She replied "Buy something of your own choice. I am in a traffic jam in a taxi. I'll come soon. See you. x"

We reached our home quickly. Yana fell asleep in the tube, Ivan was carrying her in his arms home. Henry was sleepy too. Ivan had to go to the shop. I wrote him a list and sent him inside. Having written at the same time, all that we needed, for tomorrow also. "Might as well use his strength and help while he is with me" I thought.

Time for a Change

After putting the children to bed and Ivan was at the shops, I had time to myself to think about all that he said earlier today to me. How does he see me? I thought. Well done to him for being so brave to speak aloud his inner most sincere serious thoughts! Well, well life is strange? He fell in love with me when I was seven months pregnant! This is pure crazy! I want him to hug and kiss me so much. Although I still didn`t answer him or give him any encouragement. I took a deep breath. Poor boy! If I have sex with him, then what? Sooner or later there will be heart ache for him and I as we will separate. He will find a girlfriend of his own age! I will keep trying to fix relations with my husband. Or should I start all over again with a new man in my life?

All these thoughts were running around in my head as I was peeling potatoes. Then the phone rang.

"Hello" I said discontentedly as I was pushed back into reality.

"Taya, good evening" it was Mary.

"Good evening" I answered.

"How are the children? What are they doing?" she asked anxiously.

"They're sleeping now, thanks" I replied.

"It is only nine o'clock. I thought that they sometimes go to sleep later. Pasha and I miss them, we wanted to come" she said disappointedly.

"I will see you tomorrow. We are relaxing now, watching the TV. I'll call you in the morning" I promised her and hung up.

The doorbell rang, it's probably Ivan I thought without looking through the peephole and opened the door. In front of me was Anya`s Alex. "I`ll see you damned" I thought.

"Gosh, Alex hello, come in" I greeted him.

He was holding a rose. "Is Anya at home with you?" he asked hopefully.

"No, not yet but she is in the way" I replied feeling restless.

"Where are your children?" he asked trying to look around the apartment from the hallway.

"They are sleeping now so do keep your voice down" I said in an irritated tone.

Just a second later my sister arrives. I did not have time to text her a warning or to try to get rid of him. She immediately saw Alex, but didn`t appear surprised. She greeted him.

"This is for you" he gave her the rose.

"Thank you" she took the rose but looked at him indifferently.

The front door was open, Ivan arrived from the shops laden down with groceries.

He smiled "Hello to everyone! Why are we all in the hallway?"

I introduced Ivan to Alex and added "Come in, let's not remain standing in the hallway".

Ivan and I went to the kitchen. He was unpacking the packages and arranging items in presses and the fridge, with my supervision.

Anya along with Alex were in the living room. They were talking with difficulty and the atmosphere was strained.

I was making a salad, Ivan was frying potatoes. He was concerned about cooking the herring. My sister joined us in the kitchen.

Time for a Change

"What are we having for dinner?" she enquired, looking at what we were cooking.

"A bit of this and a bit of that" I replied.

Then Alex joined us in the kitchen too offering his help with dinner.

"You cut some bread, please" I asked him.

We've prepared everything quickly and it smelled delicious. Hunger is good sauce. We sat down at the table to enjoy our bottle of brandy, fried potatoes, salad, chicken wings and bread sticks.

"I won`t drink" Alex announced strongly.

"Ok" answered Ivan, filling up glasses for three of us. The brandy was very good. Anya and Alex were tired and hungry after work. Ivan and I were just hungry.

Getting straight to the point I said "Why did you call to visit us this evening Alex?"

Between mouthfuls he replied "I work now here, not far from you. I was redeployed to the left bank of the city"

"I see" I acknowledged but I was thinking "poor Anya, now he will come to see her with or without a reason"

The men began to discuss cars. Ivan informed us that his restaurant's interior is decorated like the interior of a limousine. You get in, like you do to a limo. There were cream leather seats, tables like in a limo are separated from each other by walls, like a compartment. The windows are made so that when you look through them you see a view of New York by night. It's very cool.

"I have already invited Taya, to come and see. Please, Anya you come as well, when you have a day off" Ivan was inviting her.

By now it was late, time for the men to go, so they called a taxi.

Ivan came up to me and asked in my ear, so that no one would hear "when will I see you again?"

Smiling I replied "I'll text you, thank you for today".

They had left. Anya and I sat down in the living room each of us with our own private thoughts.

Anya was the first to speak "I`m so tired, not so much physically but mentally and emotionally too" she sighed. "We still have to apply for a divorce. This part is going to take so much strength. It's a nightmare! I'm not looking forward to this at all".

"Are you sure you don`t love him anymore? Are you ready for this next final stage?" I asked her with sadness.

"Oh, I do not know" she sighed. "I`ll wait until you will leave. I don`t want to spoil the summer for you and I want to enjoy my time with you too"

I hugged her. I felt that she was very sad, I was sad too.

"We met Oksana today and that went well. Then we went to the Botanic gardens" I began to talk, I wanted to share with Anya what Ivan had told me today but she interrupted and changed the flow.

"How`s Oksana?" she asked.

"She had a good flight". I decided to plunge right into the facts of Ivan's confession to me today, before I lose my nerve. "By the way, she liked Ivan, funny, huh? He also told me he loves me today in the Botanic

Time for a Change

gardens. He told me of all his feelings for me. And how he has been suffering and struggling with his feelings. For a year now since he first meet me! He is ready for any plans I want with him in my life!"

"What did you answer?" my sister looked at me curiously.

"I said nothing yet, just listened to him. I said, I would think about it" I replied.

"But what have you decided?" she asked. Anya knew me too well. She knew I've decided on my plan a long time ago. It's only Ivan who doesn't know yet.

"I like him, even more than that he drives me crazy with desire. But, honestly I still haven't decided what happens next? Should I start anything with him at all?" I say defeated.

"Who cares what tomorrow will bring?! We are here and this is now. Taya appreciate your life! Appreciate yourself, appreciate your youth! Of course, I'm surprised that you like him! What do you see in him? Honestly, I still don't understand. He seems to be an average guy. Yes he has a good body and average intelligence. Is he good company for you? You have him around your little finger. Is that the type of man you really want? I know you will quickly get bored with him!" she warned.

I love my sister for all these honest words. She always could tell me the truth, straight up.

"Anya, of course, I don't know him at all. But his innocence, it attracts me also his energy and freedom. I feel myself with him young and carefree. I my current life I permanently have to think and care about everyone, to handle everything. It's been like that for the past ten years. You know what Tim is like.

He won`t move his ass, not once. Yes, he's a genius at work, but at home that's a different story entirely. Who knows what will happen next. Thank you for your support in my life always. Now we are both over tired and its way past our bed time" I hugged my sister and kissed her. I went into the bedroom to check on the children.

Chapter 13

Anya was free the next day. In the morning we decided to call my parents-in-law and bring the children to them. I dialed their number.

"Good morning, my children are fully awake now and have eaten. I can bring them to you now if you like Mary" I tried to sound as relaxed as possible.

My mother-in-law, as always, started her endlessly long monologue. She informed me of all their plans for the day. Now she is busy preparing berries for jam and my father-in-law has gone to the shops. When they have time later they will accept a visit from my children, she concluded.

"Okay, I understand. You need more time to organise your morning" I asked.

"Correct, about another two hours" she said with a joyful voice.

"In two hours, it'll be very hot. I will need by then to put the children to bed for a nap. I will have to call you after that. One of you can come and stay with them while they are sleeping. Then you can take them to your place, give them a snack feed and go to

Tanya Anina

the playground. I can then go out for a few errands. I'll be back around seven in the evening" I said in a firm voice that offered no chance of an argument.

Mary agreed and we decided to keep in touch by phone.

"Anya, you can have today free to do any jobs you need to do" I offered "I'll be cleaning and doing the laundry. Then at noon, I will go to have manicure. Mary promised to stay with the children while they are sleeping" I added triumphantly.

"Well, I have nothing special to do. I'll do work on the computer so. At noon, I have to meet with a client. While you`re doing manicure, I will meet with her. And then let's meet in the city and go for a walk and a coffee" suggested my sister. Yes, let's do that, we decided.

Later that morning Ivan called me. He asked how we are and if I come to him for lunch? I explained that I am busy now doing necessary house work. Our lunch together will have to wait until another day. In his voice, I could hear he was upset. I pretended that I didn't notice. I promised him I would call him back in the afternoon then I hung up.

Anya took her eyes off the computer, she had heard our conversation. "Taya, what time does he work until?" she queried.

"I have no idea" I truthfully replied. "Why?"

"I'm completely free in the evening, if you want, I can stay with the children and you can meet with him?" my kindhearted sister said.

"Thanks sis. That would be nice. I'll call him later and find out when he finishes work" I replied excited.

Time for a Change

We put the kids to bed for their nap. I then called my parents-in-law "You can ccome now, the children have started their nap" I told my father-in-law.

He came in about ten minutes. I showed him everything, Yana`s bottles for water and milk. Pasha explained that Mary will come later, she is making dinner.

"That's no problem" I answered. "Thank you for this help" we left as quickly as possible in case he takes an idea into his head and starts discussing it!

It was hot and empty outside. I went to the tube and Anya, went to meet with her client. We agreed to meet or call each other later on.

The nail salon was close by, just three bus stops away. I had my manicure and was ready earlier than I expected. I will phone Ivan then Anya to let her know my plans.

Ivan answered quickly. Was he waiting for my call? "Hello my love" he answered cheerfully.

"Hello, how`s your work?" I asked.

"When I hear your voice, it gets better. Now it`s four o'clock, lunch is almost over and there are less people. And how are you? Have you some free time for me?" he asked hopefully.

"Well, I'm in the city. I have just my nails done and I plan now on meeting Anya" I informed him.

He replied and his voice sounded disappointed "that means you have no time for me? You're always busy. I will try to have more patience and wait until you are free".

I smiled and replied "that's just what I am calling you about. What time do you work until?"

"Till seven" he replied with new hope in his voice.

"Great, so at what time are you able to come to me to meet me? At about eight?" I could hardly contain my excitement.

"Oh yes. I'll be ready then. This is great news!"

"So it's agreed then. See you at eight at the "University" station" he agreed and we hung up.

Then I called Anya. She was finished with her client and was on her way to meet me.

We had dinner at the pizzeria and after that we decided to go shopping. I bought a new bag, summer and bright. Anya bought a belt for jeans. We were pleased with purchases and went to a cafe for coffee.

"I called Ivan" I updated her. "He works until seven we have agreed to meet at the "University" station, at eight. Are you sure you are free the whole evening?" I double checked with Anya.

"Absolutely, if you do not mind Michael will call over to me for a beer?" Anya said watching my face for a reaction.

"Of course, I don`t mind. Enjoy the beer and your evening together. I'll call you when I leave Ivan and am on my way home" I said jokingly to her.

"Oh yes do call me in advance!" my sister was making fun.

"What shall I say to your parents-in-law about where you are?" she wondered.

"Tell them I am at mums and will be back later on".

We talked for another hour. We ordered ice cream and happily kissed goodbye and wished each other luck.

On the way to meet Ivan, I decided to drop into the Vladimir Cathedral. Without knowing why, I liked to come to the Vladimir Cathedral since I was a teenager.

Time for a Change

To be more exact I liked the icon of Virgin Mary, which was paved in mosaic on the back wall of the temple. I still have an impression from my childhood that the Virgin, looks straight into my eyes and knows everything about me. I used to pray there when I was a teenager. Often going there after school, when I was anxious, lighting candles for myself and my family. Also, in Vladimir Cathedral, I stood sponsor to my godson. Year after year, returning to Kiev, I went to the cathedral and prayed.

I can't call myself a devotee, but all my life I try to keep the commandments and several times I do a fast. I confessed the first time, already being pregnant with Henry, at the same time I asked for the blessing for childbirth.

I enter the church, I humbly looked around. I bought candles and I began placing them. I began to pray for my children, my mum, for Anya, for Tim and in the end, for myself. I know I am not worthy by the fact that meeting Ivan means I am cheating on my husband and this is a sin. I repented, hoping that something will change inside of me and I will humbly accept the current situation with Tim.

But I'm only human! A very ordinary, sinful person. On leaving the cathedral, I stood for a moment thinking, still trying to understand myself. I walked on then and went to meet Ivan, my spirit blaming myself for my body's weakness.

Ivan was waiting for me with a bouquet in his hand. He happily gave me the flowers and kissed my cheek "Hello, Snow White" he greeted me, "What happened? Why are you so sad?" he added concerned.

I smiled, took the bouquet and said "thank you" and took his arm. We went to the old Botanic garden. The garden bloomed with roses. The fragrance was a sheer delight.

"And how many Botanical gardens are there in the Kiev?" Ivan asked as he was surprised to find himself in another botanical garden.

"Only two" I answered. "This is the old one. It's not that big, but I like it too". We walked through the alleys, holding each other hands.

"You look great, that summer outfit really suits you. But, you did not answer me when I asked you earlier why you were looking so sad?" Ivan looked worried.

"No I'm not sad. Sometimes I have that expression on my face when I am thinking about something" I said trying to give him reassurance.

"Tell me what thoughts disturb you?" he was looking into my eyes now.

"Ivan, so many thoughts are haunting me. The main one is of you and your love professed for me!" I sighed.

"Taya, everything will be fine! I'm here with you. Just trust me! I've been dreaming and thinking about us a lot. I want to make you happy" Ivan was calming me.

"Don't you understand? I'm married! I have lots of responsibilities. Sometimes, I even can't manage my own time! Tim arrives in two weeks and then I will have even less time. Then we plan on a holiday on our own to Turkey. After that we will return to Ireland! Don't you understand we have only a few times to see each other? How can I tell you about my love? About our happiness? Ivan! I'll be going away and you will be left here all alone with your thoughts, dreams, disappointment and pain. I can not consciously hurt you" I cried.

He tried to stop my monologue "Ivan, I haven`t finished. You have to listen to me! You may even fall in love with me more than now. You will want to be with me and I won`t be here. You will then be tormented with thoughts and torture yourself. Do you want all this? Is it going to be worth all that?"

I was looking at him with the hope that he would agree and see the madness that our affair would cause and then he would put a stop to it all now. If he could do this difficult brave act and walk away it would save us both a lot of pain. I didn't have the strength to end this between us and my resolve weakened every time I saw him. At the same time I was fearful that he would end it. Then I would be left in a void and be tormented forever, wondering what may have been between us.

"Come here to me, I want to hug you" we stopped in the middle of the alley I cuddled into him like a child. "Taya, I'm not a teenager! I am aware of and understand how hard it will be without you next to me forever. For now I'll wait for you and our meetings. You will still keep meeting me, won`t you? There still two weeks left, fourteen days of happiness! Taya don`t forbid yourself to love me and me to love you" he was patting me on my head, my shoulders and kissing my forehead and the top of my head.

I was totally confused, I felt like a child who is comforted and loved. "Ivan, I love you and want to feel your love for me. Don`t let me go" I was whispering into his chest as he cuddled me.

We hadn't notice but we had reached a restaurant at Gorky Street. The restaurant was cozy. We ordered coffee and hot sandwiches with salad. While we were waiting for the order, Ivan was telling me about his work, about funny and weird customers, whom he had to serve.

"Do you enjoy being a chef?" I enquired.

"Yes, I`ve always wanted to be a chef, even as a child. In the army I was also a chef" he shared with me.

"I`ve always thought that only girls dream of becoming a chef! At school, we used to have huge pots in the dining room. I was horrified, how someone could lift it up? And often wondered how they knew how much salt and pepper to add?" I mused.

My mood has improved, I was having fun and I liked to talk about everything in the world with him. The sandwiches, salad and coffee were delicious as we were hungry. We also ordered an ice cream with amaretto. Suddenly the lights went out and all the people who were in the restaurant froze with fear for a second.

The silence and the voice of the manager came then in the dark, "Sorry, the lights will be switched back on soon. In the meantime we will light more candles on your tables and around. Please continue to enjoy your meal".

In the darkness I felt Ivan's breath near me then his lips next to mine. Suddenly and easily we were kissing. Well, well, he had dared to kiss me in the dark in the restaurant! He is so funny I thought. What a cool kisser he is! "That`s it Taya, you're lost!" my thoughts were running through my head.

Time for a Change

The waiters lit candles. Here and there lights were flaring up and people continued to have their meals and continue chatting again.

"You are very tasty" I said, looking slyly at his lips.

"I never thought I would be kissing the Snow White" he said quietly. He began kissing my hand. "Taya, you're beautiful. I love you. I'm so happy to have you near me" inside him everything spoke of his happiness and love.

I felt happy and ease too. Smiling and winking at him I said "I am happy too".

Suddenly then the lights came back on. We were brought our dessert and we fixed our eyes on each other. "We have to cool down" I joked.

I called Anya for an update on the children. She told me that my parents-in-law are now gone home. The children were now well asleep. Tim had called in the evening! He had wanted to talk to me and would call back later. Michael is now with her and they are enjoying wine. In summary all is good and I don't need to rush home.

We walked out of the restaurant. It was already eleven o`clock. "Let's go to a night club, just for a couple of hours!" I naughtily suggested.

It was Thursday night. There were not too many people about. The music for tonight is retro, 80`s style. We ordered cocktails and sat down at a table.

"I propose a toast for you, my love" Ivan smiled as he held his glass in the air.

"To us" I responded sipping the cocktail.

"Promise me you will come to my restaurant tomorrow" Ivan pleaded.

"Ah sorry I can't. Tomorrow I`ll be at home alone with my children. I should be able to come on Saturday to you with my friend. I just have to meet with her at noon. Is that Ok?" I offer sweetly.

"Ok so. I will settle for that" he replied cheerfully, adding "I'll cook you something special. What would you like?"

"Well, some salad, but an unusual type. I like Italian or Spanish cuisine for the main and a delicious desert too. I will leave the rest up to your experienced hands!" I laughed playfully.

We finished our cocktails and went to dance. The music was not very good, but we didn't care. I was flirting with him, hugging him while dancing, touching him accidentally on purpose. Then we were kissing again. He was gentle, but passionate, I was melting in his arms. We went out to smoke, by now it was after midnight. I checked my mobile, there were two missed calls from Tim.

". . . The indifference has a soul of a frog. Eyes are like ice-holes in January . . ." I think aloud.

"What did you say, Taya?" asked Ivan.

"Nothing, dear, I was just thinking aloud" I answered, hiding the phone. "Let`s go to dance?" I suggested. "Hold on, I want to kiss you more" Ivan insisted warmly. He nestled me against him and we started kissing again. I felt like a school girl, a girl on a first date.

We ordered another cocktail, the music was getting better or was it the effect of the cocktails? While dancing I saw I was winding his passion up. He was feeling anxious his body temperature was rising. I was relaxed with cocktails, I felt free and happy.

Time for a Change

"It's time to go home now Ivan" I interrupted our dancing. "Can you call a taxi please" I said.

"I won't let you go alone at night in a taxi. I'll go with you, if you don't mind" offered Ivan.

"I do not mind at all. So let's go. What time do you start your work tomorrow?" I enquired tipsily.

"At twelve, I will leave in the morning and have time for everything. Are you sure you don't mind?" he asked again.

Once in the taxi, we were hugging. Ivan kissed my neck and was telling me that he is the happiest man. That it was a real surprise and joy to him our time together today!

Once outside my home, I said quietly "now it's important not to wake the doorkeeper, she sleeps in her little room. She knows everyone here. I'll open the door with my key and we'll quietly go to the elevator. Do you understand that? I don't want her telling everyone tomorrow my private business that last night I came home with some guy. That's why, not a sound!" With these words we entered the main entrance. We called the lift. We were lucky, the lift was on the ground floor and we quietly slipped into it.

Having entered the elevator, we gasped and laughed "Just like spies" Ivan gasped.

Having opened the door with the key, I was hoping that Fanny wouldn't bark and therefore wake up the children. The dog did not bark. She stayed with Anya, who immediately calmed her once she heard the sound of the key in the door.

Michael was still at our place. They were in no hurry to part ways. In the living room was laid the tea table. The romantic evening, apparently, had been a success. Beer replaced wine, cheese, olives, crackers, grapes and berries. There stood empty coffee cups.

We said hello and went to the kitchen to eat. Anya called me aside and asked "Do you mind, if I go to Michael`s place? He lives not too far from here".

"Sure whatever you decide. Are you ready for the next stage with him? Is rose and candy stage over?" I said joking.

"I think yours is over too?" she said significantly. I smiled in reply, she knows me too well!

Chapter 14

Once they left, we were alone. The children were sleeping in the bedroom. I suggested to Ivan that he sleep in the living room. I went to the bathroom, took a shower and put on my silk robe. Ivan went to the shower room to take a shower. I gave him a towel and warned cheekily that I won`t rub his back!

He came out of the shower. I looked at the clock. It was three o`clock. I felt tired and happy.

I was staying in the kitchen and pouring water into the glass. Ivan came up behind me, put his hands on my shoulders, hugged me and I could feel his intentions pressing against my buttocks. I placed the glass of water on the table, clearly understanding that he wanted me. Truth was I wanted him too. I turned my face to him and we started to kiss passionately.

Ivan sat on the kitchen chair. I sat on his lap, my legs akimbo. My robe fell on the floor. I was completely naked in front of him. He gazed longingly at all of me and I could feel his passion rising. We were separated only by the towel, which was still draped across his hips. His hands and lips caressed me passionately but gently. At last his towel was removed, there was no longer any obstacle to our passion. I took charge of the pace. He was trembling from my caresses. By now he was overexcited and he lost the remains of his courage. I took his hands and moved them to clasp my firm buttocks. This will help the thrusting be even more thrilling. I was kissing his chest, shoulders and neck. I moved his face so his lips could play and suck on my pert nipples. I was turned on by him. I could feel his strength and power growing. In one smooth movement he entered me. I kept sitting on him, moving slowly. With the tips of my toes I was touching the floor, standing up and sitting down. I was his rider. The sex was hot and fast, it seemed, the chair was about to collapse. Chair legs were creaking, no one had such a dinner on it before! With wild abandonment we both exploded in our passion.

Sitting still on him, having put my head on his shoulder I was gently kissing him. I was thinking "Taya you haven't imagined it would be like this! Yet this is how it happened. You have just had wild sex, in your own kitchen and with a twenty one year old!"

He was patting me on my back, without saying a word, diving his hand in my hair, cuddling me and holding me still. For several minutes we remained in this state of bliss, without moving.

"Snow White, you're incrediablle" Ivan was whispering and kissing me again, pulling me to him passionately yet tenderly.

I kissed his forehead and found the strength to get up. I threw on a robe and went to the bathroom,

"Go to settle in the living room I will join you shortly" I said promisingly, leaving the kitchen.

Time for a Change

Having come out of the bathroom, I went to check on the children. They were sleeping soundly.

He was waiting for me in the living room. I lay down with him on the sofa bed. We started kissing again, he patted me like a kitten with his nose buried in my beautiful hair, inhaling my scent, and listening to his whispers I fell asleep.

In the morning, half-asleep I heard the children starting to wake up. I wanted to remain asleep so much.

"Ivan, it's time to get up, the children are awake. I'll go to wash them and stay with them. You wake up, get washed and make tea" I was trying to wake him up. He was stretching lazily, hugging my waist and beckoning me to him.

"Ivan, this is an amazing romance, but my children come first. I did warn you about that. It's a fact that women with children differ from women without children" with these words, I got up and went to the children, leaving Ivan to wake up.

I washed and dressed the children and made their beds. I heard the noise of running water so I knew Ivan was now up and about. He entered the bedroom then fully fresh and dressed.

"Good morning, my sweet ones" he cheerily said and picked up Henry. My children remembered him and they weren't frightened. They smiled happily at him.

He carried Yana in his arms to the kitchen, Henry walked after him showing his toy car off as he went. Fanny curiously was spinning under his feet. Ivan started to prepare for them cottage cheese yogurts for breakfast.

I went into the bathroom, taking advantage of his attention to my children and freshened myself up. I changed into shorts and a T-shirt and then joined them. The tea was poured and breakfast was ready. I was pleased I liked the fact that he is not selfish. The children were happily chewing, smudging and making a mess. Fanny was picking up cheese pieces from the floor, which Henry was successfully dropping from his mouth. Fanny begged a cracker from Yana, but Yana did not give her a cracker, sagely shaking her head in different directions and talking with a menacing look. I took the whole scene in and was thinking, "well, well! Such a romantic family breakfast this is".

After breakfast, I asked Ivan to walk the dog. He also took Henry with him. Yana was folding cubes sitting on the kitchen floor I was washing the dishes and tiding up. A moment of sheer domestic bliss.

My eyes stopped on the chair. The chair is in the Art Nouveau style made of curved thin wood, with metal legs. Poor chair, I thought and smiled to myself. It simply could have fallen apart yesterday! I laughed remembering the noise and the scene of us naked. Imagine if the chair had broken under us!

Having placed the chairs around the table, I took Yana in my arms and we went to the living room to play.

Ivan returned with flowers considering that yesterday's bouquet, because of our many adventures has wilted. He had bought me a bouquet of Irises. Henry ran to Yana to tell her something. While the children were distracted, Ivan whispered "I love you" and kissed me the cheeks then on my lips, "I'll miss you, I`ll text and call you. OK? I love you, remember that" we hugged and he hurried away as he had to prepare for work.

The rest of the day passed in the usual routine. At last it was time for the children's nap and I too lay down in bed to rest. I fell asleep immediately. I was awoken suddenly by the phone ringing. Who could it be? I thought. It was Tim.

"Hello, how are you? Were you sleeping now? I called you yesterday. I spoke with Anya who told me you weren't at home? I called on your mobile but for some reason, you didn't answer? he asked demanding questions that required an answer now.

"Hello. Oh I didn't hear or know about your calls. I had a headache so I put the phone in silent mode. We are fine. And how are you?" I asked trying to compose myself and inject normality into my voice.

"Yes, I'm at work, I'm fine. The day before yesterday I went to the cinema. I've visited Arthur. Other than that I have no other news for you. The weather is bad. It rains most days. I miss you and the children. I want to come to you sooner. He was saying something else. I listened to him but couldn't keep my attention on what he was saying. We kept talking for a few more minutes mostly about the children, then said goodbye and hung up.

He wants to come sooner to us, I thought. Does he miss me? It's good if he misses me. His voice is calm, without any emotions. He's tired, perhaps. He'll arrive soon, in two weeks, I wonder what our meeting will be like? My thoughts and emotions start to flare up again and I can feel that I am getting upset. Keep calm, Taya, I reassure myself.

Anya texted me just then. She had gone on to work from Micheal's. She'll be home early in the evening. She's tired and wants to sleep on her return. A successful night for her also! On wanting sleep and feeling tired we were both the same this evening. I was feeling a new level of tiredness and heavy headedness too since my dreary conversation with my husband. This did not improve my mood. After playing with the children with puzzles and cubes, I was kissing and tickling them, their infectious laughter gave me back my good mood. Only my children I love unconditionally. My love for them will be eternal, I thought. I fed them and we went for another nap. I switched off the phone and hugged their small bodies to me on both sides and we three fell asleep. We woke up after four. We had a snack and went outside. We took Fanny with us too. We bought some juice, the children were playing in the sandbox, and I was reading a book. I didn't see my mother-in-law come near me, "Good evening, and are you already outside? Well done" she said with fake praise.

"Good evening" I nodded to her.

My mother-in-law Mary has a great talent of speaking slowly. So slowly that anyone could enter into a hypnotic state listening to her! She is the type of person who never does or never goes anywhere in a hurry. I think she enjoys annoying others with her extreme tardiness and tediousness. We sat with her and talked for an hour and then thankfully left in different directions. My children and I went again to the store and then home.

I called Ivan, "Hello dear. I didn't call you earlier as I fell asleep with the children. We have just returned

Time for a Change

from our evening out. Now I am free to talk to you. How are you?"

"Snow White, my love, I'm so happy to hear your voice. I'm fine. I think about you all the time. I'm a bit busy here now. Can I call you back later? I kiss you and love you" he said gently and was gone then.

I cooked the dinner and my sister came home. She looked pleased but tired. We sat down to eat, in the living room. The children were happily watching cartoons.

"Well, did your husband get through to you this morning?" she asked.

"Yes, he got through. I said that I had a headache and I set my phone in silent mode. In short everything is OK" I was happily reporting to her.

Anya nodded her head in approval.

"So, how was your romantic dinner?" I asked dying to hear all the details.

"As good as yours I bet. It ended with an orgy of love!" my sister laughed.

"So, we both had a fun time!" I was making fun. "And was it worth it?" I was curious if Micheal was a good lover.

"It wasn`t bad at all! He is a bit shy, but an excellent student!" Anya confesses proudly.

Suddenly the phone rang, it was Ivan.

"Taya, sorry, I couldn`t call back earlier. I was busy, now I`m free and sitting here drinking my coffee. How are you?"

"I'm great. Anya and I are having dinner together and talking about you" I was joking.

He pricked up his ears and asked "and what exactly are you talking about?"

"Well, you know what? Romantic dinner and our dessert" I continued teasing.

"And did you like your dessert?" he playfully asked.

"Very much Ivan, I want more! Kisses. I'll call you" I said and hung up.

"And how was your dinner?" asked my sister, it was now my turn to tell all.

"It seemed he got either overexcited or worried! He is certainly tender, but kind of timid. He apparently was at a complete loss. Maybe it was his first time? In short, I had to take over the pace but everything worked like clockwork" I was saying jokingly.

"Taya, of course in skillful hands, an icicle would melt!" Anya was making fun.

"He is not an icicle! Stop it!" I felt offended.

"Poor Ivan, he became numb from happiness" Anya continued joking.

We were discussing last night's activities further. We were laughing, joking and teasing each other and our new lovers. Our mood was excellent as a result.

The night was stuffy. In the morning it will start to rain. This is good, I am thinking. The city will cool down and it will be easier to breathe. The children slept restlessly, my daughter was crying in the morning, I took her to my bed and she fell asleep again.

In the morning Anya wasn`t in a hurry, she remained in her good mood. We were getting dressed. Fanny was running happily because we were all ready to go out and she too wanted to go. The children were running after each other and Fanny in the apartment. They have gotten used to her and become friends. The dog too has become more patient to them in their wildness.

"I am going to meet with Lily in the afternoon. I will take my children to our mother. She is happy to mind them as she is off today. Then she will be working for the next three days" I inform my sister of my plans for today.

"Are you going with Lily to Ivans' for lunch?" asked Anya.

"Yes, he invited us. He plans on cooking something special for us. He wants to show me where he works and I have to meet with Lily, so I will combine both" I triumphantly told her.

Having left my sister at home, we went by taxi to my mothers'. Unfortunately, the city was busy with traffic, probably they were somewhere repairing the road or it was a car accident. Instead of twenty minutes we were driving forty minutes!

Mum was finishing cleaning the house. As always, she was glad to see us and I promised to return for my children about five.

Lily approached towards me in her new car. I didn't recognize her at once. But she honked me. She was in a black SUV, Mercedes!

"Hello, so, do you like my new car?" she asked happily.

"Wow, Lily, it's a cool car" I said kissing her cheek and hopping into the plush passenger seat.

"Hello darling, you look great. Listen, let's go for lunch to a good restaurant, it's in the town center. My friend works there. I can introduce you to each other" I suggested.

Lily happily agreed. The restaurant had a car park on its grounds. We parked the car and we went inside the restaurant.

The restaurant was modern in style. Indeed, just as Ivan was telling us before, the hall was decorated like the interior of a limousine. This created the impression that you were entering a huge limousine. The tables and chairs were upholstered in soft, beige leather. It created an atmosphere of respectability and comfort. It was very busy. We were shown a very nice table in a quiet area. Ivan had reserved it for us. I felt very special indeed. The windows around were blacked-out but had night views of New York, Milan, Paris, London, Beijing. It was amazing they were surprisingly real in appearance. I do not know what material the designer used, but he had created a 3D image. The design was very unusual. We were looking around, taking it all in.

"How did you find out about this restaurant?" Lily asked amazed. "It's brilliant. I've never been here before".

"To be honest, it's my first time here too. It only opened recently. Do you remember I was telling you before about Ivan, from Koktebel?"

"Of course, I do. You liked him a lot if I remember correctly!" she smiled.

"Yes, that's the one" I smiled back at her. "Well, he works as a chef here" We are in touch lately and he invited me here when I was free. Of course, I promised him I would drop in for lunch sometime. So, today is that day" I said mysteriously. I took my mobile phone and dialed his number.

"Ivan, hello, when you`re free, can you come out? I need your chef`s advice. I do not know what to order?" I said with a sweet flirty voice. It's true I missed him and wanted to meet.

Time for a Change

"Taya, you're here! I`m on my way to you now" he said and hung up.

"Yes, from all appearances, looking at you, everything seems to be ok between you two?" Lily was making fun, watching me while I was talking on the phone.

"Lily, I`ve taken your advice, we only live once" I said pleased with myself.

Ivan left the kitchen and headed for us. The waitresses were looking at us curiously. He kissed me on my cheek and sat at our table, "this is such a lovely surprise" he said smiling.

"This is Lily, my friend. And this is my friend Ivan" I said, pleased that seeing me was a lovely surprise for him.

"Ivan smiled and asked "So, what will you both eat?"

"Now it's your turn to surprise us" I said teasingly. "I would like something with fish and tasty". "And you Lily? Do you trust the choice of the chef?" I was making fun.

"Of course, Ivan, at your choice, but not spicy" she said.

Ivan departed then with a bow for the kitchen.

"So, what do you think of him?" I asked for her opinion. At that moment we were brought two fresh juices. The waitress was looking at me and Lily with a curious expression.

Lily and I did look very impressive and stylish. Lily was wearing a black maxi dress with a very low neckline, which highlighted her beautiful breasts. She had accessorized it with bright coral jewellery. I was wearing a turquoise silk tunic with a v-neckline.

It had a wide three-quarter sleeve, the bottom of the tunic was tapered in. Teamed with denim leggings, it complimented my slim figure and my new hair color.

We thanked and smiled at the waitress. Now even more confused, she left us.

"Well, he is a fine man. He doesn`t look like a chef? His muscles would remind me more of a fitness insrtuctor. He is cute! He can't take his eye off you!" Lily was saying, sipping her fresh juice.

"In twelve more days, Tim is arriving! I've talked with him a couple of times on the phone. The same boring conversation between us. At least with Ivan I feel alive and needed again" I was confiding to Lily.

"And what are you going to do now then?" she asked with interest.

"I do not know yet. I have to go for two weeks vacation with Tim to Turkey. During that two weeks with Tim I will have a lot to reflect on. It could work out for the best yet? Ivan expresses his love to me all the time now. I do want him, I'm not bored with him and he`s not bored with me. Well, you understand this is all nonsense! I don't think he would or that it would be fair to ask him to put his life on hold waiting for me to decide what I will do. I don't need or expect his faithfulness! He has a whole life ahead of him. He should meet someone else and fall in love and get married and live happily ever after. Our relationship is just a bit of fun and naughtiness" I said. "This fresh juice is delicious?" and I drank half a glass in one gulp.

Lily was looking at me and smiling, "don`t take on stress with all this Taya. I know you for a long time now and I know what you are like. You will sort this out. You are a wise woman. Keep his love, if you need it now, and don`t think about anything else. That's my advice to you".

"Thank you Lily, I appreciate your advice always". I called the waitress who was serving our table and ordered a bottle Prosecco. "Let`s drink wine and eat fish" I was saying. We were brought a delicious salad with shrimps and arugula, yum.

I liked the flavours of the salad. Ivan brought a cheese plate for himself and sat to join us.

"And what about the other customers?" asked Lily.

"My main and most important customer is at this table" he replied without hesitation winking at me.

"Do you like the salad?" he asked anxiously.

"Oh yes, the salad is delicious, we were hungry" I said truthfully.

For the main course, there were fish balls with spinach and asparagus in a white-wine sauce. Ivan stayed with us for about ten more minutes than he had to go back to the kitchen.

"He cooks great food" said Lily admiringly "I don`t usually like fish much, but these fish balls are just so tasty".

The fish balls were really tasty. We were eating and talking enjoying ourselves.

Time was passing fast. Lily had some other plans for the rest of her day. It was time to part ways. We asked for the bill. The waitress said nicely that our bill was paid for! Ivan had asked her to inform us that he was busy now and would call later.

I sent him a message in which I thanked him for our delicious fully paid for lunch. I too promised to call him later.

Lily took me to my mums.

Chapter 15

Mum and I were having tea and chatting "Taya are you all right?" she asked concerned.

"Yes, why?" I replied shrugging my shoulders.

"Have you planned where you and Tim will go for vacation?" she enquired.

"To Turkey, to Kemer, perhaps? Imagine how Henry will like the swimming pools, slides, playgrounds and sandy beaches".

"And are you sure you can look after Yana?" I asked my mother.

"Don't worry, we'll sort it all out. Either myself, Anya or Mary would look after her" mum said. "They won't get to see her again until your next holiday home here next year. They need to spend more time with her and get to know her and her them also. After all, they are her grandparents" she added factually.

"Yes, I agree with you fully".

The children woke up then and had a snack. We left then to go home. My mum was busy with her own household jobs that needed to be finished as she will be working for the next three days.

In the evening Ivan called "Taya, hi. I hope you are not upset with me that I couldn't come out to say goodbye to you and your friend? It suddenly go very busy for me and I had to attend to a huge order" he was apologizing.

"Hello my dear. No, I didn't mind at all. I fully understood. You were in your work place, so don't worry. The lunch was just delicious and you were too kind to pay our bill too. Thank you very much" I replied sweetly but sincerely.

"And what are you doing now?" he wanted to know.

"Nothing too interesting. The usual evening time routine with the children. It`s already eight o`clock, I`ll bathe them and put them to bed soon" I answered yawning at the thought of it all.

"Maybe I can come to help you? That's if you do not mind?" he offered.

"And where are you now?" I asked, slightly surprised by his offer.

"I am downstairs! If you go out onto your balcony, you will see me. I miss you and I want to be near you as much as possible for as long as possible!"

"Ok" was all I could manage to say in my surprise. I dashed to the bathroom, to spuce myself up quickly. This is crazy, he is crazy! I was thinking as I put my make-up on.

After a couple of minutes, we were kissing passionately in the hallway. My arms were embracing his neck, I felt like I was waiting for this moment all day. Maybe all my life?

"I am so glad to see you, to hold you close again" I whisper between kisses.

"Snow White, not only you can spring surprises, I can to!" he was nuzzling my neck.

Inside once again and we set to bathing the children. He was such a great help. He enjoyed playing with them as much as they enjoyed splashing with him. Ivan was shining with happiness.

"Where is Anya?" he asked "It`s already half past nine?"

"She is off today, so I don`t know. I will to call her when we finish up here". I hadn't realized it was so late and now I was worried as to where my sister could be?

Ivan wrapped Henry with the towel, I wrapped my daughter, and we went to the bedroom.

I called Anya, she was at her friend Micheal's house and wasn't in any hurry home, or maybe she won't be home tonight she couldn't say for sure! But at least she was safe and happy. I could relax now. The children were by now sleeping peacefully.

"Let`s go to the kitchen to feed Fanny" I offered.

I didn`t know what to do, I was at loss, like a young girl. I went to the kitchen, switched the kettle on and took out the dog`s food.

"Taya, do you mind if I take a shower?" asked Ivan embarrassedly "I came straight from work to you and didn't have time before now to have one".

"Sure, no problem. There`s a blue towel, take it" I said, not looking at him.

He was taking a shower. I fed the dog, made us tea and went into the living room. He entered the room all fresh and cheerful and so damn attractive!

I got up from the couch and said "now it's my turn to have a shower. Will you wait for me?"

He was standing in the doorway, closing the exit by himself "Snow White, I request one condition, that I wash you?" he said, throatily. I saw the way he was looking at me, his passion rising inside him, like a storm.

"Come on so" I took his hand and led him into the shower. He was undressing me, taking off my tunic first. Then with shaking hands, tangling in the bra clasp, but he managed it. With his two hands he slipped off my leggings, I didn't need to help him. I saw how he likes to undress me, how excited he was by every touch. He openly stared at me, my whole naked body. "I could squat on my haunches at your feet forever" he was whispering.

I stepped into the shower cubicle and turned on the water. I stood under the shower looking at him. Having poured shower gel in his hand, I turned my back to him. He slowly and seductively began to wash me. After washing my back, he turned me around to face him and began to wash my tummy, my breast, arms and legs.

"Ivan, you're not only a chef! It turns out you're also a good washer too!" I was joking and splashed him with cool water.

"Taya, only yours, all just for you" he was answering, caressing me, he was trembling, gazing devouringly at me.

He wrapped me in a towel, carried me out of the shower in his strong arms and brought me into the living room. He put me down gently on a chair and set about making a bed. I was sitting and admiring him. Not taking my eyes off him, remembering our first time. A shudder electrified through my body, I wanted him again and now with all my being.

- "Our bed is ready, Snow White come to me" he whispered.
- "I lay down under the blanket, snuggled to him caressing his hair at his nape. I lay down on top of him, having raised myself upon one elbow, kissing him on the forehead, nose, chin, ears and neck, a huge wave of tenderness rolled on me. He lay on his back, with one hand caressing my breast, the other was on my butt. He hastened to enter into me quicker, his love making was discontinuous and timid.

"Don`t hurry, Ivan, we have the whole night" I was whispering reassuringly. I need him to realize that a lot more can happen before the end point.

He agreed, even though he didn't fully understand all that I was offering or speaking about. Timidly caressing me, he was worrying. I felt like a doll that he desires, that is cherished, yet he is afraid to play with. This feeling didn`t encourage my excitement, but rather annoyed me. And then I got the idea. What if he is truly inexperienced? That night in the kitchen, it doesn`t count, because then, I took up the running and only then, it worked out.

"Ivan" I said, kissing him "don`t be offended but tell me honestly, did you have much sex before?

He moved away from me, looked at me with a perplexed look and said "I told you, when I was seventeen! I`ve slept with my then girlfriend a couple of times after the nightclub. That`s all. And then my time with you!"

I hugged his neck and kissed him. I began to speak and teach him at the same time. "Ivan, don`t worry I

Time for a Change

will explain everything to you". Listen, I'm a woman, this is my body. Put your hand on my breast, caress my body like this, slowly and gently. Rub my tummy, slowly, going slowly down to the private area. Not fast, you have to feel me, my energy, my excitement, fuse with me. Don`t be afraid, the movements should be light. And remember, you have a lot of time, don`t rush. Let me enjoy you, as you feel me. I too will feel you" I continued kissing him to encourage his tour of my willing body.

With this he calmed down and after a while, caressed me more confidence. His sexual drive was awakening in him. He saw I liked his caresses, my body reacted to his lips and hands. This gave him a second wave of emotion and pleasure. Seeing this, I gave him time to rest. Ivan got overexcited trying to control himself so he needed to learn to pace himself.

"Lie down" I whispered to him, "close your eyes, do not think about anything, just feel the feeling of how it is with me naked next to you".

I sat at his feet and begun to massage his feet and legs, slowly rising higher and higher. He flinched when I touched his penis.

"Ivan, remember that you can only truly feel if you relax! I will caress you because I want to send you to heaven".

He relaxed obediently. I was kissing and caressing him. He had a terrific body. I sat on top of him, he put his hands on my hips and I started to move on him. First slowly, then quickly, as I teased him. He felt me, he finally stopped panicking, his power now in full swing. We were changing positions now and enjoying each other. Then Ivan couldn't hold back any longer.

In his ecstasy he had lost his mind. His final burst was loud and long.

When it was over, he buried his head into my chest and whispered, "Snow White, you are a magician, you just don`t know how good I feel with you".

"I also feel good with you" I replied smiling into his chest.

We were resting in each other's arms for a while feeling completely relaxed. After a while we turned on the TV and were watching a concert. Ivan went off to the kitchen to make tea and sandwiches, which he brought to us in bed.

Later on I asked him "Shall we sleep now?"

"Are you sure you want to sleep, my love?" he asked as he began to kiss me passionately.

We started to make love again. For this second time, he didn`t need any instructions! I enjoyed him fully as he smoothly went through the steps as before but with his own extras. Wow, I smiled in the dark, he learns fast.

"Kissing my tummy he turned his eyes to mine and whispered "Do you like how I show you my love now?"

"Oh yes, I really like it. Do continue please! I really did like it. I was drowning in his love and caresses. That night he showed me time and again the pleasures that a man can give to a woman's body and we were student and teacher no longer.

We slept on and off for only a few hours here and there. We were crazy for each other and couldn`t break our hold and when we slept we were entwined together. It seemed that this night would never end and I wished this was so. But then it was morning,

Time for a Change

Ivan had to go to work. I didn't get up to see him off. He went to the shower and hurryingly got ready to go to work. He kissed my sleepy face, whispered that he loved me and that he would call. Shutting the door quietly, he left.

I woke up later feeling tired but happy. Having made myself coffee, I began to start my everyday household chores and care of my children. Ivan sent me a text message. I was pleased. Anya also has sent a text saying that she'd be home soon as she doesn't have work today. That's good, I thought, we will have some sisterly time together.

Anya came home, we chatted for a while about this and that. Anya was tired so she went to sleep. I walked with my children outside in the evening. When we returned, Anya was already awake and was sitting having her dinner.

"Hi" I said to her on entering our apartment. "Did you have enough sleep?" I was positioning the children to watch a few cartoons before their bedtime, as a treat.

I then went to join my sister I the kitchen. "Ah yes, I did, I needed that, thanks" she answered with a contented smile. "What shall we do together for the evening?"

"Now I'm tired" I said regretfully "I just want to take a bath and go to sleep after. I'm serious Anya, I never hardly got a wink of sleep last night! Ivan may have arrived to me an inexperienced lover but now he is and expert in the technique of love making. I gave him a master class! Thankfully he is a bright student and I got lots of revision from him!" I said smiling slyly. "Now, I'll go for a nice long soak and then to sleep. Will you put the children to bed for me?" I implored.

"Yes of course" she replied "Consider it done. Go and enjoy your bath and your sleep. Sweet dreams!" she added teasing me.

I felt that I needed an aroma bath. I took a glass of milk, added 5 drops of rose oil with 5 drops of sandalwood and 7 drops of orange. This combination of oils is guaranteed to relax and remove any anxiety and stress. The bather's body will be filled with peace and harmony. This is what I needed now so much. The aroma was divine. It felt so good to relax in a hot bath and inhale the sweet citrus flavor. I lay there, for several minutes, remembering how good it felt to be loved and desired again as a woman.

Anya knocked on the door and asked gingerly "shall I make you some tea?"

"Yes please do" I said. "What a caring sister I have" I thought to myself. I love her so much!

Anya brought me some tea. I stayed in the bathroom for a long time, drinking lime tea and dreaming. When I got out of the bath the children were already asleep. Anya was working on the computer. I went to bed and fell asleep immediately. Aromatherapy sure does work. As I fell asleep my thoughts were flying off into the distance. I am happy, that is most important at this moment for me.

Chapter 16

The morning has started as usual, too quickly and early. Anya was gone to work. The dog was barking for a walk. Henry, taking Yana`s toy accidentally hit her on her head and she was crying until eleven. I tried to calm them all down. We took the dog for a walk and I struggled to keep my patience with them. Thankfully my mum will come to visit me in the afternoon. I continued to do my housework and do the laundry. Mum arrived at noon.

As I was cleaning I was thinking "Taya, you've really get the hots for him. What is it with you?" These thoughts were making me happy and sad at the same time. I had a week before the arrival of my husband. All things must pass! Tim would come and my passion and adventures with Ivan would be over too! But, I don`t want to give up on Ivan. I feel so good with him. What to do? What is to be done?

Mum and my children were going for a walk. I was at last alone but could feel a headache coming on. I needed this time alone. But my sister arrived not long after they had left. She was in a good mood.

"Hello to everyone!" She shouted from the hallway.

"Hi" I answered with as much enthusiasm as I could muster.

"Where is everyone?" She asked disappointedly as she entered the room.

"They are gone for a walk" I replied.

"Why are you staying at home alone?" she looked sadly at me. I shrugged my shoulders and replied "I`m thinking".

"Taya, let's eat now then feed the children and mum on their return. We can send mum home and call a babysitter and go out to a pub! I know a great pub, with fabulous music. Shall I call to book a table for us? Around ten o`clock is a good time. What do you think? You have to stop feeling sorry for yourself. Tim is not bothered that he has hurt you, so why are you giving him any space in your head? Let's get up and go to the kitchen. By the way, let's drink some of the wine that we have left". Anya took a half-filled bottle of wine she kept in her stock. I opened the fridge to check for salad and fish cakes. It turned out that I was hungry though I hadn't felt hungry at all.

"So, how's Ivan doing?" continued my sister.

"Fine, he`s working" I added sharply.

Mum returned from their walk. She wasn't hungry. We had some tea with her and talked about our plans then she went home.

At nine o`clock the babysitter arrived. The children had fallen asleep quickly. Anya had booked us a table at the pub. We prepared ourselves for going out to the pub. Anya did my hair and also hers. We were dressed in short dresses in the style of the seventies. Anya was wearing a bright orange one. This color suited her

Time for a Change

perfectly as she is brunette. To this outfit she added black suede toe shoes. I was wearing a bright green dress and gold soft leather sandals with a platform. I made me taller by at least 10 cm.

We left our apartment quietly as our taxi was waiting outside. We entered the life and on the ground floor, the lift doors opened. Standing before us was my mother-in-law! "Taya!? Anya!?" she stated disapprovingly with her eyes wide. "Where are you going so late?"

Thinking quickly on my feet I gasped "Fanny, Anya's dog, somehow slipped out of the lift! We are looking for her. Did you see her? Mary, get into the life quickly so we can continue to search for her. She's not on this floor. Wait I hear her barking, she's on our floor. We must get her quickly before she wakes up all our neighbors. Such a foolish dog!" My mother-in-law, surprised with this story, was standing with us in the lift and trying to understand what was going on? "Mary" I was saying to my mother-in-law "we just came from a birthday party, and went to walk the dog. Then the stupid dog jumped out of the lift".

Mary, shocked, go off then at her floor. She was trying to make sense of all I told her. "Good night, say hello to Pasha" I said as the lift door closed.

Anya started to laugh quietly. I stood there in muted horror, then I laughed too. Anya between laughter said "Well, that was unexpected! What took her outside at ten o'clock? And then to bump into us! How did it cross your mind to talk about the dog? Well done! Taya. You are some actress".

"It would be even funnier now if my father-in-law would appear next!" we were joking.

The incident with Mary had shaken us up but we were now ready for our adventurous night out.

Our taxi quickly brought us to the pub. We went inside, it was noisy, lively. Some band performed compositions in English, the repertoire of "Scorpions". For a start, it was not bad. We sat down at our table and ordered a beer. Having run our eyes over the attendance, we noticed two foreigners sitting at the bar. They definitely weren't friends, they were just chatting politely together. They were both I there forties. Every now and again, they were looking around, reviewing the attendance.

"Anya see those two guys. What do you think? They obviously want to hook up with someone for the night?

"Let's see what happens. We've just got here so they havn't seen us yet!" my sister playfully replied.

We were drinking our beer. We felt cheerily and at ease. Anya was telling about the adventures of her friend. This friend had fallen in love with a violinist of much older than her and became his devoted admirer. Following him on around and touring with him. Love knows no age, this was not a surprise. But the crunch of the story was that he is married. He also has an ulcer, he suffers from insomnia and periodic asthmatic attacks. His wife takes care of him, cooks him soups, keeps his diet healthy. She also takes part in his everyday music life. At the same time, she knows about his mistress! She was even acquainted with her and perceived her as a muse! All this didn't bother the young mistress, instead it spurred her on to more sacrifice and devotion. So, this trio has now existed for three months and they were all getting on well together!"

I listened to this story of the usual love. Smiling, I said, "Anya, that's a good love story. Probably this old man is really talented, especially if he`s able to keep two women happy and near him!"

"Maybe he is talented. I can not understand what she sees in him I saw her today and she is beautiful. She is twenty four years old and he is over sixty! She doesn't need him at all".

"Let's have a shot and another snack. I'm hungry again" I suggested to Anya. "Ok. I`ll have a "Speed 120"" she was reading the menu. "And, I'll have a "33"".

We ordered our shots, French fries and sandwiches with anchovies and more beer.

The foreign men at the bar were looking around with bored expressions and drinking pint after pint.

"Where do you think they are from?" my sister asked me.

"I think one of them is from Australia or USA, he is not dressed like a European man. The other one is most likely English or Scottish. He`s definitely not Irish!" I stated authoritatively.

They noticed that we were discussing them and they smiled broadly back at us. We smiled at them in return. Let's see what happens now that we have their interest.

Shots were brought to us, courtesy of these two gentlemen and we drank them. "Nice and strong" laughed Anya. "Which" I laughed back "the shots or the men?!"

While our food was being prepared, we decided to dance. Much to our surprise, the two foreign men also joined us. Then the music tempo changed to a ballad. These men, deciding quickly which one of them would dance with either of us, made an agreement and asked us for a dance.

The guy who had chosen me is from Edinburg. So I was right. "Good guess Taya" I smiled to myself. He was surprised that I was from Ireland. He started to joke "I could not believe that finally during the whole evening I can speak English". He had come here for business for a few days. The dance was over. Anya and I went back to our table.

"Taya" my sister said excitedly when we sat down, "he is American, from California! He here on a business trip".

"The second one is Scottish, I just knew it" I spoke to Anya. At that moment, our two new friends were heading towards us.

"Excuse us, please" they said in English. "May we join you both?"

We agreed. The waitress brought us our order of beer, fries and sandwiches. We were eating and our new friends were drinking beer and telling us about their impressions of Kiev and about the Ukraine in general. It turned out they were well travelled business men. They were asking what we did. In short, the conversation flowed and we were all very relaxed together. We were glad that they didn`t try to any moves on us and they were glad that we spoke English and kept them company. Having tried to pay for our food and drinks at the end of the evening, they were surprised when we declined their generous offer. Having said a friendly goodbye to them, we went home.

On our way home, as always, my sister and I were discussing the day's events and laughing. We had had a great evening. The children were sleeping. So following their example, we went to sleep too. That night out was like a tonic to me.

It was the last day before Tim's arrival. The children had missed their dad. They were now pointing their fingers to the sky, to all flying planes, screaming, "Daddy, Daddy!!" as I had told them he would come soon by plane.

Mentally, I was not ready for his arrival. There was no way out, he is my husband, whether I like it or not. Taya, be a patient pretty woman I told myself. This is the last day I have to myself before he arrives.

Ivan took the day off. He knew after this out time alone would not be possible. We had spoken about this a lot lately. We planned that I would take my children to my mum for the whole day. We wanted to make the most of our time together. We spent the whole day together. We went to the cinema. And then my chef was cooking me dinner and I dutifully was sitting in the kitchen and keeping him company. After dinner we walked around the park, holding hands. For a long time we didn't talk about anything, we didn't want reality to invade our special day.

In the evening, I prepared an aphrodisiac bath, adding to water sea salt and ylang-ylang with jasmine 10 drops each. The aroma was divine. I lit a few candles and I beckoned Ivan to have a bath with me. I stared at him in the dim light of the candles, spraying him with water from my hands and kissing his shoulders. I was crazy about the feel and look of his muscles. He is damn good, I thought, and jealousy crept into my heart. I don't want to share him with anyone. The longer we are together, the more I want to be with him.

My inner voice was nagging me: "You'll fly away soon. You made him a man and now you know about all of his body and all of him as a person". I was falling in love with him and I was jealous. I wanted him to be mine and only mine! But my great desire was not compatible with the reality of the situation.

As you know it is impossible to keep something you don't own. I will give Ivan the last hours of my love and passion. I will give him all this with all my heart, generously and irrevocably. Our last night of love, passed like an hour.

I requested him not to call or text me. I promised I would call him when I could. He agreed, and told me he will live in the hope to see me occasionally and spend time with me if possible. He made me promise not to forget him or our time together. Heartbroken, Ivan left me at twelve o'clock.

Chapter 17

The plane was arriving at four. Mary was cooking dinner for her son, so I didn't have too. I decided to go to the airport to meet my husband.

Tim arrived tired, but happy. He hugged me and seemed happy to see me. All the way, he was asking about the children, his parents and was telling me all his news.

"Why, do people who live together for a long time, stop kissing each other when they meet?" I thought. Well, when we met of course he kissed me, but only briefly. If people really love each other surely they desire to kiss? Especially, like us, they had not seen each other for months. I can't understand why my husband doesn't have a desire to kiss me right now, here in the airport? Routine and habit take over our lives and demolishes the place where once stood passion. This situation gradually transformed our passion and love into family friendship.

On the positive side, many couples say "my husband or my wife is my best friend! I share with him my problems, plans, worries, etc. with them". This is a lovely sentiment but we all need passion too.

I agree. You have, as a couple, to share, and it is correct too, each other's sorrows and joys. But where is the influence of love and passion! You can`t forget it, even with the problems of chronic fatigue. All these thoughts swirled in my head. I looked at Tim, and saw that he was very far from passionate kisses and from me. So what is going on with him? I thought. Perhaps, he has another woman? We had not seen each other for almost two months. And it seemed, nothing has changed.

"Taya, have you already thought where we go on our vacation?" he asked nonchalantly.

"Probably to Kemer. I`ve heard it`s a good place. The beaches are good for children. We will take Henry with us, won`t we? I waited until you arrived to confirm any flights. Tomorrow I will go to the travel agency and buy some last minute travel offers. We can depart in two days?"

"All right" Tim said.

We were talking about everyday minutiae and at last we reached the house.

My mum had brought the children home. They were looking forward to seeing their dad. It was a picture of much happiness. They were hugging and kissing him, telling him stories and showing him their toys. Tim was very happy, and was glowing with their pleasure. Here, for the sake of such moments, women keep their families, sometimes sacrificing their own happiness, I thought.

We went then to his parents for dinner. They were so very happy with the arrival of their son.

Time for a Change

Watching this joy I reflected on how for the ten years of our lives abroad, they never called, not even on his birthday nor the children`s birthday. They wrote letters to him only three times a year, on New Year's, Easter and his Birthday. I did not understand this at all. Were they not really interested in how he's doing, how his life is? Is it possible that some 2 or 3 dollars are for a phone call have more value than their son`s voice? An answer to all of these questions, I've been searching for. Unfortunately I never could find one.

Now today, they didn`t ask long about his life and work. They only criticized him if he said something they didn't agree with.

I looked at them and thought: "you haven`t seen your son for two years and you are not interested in his world. Yet you impose your opinions and your principles on him. Without listening to someone you love, your son, who is precious to you and who cherishes you too".

I did not want to join in the conversation I was looking after the children and glancing at the clock, hoping to get away home soon. Tim told them that in a few days we're going to go to Turkey, for ten days. This sparked a blitz of a new wave of moral teachings and opinions. Pasha gave his opinion clearly on our planned holiday and how there are very good health resorts near by in Crimea.

Mary chimed in to add her opinion too "your father's right. Why do you want to go to Kemer? Here, the train is near you, we went with you Tim to the Crimea during all your childhood holidays and never heard about Turkey!"

"This is probably Taya's idea?" Pasha said, looking at me disapprovingly.

"No, this is our mutual idea" Tim said. "We have a lot of friends, who went to Turkey on holiday with children and they loved it".

I stayed in silence. "I'm so fed up with you all" I thought. You even upset your own son's mind on the first day of his arrival home.

"Excuse me, I have a headache. It's probably too stuffy?" I said. "Thanks for dinner, I'll go outside with the children for a walk".

Tim realizing that I'm leaving him alone in the battlefield. My nerves were frayed. Having left my husband with his parents, my children and I went outside and I took a deep breath.

You don't choose your parents or your parents-in-law! Let Tim discuss the pros and cons, of the Crimea versus Turkey himself with his parents. I no longer have any patience to participate in these family debates, I thought.

The children were playing in the playground. They were happy, about an hour had passed. Tim came out of the main entrance of the house. He seemed all upset, tired and walked up to us.

"Hello. Well, how was your walk?" the children saw him and ran into his arms happily telling him their news.

"Let's go home, or walk for a while?" he asked.

"Let's go home, you look tired" I replied.

The evening passed quickly. We were alone. Anya went to the country, to her friends for a few days to have a rest. The night was approaching, I couldn't

Time for a Change

imagine what this night would bring to us. We were watching TV till late.

I didn't feel resentment towards my husband even the affair with Ivan didn't change my attitude towards my husband. I love him and I want him with all my heart. I want to belong only to him, to love just him. I was looking at his hands he was holding a cup of tea and drinking. I like his hands so much. The hands that, not just once, have supported me, treated me, loved and caressed me. I felt a lump of bitterness in my throat.

Tim was drinking tea, sitting in a nearby chair, and didn't seem to notice, the way I was looking at him and didn't feel my mood. I went to the bathroom and then the bedroom, having wished him good night. Of course, I did not sleep. I waited for him, turning from side to side. I heard he was taking a shower.

He lay down on the bed and hugged me "do you sleep?" he asked, kissing me on my cheek.

"No" I replied not giving him any encouragement.

Without saying a word, he was kissing me and we started to make love. It was quick sex, more like a physical necessity than anything else. Then he fell asleep. I was lying and thinking, perhaps, it happens in many families, satisfied husbands sleep and thousands of women lie and look at the ceiling, feeling worthlessness of their husbands and disappointment in themselves. Sighing heavily, I got up.

I went to the kitchen to drink cognac. I poured fifty grams and I drank it in one gulp, bit on an apple and went out onto the balcony. Yes, nothing has changed. He performed his bedroom duty. I was telling myself, watching the city at night. "What needs to happen between us, to make things as they were before? After all, he is a very hot man. Before, he liked to make love and had a real appetite for it. I remembered thinking at the time I was the happiest woman. But, everything flows away, everything changes. Enough, Taya stop torturing yourself, go to sleep" I said to myself and went to bed. I calmed down and with thoughts about the upcoming trip, I tried to fall asleep.

Two days passed quickly. I bought the tickets to Kemer. Mum took a vacation and planned to take her granddaughter for a week. Anya didn`t return from the country. She was having such a great stay with her friends there. My parents-in-law were coming to visit us, but I wasn`t at home. All these days were filled with duties and gatherings to prepare to leave. Ivan and I were texting and calling each other.

It was the last day before our departure.

Tim went on business, to meet with friends he informed me.

To be more exact, with a female friend, whom he had a long-standing friendship with. Before we met, she was his girlfriend, but he hadn't proposed to her, ever. But with whom, he keeps their friendship alive for fourteen years. At first I was bothered with it and we even had quarrels about it. Then I put up with or got used to it. I never invited her to our house and turned a blind eye on their friendship. Believing in Tim`s love and faithfulness to me. Today I felt an unpleasant feeling that he was going to meet with her again.

So that day I was at home alone with my children, when Ivan called me," Honey, I'm at your door. Can you come outside for just a few moments? I miss you

Time for a Change

very much. I am working in the evening and decided to visit you. I know you can`t leave for long. But, I'll be waiting for you downstairs. Come out when you can!" he was speaking on the phone, with clear excitement.

"Ivan, I'm at home alone. Tim is gone out on business and won't be back until after lunch. Take the lift up to me" I said, completely surprised and excited too by Ivan's presence so near me.

Such a boomerang! Tim has just left to go to his "female friend" and Ivan comes to see me. Such a madhouse! It boosted my spirits. I was so glad to see Ivan, even more so, now as I will be gone away for ten days.

Ivan arrived all hysterical and shocked. "Taya, you are not going to believe me! I`ve just got acquainted with your mother-in-law, Mary, in the lift!" he blurted out, waving his hands.

"What do you mean by got acquainted?" I was surprised. "How do you know it was definitely her?"

"Unfortunately, it was definitely Mary! I went inside and she got in after me, this old woman. I even held the door for her! She was carrying bags. The concierge asked me "Which apartment are you going to?" I answer number seventy and I called your surname".

By this time old woman called an elevator and was staying and waiting for it. I walked to the lift, and she asks me,

"Who are you visiting at that apartment?"

I answer her "What business is it of yours".

She says "My son and his wife live there!"

We enter the lift then with your mother-in-law, Mary! So as confidently as I can, I reply, "I go to see Anya".

"Young man, don't you know that Anya is in the country already for several days with friends?"

"Taya, you didn't tell me that Anya is in the countryside!, I really didn't know. I answered her that it didn't matter that she is in the countryside. I have to give her a CD for work. Taya's is at home, I'll give it to her. I called ahead to Taya and she will give Anya the CD. Mary looked at me suspiciously and asked "what's your name?"

"I lied and replied Alex! She reached her floor, scanned me with her eyes again and walked out of the lift. Please give me at least a sip of water" Ivan was mopping his brow.

I poured him some water and after thinking for a moment I laughed.

"I can't believe it! For such an old woman she is so curious. Don't worry, you told a good lie. Anya will cover me. It is a believable story".

I hugged Ivan and nestled him to me. "Ivan, I've missed you so much. I was thinking about you lots. It's just so great that you came to see me".

He entered the living room, hugged and kissed the children. They recognized him. Henry was asking him about the fish, which Ivan had promised to catch for him. Yana was spinning around us. We stayed with them in the living room and played. After a while I fed them and put to bed for their nap. It was already noon, in two hours Tim will return home. Ivan, didn't ask me about my husband and I didn't offer an information either. I told him that we are taking Henry with us, mum will take care of Yana for us. We will be back in ten days. After five more days, we then fly to Ireland.

Time for a Change

Ivan was devastated to hear this short time frame. He listened to me with sadness in his eyes.

"Taya, I will miss you very much, even these couple of days, I barely lived without you! You're talking about ten days and then maybe about a year! I love you, Taya, you are my girl! I miss you every second! I came here hoping to see you and spend some private time together. Unfortunately, I managed to meet your mother-in-law too?" he said his heart breaking. With a worried look he added "what if she didn`t believe my story and will tell your husband that she saw a man visiting you? Or maybe she will ask the concierge whether she saw me coming here before?"

I was hugging and patting Ivan`s hair "Ivan don`t think about anything. Who knows you could be Anya`s boyfriend! Who cares what she thinks?"

I suddenly realized how much I missed Ivan and I absolutely don`t care what anyone says. "Let's go into the bathroom?" I beckoned him.

"Taya, what if your husband should arrive home earlier than planned?" whispered Ivan.

"Ivan, he won`t come! He definitely won`t come! He's very busy. Let's not talk about him. I want you, I really missed you" I uttered between passionate kisses.

We were kissing, standing in the bathroom, I was in a summer dress, from which Ivan, set me free in a matter of seconds. His hands domineering, were caressing me, as if for the last time, fiercely, passionately but gently. He was showering my body with kisses, he was standing on his knees in front of me and kissing my tummy, pulling me to him and repeating "Snow White, I don`t want to believe that you will fly away and I will be without you, without your smile, without your voice. How will I live without you?" he was whispering. I was toying with his hair and trying to answer something in response.

Without giving me time to come gather my thoughts, he lifted me and put me on the washing machine. I wanted to feel his love inside me so much. Throwing my legs around his waist and I nestled into him. With eyes closed, I could feel that he was lifting me like a feather. My arms were around his neck, kissing him. I could see that his longing was as intense as mine. In one smooth movement he entered me. He needed no instructions on rhythm or pace now. We were enjoying each other, all anxieties far away now. I felt once again a desired and a beloved woman. In return I was giving him something that belonged only to me, myself! All my accumulated tenderness, passion, power and love I gave to him then and there. We mounted and surrendered to our passion.

We lost all track of time and reality. Kissing me he continued to say "Snow White, I love you" kissing my shoulders, breasts, hair. Having disheveled all my hair, he laughed "You're a fantastic woman and you`re mine! I feel it and I know it! Do you hear, I will wait for you forever, even for a lifetime!" He gently removed me from the washing machine and put me on my feet. Burying my head in his chest, for the last time, I inhaled the smell of his body and perfume.

"Yes, Ivan! I'm yours, it's true! I'll miss you" I said, putting on my dress again and straightening my hair.

Coming out of the bathroom, we returned to reality. Time had passed too quickly. Tim could return at any moment. I went with Ivan to our door, kissed goodbye and parted ways.

Chapter 18

My husband came back in the evening, cheerful and happy. It was clear that he had enjoyed his time with his friend. He mentioned that I looked good. He ate his cooked dinner and went to sit down, to watch TV.

I was busy with the children when my mother-in-law called. I vaguely heard them talking. Tim listened to her for a long time and then promised to find out everything. I knew immediately she had come to report to him about my gentleman caller that day!

"Taya, my mum has been telling me that today while I was out" he started, looking at me questioningly "some young man came to our home? Mum saw him in the elevator. She thought he looked suspicious. He told her that he was coming to see Anya on business, but my mum had her doubts. Anya, is not here for several days? Why did he come to her, if she isn`t here? What kind of business?" Tim was looking at me suspiciously "Who is he?"

"He is my young lover" jokingly, I replied. "That's what your mother wants to believe. Isn't it? If she doesn`t believe that this man brought Anya CD from work. Yes, all the time while you were in Ireland, I had a lover, a young and handsome one!" I kept joking.

Tim was looking at me, not knowing whether I was joking or telling the truth.

"We regularly have sex! He is in love with me! In me he sees a sexy beautiful woman, the one that you no longer notice" I scoffed.

"Taya, you're joking, right?" frightened, he asked.

"Why do you look so worried? You no longer see a woman in me, you don`t care about my thoughts and desires?"

"Taya, please don't mock. Is he really your lover?" Tim repeated his question with a serious tone now.

"No, Tim, but you can tell your mum that he is my lover! I'm telling you, he`s Anya`s workmate! You don`t believe me, do you? That's your problem. If you don't trust me then don't go out all day to your private business meetings. Stay here and watch me. I didn't ask you where you went all day and what you did from when you left until you returned. I went then to attend to the children.

He called his mum on the phone, talked to her and then he came to me.

"Taya, I'm fool, I'm sorry. Mum is old and gets confused easily and I believed her. I'm sorry" Tim seemed to speak honestly. He put his arms around my shoulders. "I'm fool, I don`t know what came over me!?" he continued "I was jealous. I just arrived back and you are all blooming, rested, happy and beautiful. Let's start from the beginning. We`ll fly away to Turkey and forget our quarrels and bad things" he was patting my hair and looking into my eyes with regret.

I felt sorry for him.

"My dear wife, I love you, I promise, we will be fine". And having kissed me on the cheek, he took Yana up and carried her to the window, to show her cars. The conversation was over.

Such an old interfering mother-in-law she is! I was thinking. She hoped to separate me and Tim with a scandal. I don`t understand what is going on in their old minds? She had to tell her son and upset his nerves. She is so stupid! Doesn`t she realize that I would get out of it someway. Little does she know the real truth! I will have the last laugh, wait and see.

Saying goodbye to my family and kissing my daughter a thousand times. We got into a taxi and went to the airport. I was wearing a white linen pants and a peach-colored T-shirt and brought a white linen jacket, just in case it was chilly.

Henry, crazy about airplanes, was watching from the window of the holding room. The day before we had bought him a toy plane, he took it with him and drove it on the floor.

In the plane, we sat three in a row. My son sat half of the flight beside the illuminator and then crawled closer to me, exchanging places with his dad. I sat near the passage way. At this time, they were carrying out meals and Henry wanted a tomato juice. As soon as he picked up the juice, whether Tim turned somehow or maybe Henry jumped but the whole tomato juice spilled on my legs and stomach. I had neither words nor expressions, what a mess. My linen trousers were no longer white, but red-orange. I rushed to the bathroom, washed it and wiped it. The trousers were ruined and I was all wet.

Having suppressed my anger and with my eyes blazing, I sat quietly till the end of the flight. Tim apologized, not knowing how it happened. No matter what he said my mood was spoiled.

When we arrived in Turkey it was so warm and sunny. We got to the hotel quickly. Along roads, rhododendrons were blooming, camels were grazing and the Turks were trading all sorts of things. The hotel was located on the front line and had its own beach.

We quickly settled down and changed our clothes, we immediately headed off the swimming pool.

At the hotel area, there were five pools. Henry and Tim left to swim and I went to walk for a look around. I liked the hotel, it was buried in the green grove of eucalyptus trees and other conifers. I was happy with the choice of hotel, I am pleased we will be staying here for ten days.

My favorite thing to do at the beginning of a holiday is to have a Spa treatment. I especially like a whole body scrub and skin wrap. Following this treatment my tan sticks very well and lasts much longer. Such scrubs and wraps deeply clean the skin, removing dead skin cells and stimulating lymph flow. This removes toxins from the body, after this procedure, I always feel comfortable. My skin becomes velvety and fresh.

On the first day, I signed up for the full evening in the Spa. Timothy and Henry went to jet-ski, I went for my relaxation treatments.

Time for a Change

At the reception, much to my surprise, a young twenty five years old cute Turk was waiting to give me my treatment! He`s a masseur and beauty therapist who gives the scrub and wrap treatments. I am shocked as I never had a male masseur work on me before. Usually it is only women that I am familiar with in this job.

He explained that first I would have a sauna treatment and he would prepare the treatment room for me in this time. The treatment room was small and the interior was in oriental style. In the corner of the room there was a shower stall, without doors. He gave a towel and asked me to undress and take a shower. I stared at him, wide-eyed and suddenly shy of exposing my body in front of him. I stood and stared, waiting for him to leave the room. He didn't seem in any hurry to go and explained in broken Russian, with a strong Turkish accent "at this stage of the treatment, after you shower can you please come over here to the couch and be naked. I need your clear skin to begin the skin scrub before the wrap".

I couldn't do all of this in front of him, a complete stranger, even if he is a masseur. I had to ask him to leave while I undressed and showered. I reassured him I would call him when I was positioned on the couch and draped in my towel.

He lowered the lights, the room was dim with only aromatherapy candles lightening. He turned on relaxing sounds of surf waves. I was lying down on my back, on a soft towel. He took aroma therapy oil mixture in his hands and beginning from the tips of my toes, slowly applying the mixture to my body. I closed my eyes and tried to relax as his hands glided expertly over my fully naked and glistening torso. He worked in silence.

I lay there in silence too, but I couldn't relax. There were so many thoughts swimming in my head and I couldn't settle them. His firm but gently massaging was so distracting to me and now he became an object of curiosity for me. I wondered how many other women's bodies he has massaged in such a manner? For sure he has expert hands and a calm energy. He is cute too! I wonder if he was ever offered sex by his clients? Some women would chance to ask I'm sure.

He asked me to turn over on my back and continued to apply a scrub. Then, having left my body to rest for a few minutes, he offered me a drink of cool water.

The next stage this process was the massaging scrub purification this lasted only a few minutes. He then asked me to take a shower and turned on the water for me. Giving me some level of privacy he turned away and began to mix more oils. I pulled the towel around me as I would then be covered as I walked over to the shower. I washed the scrub off and dried myself and returned to lie down on the couch. This time it was the mud thermic treatment. I was slowly getting used to his presence in the room, I wasn't as self-conscious anymore and his silence helped to calm me. He took the thermic mud and again began to apply it on me, having warned me first "Madam, you may find this prickly, but that's normal so don't be alarmed. I will not apply it to your face".

I smiled my understanding to him. Although my face was untouched he already had touched me everywhere. I was thinking lying and feeling his hands

Time for a Change

running around my body. Several times I shuddered, the feelings was strange, small tingle mixed with excitement. Maybe he pressed some special places on my feet? Sly Turk! I smiled to myself.

He evidently noticed my smile asked "Madame, you are enjoying the treatment, yes?"

To tell a lie in response was pointless so I plainly answered "yes, thank you, I am".

In his Turkish accent in broken Russian he continued "Madam, I am doing you a massage with sea mud. I like your body, it is elastic and Madame's muscles are beautiful and contouring. Sometimes such big women come and their bodies look like wafers. I've already work here for six years and a body like Madame's I see rarely".

He lies for sure, this charming Turk! I thought but I replied nothing. He then closed the thermic capsule and went into another room, having promised to come back in a few minutes.

I was lying and now relaxing in the warmth. The temperature was slowly rising, after a while it seemed that mud was boiling inside the capsule. I felt a little creepy. At last he came back and the first thing I asked him to do for me was to reduce the temperature and also to give some cool water again. He obediently did both requests for me. The temperature in the capsule was slowly decreasing. I was comfortable and I didn't notice the time passing. At the appointed time he returned and freed me from the temporary encasement. Again he directed me to the shower. I did his bidding and when I came out, he handed me a robe.

He brought me freshly squeezed juice "Madam, did you like the treatment?" he asked, smiling sweetly.

"Yes, thank you. You have expert hands" I answered honestly.

"I`m not like the others. I don`t smoke, don`t drink and don`t walk at night. May we meet tomorrow or later today to walk and talk together? I like you" he looked at me with wide expectant eyes open and definitely hoped for a positive answer.

"Sorry, I`ve come here to rest, not to find a holiday romance. I am here with my husband and child. I wish you luck in finding a lady friend!" I got up quickly then and left.

"Madame, if you want to have another massage, please do come back. I can do and I will give you a discount" he suggested me as I left, throwing up his hands in confusion.

I will think about it" I smiled and went to change into my clothes.

Well, Taya, your adventures continue, I smiled to myself. I actually wanted to say to him "grow up and learn Russian"

The days passed easily. My relations with Tim at last seemed improved. We talked all day, went swimming, laughed and ate together. He had started to give me nightly sensual massages of his own free will and enjoyment. A few times when we went to the nearest town, he bought me gifts. Our sex life had returned and it was as full-blown and colorful as ever before. Henry tired from swimming and his days activities slept well every night. So then we had private time to enjoy each other. All of this compensated in some way for the sexual drought we had just passed through. Any thought of Ivan didn`t come into my

Time for a Change

head. I loved my husband and it was bringing me joy and satisfaction.

From our holiday in Turkey, we returned all rested and tanned. I closed my eyes, pretending I'm sleeping. Thoughts haunted me. Feeling of guilt in front of Tim was gnawing inside me. Thoughts like a short film flew through my mind, about our ten days of vacation. Have I rested? Yes, I have, had enough of sleep and swim, got a great pleasure from our son. Tim was reading. I remembered our last night before we left, we were sitting on the terrace and smoking milk hookah. I was drinking wine, he was drinking brandy. He was looking at me tenderly and lovingly, having taken my hand, he was looking at my hand and then he kissed it.

"Taya, I'm so happy that everything has clicked into place again for us. You're so sexy and beautiful. All these days, I admire you in the pool and on the beach. Forgive me, please. I don't know why we were so distant and strained from each other in recently. I must have had a midlife crisis?" he joked.

"I will try to understand and move on together from the hurts of our past few months" I said sincerely. "The most important thing is that we are together. I want to live with you, I'm your wife. I hope we won't be like pieces of ice to each other ever again. Tim, if we don't make the effort to change, then we will become strangers and will separate" I added truly and sadly.

"Taya, you and the children, are everything to me in this world. There is nothing more precious" he leaned over and kissed me gently but sincerely.

I was filled with peace and happiness. I've always wanted to make people I love happy and now Tim has made me happy. Yes, our relaxing Turkish holiday experience is behind us and soon we will be back in Kiev. I need as soft and as quickly as possible to break the relationship that Ivan and I have. I only have five days left before leaving for Ireland. I was looking forward to landing. I`ll be glad when I`m at home so I can see my daughter, my little star, I was thinking and looking lovingly at my sleeping son.

At home, everything and everyone was fine. Yana, the whole week, was with my mother in the countryside. She bathed her in an inflatable pool, she loved splashing in the warm water. Yana too was tanned and looked healthy. When she saw us, she held up her two tiny hands, she was eleven months old. "Mumy, mumy" she chirped continuing her childish babbling. I was kissing and hugging her many times. Henry was showing her his robot and telling her about the sea. The whole family shone with being together again.

We spent the entire evening exchanging holiday stories and experiences. We gave them our souvenirs and gifts. I heartily thanked mum and Anya for their help with Yana. Mum saw in my happy face, all the answers she needed and without a word, understood that my husband and I had fixed our relationship.

Chapter 19

Our departure date home to Ireland was coming fast. All these days I was rushing to the shops, buying presents for my Irish friends and packing our suitcases. I met on last time before our departure with Tim`s relatives and my friends. All these busy days and events consumed me and time slipped away. I did call on the phone to Ivan a couple of times and chatted with him for a few minutes. But there was no time for us to meet up.

"Our flight is tomorrow evening" I was saying to Anya. "I should try to meet with Ivan. Even for half an hour. I'll go today to his work to say goodbye". I was surprising myself with my calmness and apparent indifference.

Anya was making a flower, sitting on the couch. She raised her head, looked carefully at me and asked, "Taya, and will you leave him fully? Or what? You drove the kid crazy. So now you just kiss him goodbye?" she asked astonished.

"It's the only way now. I won`t accept any promises from him. God grant, he`ll meet a nice girl, and forget about me. He'll be happy and in love again. I'll see him now aiming to break our relationship. I have to finish this affair. I really do like him. I feel when I am with him, like a teenager, all cheerful and carefree. Like a butterfly I was fluttering all summer. It is sad to give up on him. But I have to!" I retorted.

What shall I wear? I was thinking. I came across a thin cotton white dress with printed blue flowers. Length of it was above the knee. It effectively emphasized my tan and blond hair. I gathered up my hair, pinned it up with light blue barrette, put on some light natural make up and came to Anya to get her opinion on how I looked.

"How do I look? Not bad for a last date and memory?"

"Wow, you look like a sex bomb! Poor Ivan! How can he resist you? In your case, you need to wear a burqa, for him not to see your seductive body" jokingly said my sister.

The restaurant was full of people. I sat down at a table and called the waiter. I ordered fresh juice "please tell Ivan that Taya is waiting for him. Thank you" the waiter left to deliver my message.

A few minutes later, Ivan appeared in the saloon. He came up to me, smiling happily "what a surprise my darling! You look adorable, all tanned and rested. How is Henry, did he like the sea?" he kissed me on my cheek and sat down. "I missed you very much. Can I meet with you privately before you leave?" he asked hopefully.

"Ivan, what time do you have a break here today?" I asked meekly.

"I can take it right now for a few minutes if you need. Wait, I'll go over to agree it with my workmate. Are you in a hurry?" he anxiously added.

"No I`m not in a hurry today. It's just that we leave tomorrow!" I said without making eye contact with him.

"Wait here. I'll bring you a fresh juice and we can talk" with that he left. I felt the eyes of his work colleagues on me. A random thought flashed through my head, that, maybe one or all of the waitresses here have the hots for him? At this thought, Ivan returned with my fresh juice in his hand. He sat down next to me "You are telling me that you are leaving tomorrow?" with sadness in his eyes and he was nervous.

"Ivan, you knew it was going to happen sooner or later" I was choosing my words as carefully as I could as I didn`t want to hurt him. He was looking past me. I finished my fresh juice.

He got up "let`s go" he said and took my hand. I obediently followed him. We passed through the back rooms and went out to the backyard. Not fully understanding what it is he wants or what he wants to do. I stood there silently and waited until he said something. He was smoking.

"Taya, when will you come back?" he was looking straight into my eyes.

"I don`t know for sure, maybe next summer. I have to work. Understand that this is my life, my way to earn a living. Here, I come only for a visit. Ivan, please listen to me, try to forget about me, about all that was between us. I free you from all your promises. Find a nice girl and love the one who is worthy of your love" I said as I mustered up my courage.

Ivan was looking at me as if I was crazy. Suddenly he was in front of me on his knees and kissing my hands, saying "Snow White, listening to what you are saying. What nonsense are you talking?" I left his last sentence dangling in mid-air "Ivan, please get up from your knees, don`t make an eighteenth century scene!"

He wasn't paying any attention to my plea and continued "I love you. Understand, you can`t love someone and then forget it. If this love is not good for you now in your life, I told you, I will wait for you. You can text me messages and I will text you too. I would like to call you and hear your voice occasionally. I spent these past days thinking about you and only you. I was waiting for your return from Turkey. I will wait with the same patience for your return from Ireland next year too" he implored.

"Ivan, I beg you, please get up from your knees" at last he stood up, his eyes were clouded with grief. I couldn`t look at him, my heart was breaking "Ivan, I'm sorry. I felt good with you, believe me. I was the happiest woman with you for these past few months. I wish you happiness always. Ivan don`t forget I'm married and nothing can change that. Nothing! As much as I may want to be with you, I can't be"

"Taya, I'm not stupid, there is need to explain obvious things to me" he started kissing me. As we were kissing, I realized I couldn`t just brush him aside and break this relationship without pain to both of us. He gave me a final hug, I didn`t resist it. Such actions are necessary to give people hope. Sometimes this is more important than ideals or principles. Kissing him gently good-bye, I left. I promised him to call once I was back in Ireland.

Time for a Change

"See you soon, my darling" Ivan whispered as I left "I'll be waiting for you" and he returned to the restaurant.

I was going home to Tim and my children and I was all upset. I couldn't just brush off Ivan. Instead I gave hope to him, I felt sad in my heart. Tomorrow we depart Kiev.

In the evening, we went for dinner to my parents-in-law. I had asked Anya to call me after about half an hour, with any excuse so that I have to return home. Their grandchildren and their son is enough for them. Mary cooked the dinner, she was trying to impress her son. Tim is a vegetarian, for about twenty years now. She cooked his favorite stuffed peppers with a selection of salads. "Well done, Mary!" I thought. At first, the conversation at the table was neutral about the weather and about the heat. Then the conversation went smoothly into another topic, about money and savings.

"Well, Tim, ask Taya, why does she buy two kinds of cheese?" Mary slyly asked addressing her son.

"Taya, why do you buy two kinds of cheese?" jokingly teased my husband.

"Simple" I brightly replied "because Henry likes cheese with large holes and I like cheese with small holes" playing along, I answered.

"Now, mum, do you understand? That's why my dear sweet Taya buys two kinds of cheese" replied Tim triumphantly.

"I consider that a waste of money" my mother-in-law continued and not leaving me alone "she constantly is buying cakes, pastries, children chocolate, cake cheese and drinking yogurts. Here, your father and I drink buttermilk. We consider there is nothing as healthy. Your Henry will never touch buttermilk! One time, I tried to give him buttermilk and he told me "Granny, no! This is smelly milk! Give me what my mum gives me in small bottles" You and all other kids all their lives used to drink buttermilk. Now, you give yogurts! Do you know how much yogurts cost? And cookies and candies, she spends money for all of this" my mother-in-law was saying bitterly, without paying any attention to my presence.

For all the outward calmness I showed, I could feel anger rising inside me. Irritated I was thinking "why hasn't Anya called by now to offer me escape?" I had lost my appetite for dinner.

"Tim" continued Mary "if only you could have seen Taya and her sister, they were drinking wine and beer all summer! They could drink a whole bottle in one night! Because you were not here, I was checking in on them to check if everything is going ok for them. Imagine my shock" she significantly paused and then continued "there they were in the kitchen and the opened bottle of wine and wine glasses out for all to see! The bin was full of empty beer cans! There was also lot of different and expensive kinds of food in the fridge! She has items such as smoked fish and baked ham. Also two kinds of sausage meat, cheese and fruits. I can't remember all. As you were working hard in Ireland, she is here spending it all foolishly" she bleated.

From her arrogance, my eyes popped out. Keeping my emotions under control, I was hoping for support from my husband. As of yet none was forthcoming.

So in my own time I asked mother-in-law "Mary, did you go to check the bathroom too?"

Time for a Change

"Yes, as a matter of fact I did" and without any feeling of invading my privacy she continued with her rant "you could buy more cheap washing powder. You wash with "Ariel" aand you whirl those clothes a few hours in the washing machine. You should take it all and wash with your hands in several waters, as we used to do. Yes, in general, you wash half-dirty laundry. In my day children had a pair of tights, socks or pants on for several days before washing".

"And my underwear, have you had them also checked for dirt?" I asked in disgust.

"Well, there is nothing to check? I fumbled a couple of times among your rags. You have dozens of underpants, all transparent, like pieces of ropes. How do you cover your ass with it?" she scoffed.

My father-in-law was almost silent during this exchange. Timothy decided to stop this empty talk "Mum, please stop! Taya is a grown up person and she works as much as I do. She has the right to spend her money, at her own pleasure. I also was drinking beer and wine in Ireland. So does that mean that I am an alcoholic or an over spender?!" he retorted "whatever she chooses to cover her ass with, is her business. I quiet like her sexy "pieces of ropes" as you say" he smiled and winked at me. This made me blush with pride.

"Well, whatever, as you say it's her business and she is your wife" said Mary with irritation and got up to clean the table.

I suggested to Tim to go and help his mother that I will go so that I can continue to pack suitcases. Thanking all in general for dinner I stood up to leave.

"How about tea and dessert?" my father-in-law suddenly perked up and addressed me. He had been like an old rooster all during our conversation, seeming to be asleep, sitting on the fence.

"I`ll have my tea at home. I`m too full now, thank you" and I left Tim and the children there for the remainder of their evening together.

She gets even crazier the older she gets, I am thinking on my way home. Imagine, when I am her age, I poke in my daughter-in-laws fridge, trash and delve into her children`s dirty laundry! I remember then a story that my mother-in-law told me after I married Tim. I noticed that she didn't like her mother-in-law, her husband, Pasha's mother. I had warm relations with Tim`s grandmother from the first time I meet her until her death.

"Taya" my mother-in-law Mary used to tell me, "can you imagine when Pasha and I got married we lived together with his mother. When I was doing our washing, she stood over me, like a supervisor and gave me instructions and criticism on how to wash Pasha`s shirts? The first few times, I said nothing, and then one day, I gave her a piece of my mind. We had an argument. She told lies about me to Pasha, but he paid no attention to her. We never spoke to each other much after this event.

After hearing this story, I felt sorry for Mary. But it was clear to me that she never learned from this experience as she treated me with the same level of suspicion and indifference. I have to accept and endure my situation. We will be flying back to Ireland tomorrow and I can forget about them, like a bad dream, for another year.

I entered our apartment, Anya was sleeping sweetly. Poor girl, she fell asleep and didn`t call me. I quietly went to the kitchen and switched on the kettle. I poured myself tea, called my mum. We agreed that she will come to us in the morning and say goodbye. Tim came back with the children and Anya woke up. We asked Tim to run down to the store for wine, cheese and cake. That the evening, after putting the children to bed, Tim was playing on the computer and my sister and I again took the wine glasses and poured some wine. We toasted all the good things that had happened during this summer: our vacation time, to the children, to our mother. Of course, to us, the two over spenders and drunkards according to the definition of my mother-in-law!

Our mum came in the morning. She was playing with the children, kissing and squeezing them. The children adored my mum, she always gave them some gifts. Today, Henry received a gift of a new small truck and Yana got a doll.

Our taxi arrived on time. Tim's parents also came then. Mary was hugging her son and crying. Pasha, fussing as usual, kept reminding us continuously about passports and tickets.

I hugged mum and crying said to her "Mum, thank you for all your help. I love you. I'll call you as soon as we land" I hugged and kissed mum for the last time, feeling a lump in my throat and hardly holding back my tears. Her eyes too were full of tears. I knew my mother would cry when she will be alone that day and for the next few weeks on and off. Being a strong woman, she never cries in public. Anya didn't go with us to the airport as she had to work. We said our good byes through more tears "take care, I love you, thank you for everything" I said to my sister. "I love you too,

I'll be waiting for your call, take care of yourself and your children" she broke off unable to continue.

Finally, I hugged my parents-in-law and thanked them for their help.

Chapter 20

Several hours later and we arrived in welcoming, rainy Ireland. We quickly passed through customs and went out of the airport to the fresh air. The kids were tired and naughty too. We hurried to get home. Tim, before he left for Kiev, had asked our neighbors to water the flowers and look after our house. I was glad now to return to my own home. We brought the suitcases inside and for the first time in hours we felt relaxed.

I hugged my husband and happily asked "do you want some tea and biscuits?" I opened a pack of biscuits and we sat down to have tea.

When you come back from holiday, the most tiresome thing is the unpacking. During the next day I was sorting out our clothes. Of course, if I was alone, I`d have this sorted very quickly. But the children were helping me, they were playing a game with the clothes. This game involved making various parcels from the clothes and carrying them all over the house. Some kind of game! It took me ages to track these stray parcels and get the washing started.

While unpacking, I noticed that Tim had bought around a dozen CD's with computer games on them. That's a lot of computer games I was thinking and then the thought struck me that maybe some work colleague had asked him to bring them back for him. And without giving it another thought I continued to unpack the suitcases.

Now that we were home the time was going by quickly as we settled back in. Henry and Yana went to the new crech. They liked being with other children and they were happy. I returned to my busy work schedule. A lot of documents, all for translation, formed a backlog on my desk. Also in September a wave of refugees arrived.

Our plan was that in the mornings I would bring the children to the creche and from there go on to work. Tim would pick them up from the creche in the evenings. They would eat at home and play while waiting for me. It would be busy but we can manage it.

There was however one big exception. As Tim is a vegetarian, he completely refuses to give our children any meat. We had strong disagreements from time to time because of this. It was impossible to change him in this matter. I let them eat everything, both meat and fish. My belief is in nutrition. Now that I was returning from work late in the evening, I began to prepare the dinner the evening before so it only needed to be heated when Tim came home with them. Often this prepared dinner remained untouched in the fridge. On questioning Tim "did the children enjoy their dinner today?" his calm answer was "Oh, I cooked them spaghetti" or sometimes a different answer "they

Time for a Change

didn`t want to eat so I gave them cookies and put them to bed".

Such answered made me angry. But since I am a person who believes in solving problems in a peaceful way, I held back. Until one day I came home earlier and saw the following. My husband wasn`t expecting me home, I hadn't called ahead to him. I wanted to surprise them, but it was me who got the surprise. I came home, Tim was sitting at the computer and Henry was climbing on the kitchen chair to get cookies.

"Mummys home" he exclaimed happily, having forgotten about cookies he got down off the chair. Yana, too, ran out of the room and gave me a tight hug.

"Have you eaten yet?" I ask my son.

"No not yet. Dad is sitting and playing on the computer. I asked him to feed us and he said "I`m coming but he doesn`t come" so I put the chair here and reached up to the shelf all by myself" he proudly reported to me. "For biscuits" he concluded.

I kissed him on his cheeks. "Now, we`ll eat. I`ll just wash my hands. I`ll give you lollipop instead of cookies, if you`ll eat all your dinner" I cheerfully added.

Tim was so wrapped up in his computer game, that he didn`t hear me arrive home. Some thirty minutes later he became aware that I was home just as we were finishing our dinner.

"Oh, you're home already?" he was genuinely surprised. "I never heard you. Since the children were so quiet, I went to play on the computer" he said innocently.

I didn't reply to him. I was disgusted by his behavior and I didn't want to release my anger in front of the children. After the children were in bed and settled. I went down to the living room to talk to my husband. "Firstly, tell me, to whom did you bring all these CD computers games for?"

He looked at me as if I was crazy and calmly replied "for myself, of course!"

"And, do you have time to play all of these games?" I continued questioning.

"Oh yes, the children are busy by themselves and I play. You know, now I'm playing such a cool game. You have to choose a strategy" he began to explain "and then..."

I interrupted his speech, I`ll be damned if he thinks I am going to listen to his explanation about his games. "Tim, you are the father of two young children! Can you fully you understand that? They want to spend time with you, not to see your back at the computer! And instead of giving children cookies you can heat up the cooked dinner I leave prepared for the in the fridge" I was so serious with my words.

He calmly looked at me. I hated his ability to remain calm at all times.

"In the fridge, there are only meat dishes" he was mumbling.

I opened the fridge in anger saying "open your eyes! There are yogurts, cheese and vegetables. Is it difficult for you at least to make a sandwich for the children?"

"There are sausages there too! I don`t ever want to touch meat with my hands" he announced.

"We had a deal, I cook the dinner in advance meal and you feed them. But now you don't even feed them and all the wasted food is flushed down the toilet! Do you think this is right?" I sighed loudly. I hated his vegetarianism and above all else I hated his selfishness.

"No" he said, "I won't give them meat or sausage. You poison them by yourself if you want?" and he went back to the computer.

Such a moron, I was thinking, staring after him.

After this argument, we didn't talk for several days, there wasn't anything to talk about. Every evening, I came in from work and it was the same scenario. I am greeted with the smiles of my children and his back facing them and him on the computer. Our relationship is doomed again. Following this argument, I asked in work if I could finish before five every evening. Now, in the evening I was at home, I would feed the children, bath them and read them fairy tales before settling them to sleep. Then I had to work late into the night as I had to translate the remaining documents from my office work.

Tim was working during day and in the evenings he was playing his games. He was oblivious to us and our needs. More and more he was staying up until to two a.m. As a result in the mornings, he was sleepy, grumpy and unhappy. At weekends, he was sleeping all day and playing these games all night. In such a vaccum I had exist and pretend to be happy for the children's sake.

Tim refused to help me with any domestic chores, using the excuse that he was tired. He just said this excuse so he could escape to his computer. He was complaining to Arthur that I don`t understand him or give him any personal space.

In my loneliness, I was recalling Ivan and our sunny summer of love. Ivan was texting me occasionally, he was reassuring me of his constant love for me and that he will always be waiting for me. I missed his companionship. Sex with my husband was out of the question, he just wasn`t up to it. He was too busy working out strategies for the game, taking notes and playing more. Tim seemed quite happy with this situation. I thought I would go crazy!

Chapter 21

The day before New Year's Day, Yana became sick. We treated her at home, thinking it was a virus. But her condition worsened and we both were taken to the hospital. The results of her tests and examinations showed that she needs kidney surgery. We were advised the sooner the better and that there is no other option. Otherwise, she`d lose a kidney.

In Ireland, this operation cost about 30 thousand Euros. We started to search for clinics in Kiev and found a children's surgeon who specializes in this. This stress jolted Tim out of his addiction to computer games. He loves his daughter very much and he focused clearly on this task to sort out what was best for her. I was relived.

I took leave from my job and began to get ready to go to Kiev. We talked to the surgeon over the phone. He advised us not to think of travelling back to Ireland before five months. Tim took a month vacation from his job and we immediately started our trip to Kiev.

When we arrived there was plenty of frost and snow as it was February. At the airport, we were met, as always by Anya. The children hugged her they were so excited and looking around everywhere. They were tired after the flight. When we were putting the luggage into the car, Henry was crouching on the parking lot and touching the snow "Wow it's so cold and wet. Mummy, it's so cold. Snow, snow!" he exclaimed with excitement as he was threw a handful of snow-flakes in the air. Yana, at first looking at him, then took the snow in her hands too and tossed it around "Snow!" she repeated and laughed.

"Yes, children, this winter is very snowy and we have a sled. I will take you both for a ride in it" Anya was saying.

I was smiling, trying not to show my worries and concerns. I was looking at my sister, my husband and my children, thinking that only God knows the troubles in my heart and mind.

On the fourth day after our arrival, we went to the hospital. Yana and I were provided with a separate room en-suite. They did lots of tests including ultrasounds, CT scans, X-rays and bloods. These were all necessary for the pre-operative preparation work-up.

We met with the surgeon. He was a student of the old Soviet school, with great experience in his field. I felt reassured after our discussion about the planned operation and expectations during recovery. Because of his reassurance and experience, I was able to stop shaking with nerves and apprehension.

His name was Dr. Basil. He had made a good impression on me. I had full confidence in this man who would operate on my child. He had an excellent reputation and is of international standard. I placed my complete trust in his skill and abilities.

Looking at my daughter, my heart was breaking into small pieces. She is such a good little girl, very playful and smiling. She will have to go through a lot of pain. I have to accept that this is how it will be.

Within myself, I was in torment. I was blaming myself for not picking up in any of Yana's words or expressions that she was unwell. I felt that God had sent this punishment to me, for my fornication. He is punishing me, through my daughter. These thoughts and the gnawing guilt were constantly in my mind.

The operation was scheduled for nine o'clock a.m. Yana felt good and by now she had no fear of the nurse's white uniforms. When the nurse was taking her for surgery, my daughter was smiling and relaxed.

The operation lasted for two hours. During this time, I was sitting still, in our room, on the bed. Tim was sitting beside me. We tried to make conversation, but our voices were strange and our words seemed meaningless. I tried to read magazines, but again I couldn't concentrate and I was flipping through the pages automatically. "Tim, she will be alright, wont she?" I kept asking him again and again. Wearily, I got off the bed and went to the window. Outside, small flakes of snow were falling gently down.

Tim sat motionless, as if he was in a frozen state and was completely silent.

I sighed, I thought he doesn't either see or hear me. He too is in his own world of concern and worries. I remained standing with my empty head and aching heart. I could feel the blood pulsating in my temples, "God, please make her recover". I was reading the

"Our Father" and "Holy Mother" I remembered too the prayers that I heard from my grandmother in my childhood.

"Taya" suddenly Tim said, so unexpected that I was startled. "Taya" he repeated "Soon, the surgery finishes. The surgeon is brilliant, all will be well".

I started to cry, trying to hide my tears. I buried my nose in the glass of the window. "God, give her strength, give her health again" I was whispering.

After a while, the nurse came in and said "follow me, Yana is now in the Intensive Care, you can see her. Everything is good, the operation is over. Tomorrow night, she should be transferred to the ward. You can go home and rest".

We, in our trance like state, stood up and followed her silently. On the door, there was a sign, "No Trespassing." The door opened and I saw her. She was connected to a monitor. My sweet Yana, all lonely and pale faced, her small body so vulnerable under a thin sheet. She had all sorts of lines, catheters and drainage tubes coming from her. "You see, she is sleeping and is stable" continued to nurse "don't worry, leave your phone number with me and go home and rest. Everything will be fine. The surgeon is still in surgery but he will talk to you both, tomorrow morning".

Exhausted and drained we went home. Henry was such a pleasant distraction for us and we played with him arranging puzzles that he wanted to do. I couldn't wait for the day and night to pass so I could go back and see Yana again. The day seemed like an eternity.

That night, I had a strong toothache. I took a lot of painkillers to get me through the morning as we were going to meet with the surgeon first thing. He informed us that the surgery had been a success and he expected an uneventful recovery within a few months. He promised to transfer Yana to the ward around noon and we could see her then. Thanking him, I left to go to the dentist and Tim offered to wait at the hospital so that one of us would be there when she was transferred.

I vaguely remembered that somewhere near the hospital, was a dental clinic. To my pleasant surprise, I quickly found the clinic. It looked like a dentist with a good reputation and business. I asked for an emergency review and had only a few minutes to wait in the reception area. Then I was escorted I was sent to a room with the name "Lomov" on the door. I hope he's a good dentist and I don't have any regrets about his skills, I was thinking as I entered the room. Dr. Lomov was a young doctor about thirty years old.

I sat in the chair. I don't have any fear of the dentist and never have had. I really wanted to sort this out quickly. I was anxious to be at my daughter's bedside. After telling him my story of toothache, I opened my mouth and the examination started. He then confidently said "Your tooth needs to come out!"

I agreed "Ok, pull it out so" I consented.

"You will need anti-inflammatories too, to reduce the swelling. I will write you a prescription" continued the dentist.

I nodded, letting him know that I understood him fully. After a few minutes, my unfortunate tooth was pulled out. The prescription was written. I was now free to be at my daughter's bedside.

When I entered the ward, Yana was lying in a position like a star. She was on her tummy, arms and legs in different directions. Her arms were pierced with butterfly-needles attached to the monitoring system. From her sides were two drainage bags. One is for the drainage of blood from the wound and the other one, for urine.

She was sleeping, as they had her under sedation for now. She needs rest for recovery and healing. Following kidney surgery the recovery is a very important phase.

"How is she? Did she wake up? When was she transferred to here?" I bombarded my husband with questions on my return.

"She is doing well, they are pleased with her" Tim replied, carefully adjusting her blanket.

"Thank God" I was looking at her and crying. I felt so sorry for her. The attending physician promised to discharge her, in two weeks, if her recovery is uneventful.

Tim went home then to rest. I remained beside Yana for twenty-four-hours. Occasionally my sister and mother would relief me so I could wash and eat. Tim came every day to check in on us. Then he would leave after a few hours, to run his errands.

Five days have passed slowly like this and thankfully Yana was slowly getting better.

On one such day, my daughter had fallen asleep, so I went to walk in the hallway. A woman came up to me. I had seen her before her daughter also was a patient. They were in the next ward. She introduced herself. Her name was Irina, she looked at about thirty-five years old. She had a friendly face and was wearing a jumpsuit. She looked tired and upset as her eyes had dark circles underneath and red, swollen eyelids.

"How are you? How is your daughter?" she greeted me with a tired depressed voice.

"All seems to be going well. Yana is only one and a half year old, so she can`t tell us how she feels. The doctors are pleased with her test and blood results and Yana seems happy in herself" I cheerily reported.

"Have you been here for long time? I hear that your daughter had surgery too? How is she doing?" I enquired.

"Yes, I have been here for a very long time. It`s been four months now" said Irina, her face expressing pain and sorrow.

"It`s almost the end of winter now" she was speaking slowly, I realized she had retold this story many times before.

Sometimes as a mother you need to talk and share with another mother people. This is especially so when you have been through a trauma with your child. It helps you to deal with the loneliness and sadness. The world is full of kind hearted people. Some people are able to empathize and sympathize. I listened carefully to her, without interrupting.

"In autumn, at the beginning of September, we were on the riverside and Elena, my daughter, was playing near the water. I was preparing sandwiches, filling glasses and making our picnic. I hadn't noticed that she had wandered off, just twenty meters!" Irina sighed, her eyes filled with tears. "She just screamed! I heard her voice and ran to her. She was lying under the wheels of the jeep and the guy was sitting next to her, trying to get her out from under his wheel" Irina was crying, having taken my hand adding "Oh, God! You have no idea!? What I`ve been through!?

My girl, she's only nine years old! He hadn't seen her. She was squatting down in the long grass, examining something. The jeep practically run her down. It crushed the bones of her pelvis and legs, her stomach . . ." she paused and after some time went on. "Four teams of doctors at the same time were working in the operating room. They saved her to life, but she's disabled" a spark of hope flickered in her voice. "She's has already been operated on three times to restore the bones of the pelvis and repair her internal organs. The doctors here are wonderful specialists" she looked at the ward door, where Elena stayed. "She has gone through so much pain, she suffered so much, poor thing! How long more has she to suffer? They have planned more reconstructive surgery. She needs plastic surgery to give her labia, everything is ruined in her private parts. She's such a young girl to have to deal with all this. Will she ever be able to have children? How will she live an independent life?" Irina again began to cry. I hugged her and calmly said

"Elena, is alive, I too will pray for her! Miracles do and can happen! I'm very sorry that you have such trouble. Stay strong, she needs you. You are doing great after all you have been through. Elena is alive she will have a full life. She can continue her education, even while in hospital. She can draw, speak and read, these are all important skills for her to have. But most important now is for her to see her mother's smile. Your smile will help her to believe in her future".

"Thank you very much, sorry for off-loading all this on you" she sighed. "I am very tired I know I have to be positive. Thank you for understanding" she

Time for a Change

paused, she was going to continue talking, but at that moment, her daughter called her.

"Go to Elena. We'll meet again. We will also be here in the hospital for a long time, be brave" I told her and we went to our separate wards. Yana was still sleeping and I went and stood by the window looking at passers-by.

God, that poor child and her poor mother! I was shocked by their story. I was very sorry for this family. What can I do for them? How can I help? I heard my daughter move and then she opened her eyes. I leaned over to her. Her trusting eyes were looking at me, full of love. She was smiling. Thank God, children forget many things as they get older, so hopefully she won't remember this experience. I started to speak to her and she was telling me something as she was half asleep. We should thank God for every day and appreciate what we have, our loved ones, family and friends, I was thinking as I stroked her hair.

After my tooth had been pulled out, I didn't feel any better. I had an inflammation in my submandibular lymph glands. My gum wasn't completely healed and the pain had returned. I was taking painkillers and hoping that with each passing day it would improve. But no such luck. By the sixth day, I had such a strong toothache, I was driven to distraction. When Tim arrived that day to Yana's bedside, I immediately went to the dental clinic.

Dr. Lomov was not on duty that day. I was sent to see another doctor. After an examination, she took an x-ray and asked what Dr. Lomov had prescribed for me. I informed her and she was clearly horrified by the expression on her face. She gave me an injection to my jaw that included painkillers. She explained that my gums needed to be cleaned. She told me that I have to come to her for further treatment over the next several days to ensure that the infection doesn't travel down my neck.

Relieved from pain but upset by this new process, I returned to the hospital.

Tim left then and I stayed with Yana. That night, unexpectedly, diarrhea, vomiting and a fever started. The doctor examined her and then he called our surgeon for advice. They increased the rate of fluids through her vein and checked the drains and catheter. Poor Yana was so exhausted. She had no strength to even cry, she just moaned. In the morning, Dr. Basil examined Yana. His very presence calmed me. I could relax a bit now as I trusted his judgment fully. I dosed on and off in the chair beside her.

I waited for Tim, who was always late, to arrive to give me a small break. This always upset me but no matter how I expressed this to him he never heeded my opinion. Today, I had to go for the treatment to my tooth.

Eventually he came all cheerful and full of life; even having his computer with him so he wouldn't be bored staying with Yana! I was horrified but didn't have the strength to argue with him. I was hungry but because of my tooth, I hadn't really eaten properly for a week. I was only drinking yogurt and eating pureed foods. Angry at my husband and being tired from sleepless nights, my mood was not good. Now I was worried again because of Yana's latest set-back and complications. The whole world seemed black and dark to me, despite the beauty winter of the white snow outside the window.

"Tim, I'm very tired and I don't feel well. I have a sore tooth and my gums and head ache. It hurts so much that I can barely keep my eyes open. Can you stay with Yana until morning? I can rest at home and get to see Henry too. I have kept vigil here for the past seven days" I said with a weary voice.

"Of course I will stay. Please, after visiting the dentist, do go home and rest" he said with concern in his voice.

Surprised by his quick compliance to my request, I muttered a thank you and kissed him on the cheek and left.

Chapter 22

The morning frost cheered me. Needing the fresh air, I walked to the dentist. The smell of the hospital lingered in my brain along with the talks with worried parents of other sick children. I was filled with pity for these children and their parents. But, what can I do to help them? I am struggling with my own worries. I could feel a depression coming over me. Yana, you are just tired now, I reassured myself. Things will get better this nightmare too, will pass in time.

At the dentist, my treatment for my gum infection continued and then at last, I went home to rest.

While I was staying the week in the hospital with Yana, Anya has found a good private kindergarten for Henry. He liked being in the kindergarten and he was happy to go there.

When I arrived home, no one was in. Anya brought Henry from the kindergarten. He was thrilled that I was home to spend time with him. He kept asking when Yana would be back. I could see that he was sad without her and he misses his little sister. It is good that they love each other, I was thinking. Henry drew a picture for Yana and asked me to give it to her soon. I bathed him and played with him. This distracted both of us from sad thoughts. Tired from his happy evening he fell asleep fast. Tim called to tell me that all is well, that Yana is stable. Reassured by this and feeling calm I too went to bed early and slept deeply.

In the morning, following my visit to the dentist and more treatment, I went to the hospital to my daughter. It was my turn again to resume my daily vigil. In the corridor of our ward, I was met by Dr. Basil. He invited me to enter the staff room to have a talk with me.

"Taya, good morning" he said looking puzzled. "Where were you yesterday?" he enquired.

"At home, I went to rest and spend time with my other child" I replied helplessly.

"You know, Taya" he started, "the most important thing for your Yana, is your care. My role is complete now. It's your role to complete the care for her recovery" he said.

"Yes, thank you for all you have done for her and us. I will of course continue my care. Yesterday I had to go as I had to see my dentist for important treatment and I needed to get some sleep after keeping seven days vigil at her bedside" I felt I needed to justify my unavoidable absence yesterday adding "Yana's father was with her for the day when I couldn't be" I was still puzzled by his words.

"Yes" he replied very seriously "I am aware your husband was here for the day yesterday and I would recommend that this is not a common occurrence".

Shocked and confused I asked "Why? Did something happen yesterday?"

"Her father, did not change her nappy at all. Poor Yana had diarrhea and she needed frequent changing and cream applied so she doesn't get sore. He hounded the nurses consistently to attend to Yana. In the evening, he was absent from Yana's side and she was fretful alone. He had gone into the room of an infective patient without taking any precautions not to pass this infection onto vulnerable Yana. I accidentally noticed him in there, when I was doing my rounds. This patient has a serious infection called "Pseudomonas Aeroginosa! He went there to play a game on the PC" the doctor was so mad with this idea that his eyes popped out of his head. He was really angry at Tim. "Taya, if he infects your daughter, with Pseudomonas Aeruginosa, with her complications, I don't know then what out come to expect". He threw up his hands in despair. "So, I told him only Yana's mother can come now to stay with Yana. Please stay away so you don't infect your daughter. So Taya, the rest is now up to you! Go to your daughter now. I will drop into you again" he pointed to the door. Silently and filled with shock and shame I went into see Yana.

When I entered the ward, my husband, as innocent as you like, was playing a game on his laptop. Poor Yana was lying in silence, staring at the ceiling as he offered her no contact or interaction. "Tim, what happened? Why is Dr. Basil so angry with you? He told me that yesterday you left Yana abandoned for long spells and were I a room with a highly infective patient. He is so worried that you will spread this infection to Yana as you didn't take any precaution when you were in the room!" I was trying to remain

Time for a Change

calm but my anger was rising. How could he put Yana at such a high risk after all she had been through.

"Taya, yesterday I met a mum of a boy from the infective ward in the children's dining room. He has been there in that ward for a week already. We talked and she told me his ward number. She invited me to visit if I get bored" he said as if it was the most natural thing to do, to go visiting random sick children's mothers', in infective wards!

I barely could listen to him, hardly holding my anger, I felt like slapping him across the head to knock some sense into him.

He continued his tale "Yana fell asleep in the evening as she was given a jab. I was bored sitting here so taking my lap top, so it won't be stolen, decided to visit this boy and his mother. We talked and relaxed together so easily that time went by fast and then it was late. By the way, his mother is a very good woman. It turned out that her son couldn't get through the next level of his game. So I offered to help him. We just started to play and got on well together. Then, our doctor appeared as he was doing his rounds. He saw me there and was very angry that I was not with my own child and that I was sitting in an infective ward with no protective clothes or gloves on me. He sent me away, well, you know the rest" he stated non repentant.

I was completely shocked. My anger knew no bounds. I sat down next to daughter's bed, took her hand and silently was looking at her and smiling in response to her smile. It took me a few minutes before I came to my senses and was able to find my voice. I said in disgust "Tim! Are you an idiot?"

"Taya, why do you insult me?" he took offense to my question.

"No need to answer that question. You really are an idiot!" I continued. "You are bored in hospital with your own child? She is just recovering after her difficult surgery! How could you leave her alone at all? You know that she can turn on side only for ten minutes. Maximum! What if any of her drains became disconnected? Not to mention the Pseudomonas Aeruginosa bacteria you possibly have exposed her too because of your foolishness! Are you a doctor?! I shouldn't have to explain all this to you. It`s shameful and embarrassing behavior towards our doctor. He had a phone call at home, late last night because the doctor on duty was worried about Yana. The man puts his heart into her recovery"

I tried to speak in a calm voice, not to frighten Yana. But she felt my tone and became tense. "Were you so bored? You are so selfish you care about no one and nothing just yourself! This past week I stayed here for 24 hours a day, with a severe toothache, surviving just about on poor pain relief. You couldn`t stay with Yana for a day, without an incident" my energy was running short, at first I was talking in a subdued angry voice. Then looking at his empty, dull eyes that expressed only bewilderment, I suddenly realized that I can`t and don`t want to see him anymore. He seems all right to sacrifice his daughter for his selfishness and pride. I sighed, defeated saying "Okay, get ready and then leave"

Without arguing, he got ready and left. He seemed relieved to be able to go showing no signs of any guilt or remorse.

Time for a Change

For the next three weeks I lived in the hospital beside Yana. When I had to visit the dentist, my mother or my sister were replacing me. At last my gum began to heal, at the same time that her drains were removed. It was as if we were both recovering together.

A few days later, Elena had plastic surgery to her labia and other reconstruction procedures to her genitals. I understood that the catheter was not necessary for her as Elena can go to the toilet by herself. It seems the most general things, like going to the bathroom none of us appreciate. People don`t think about it at all until it becomes an issue.

"Elena is expecting to be discharged next week" Irina was excitedly telling me. "We can go home. Can you imagine! We haven`t been at home for almost seven months! It`s so good" Irina clasped her hands "I can`t believe it!"

Well, that's super news. You have positive news now" I hugged Irina and wishes her all the best for their future. "I told you things will get better. The main thing is to have faith, hope and courage. Don`t give up, even when you`re frustrated and can only you see darkness all around you" I said sincerely, as I squeezed her hand.

Yana was getting stronger every day. It was so great to see this. She began to eat. She could now sleep anyway she wanted in her bed. All position restrictions were lifted. Thank God children forget both good and bad experiences from their early childhood. My heart was full of love for my daughter, my beloved girl. I had waited so long for her in my life.

Elena was also getting better. Her mother happily updated me daily. By coincidence, we and Elena were discharged on the same day. Only Elena was discharged before lunchtime and we were discharged after lunchtime. Irina was all aglow with happiness. I gave her my phone number and address, she promised to call me.

"Taya, I wish you good health and that we meet again but not in hospital!" Irina was saying to me on parting. "We can visit each other" she offered.

"Yes, of course" I agreed "I wish you, too, health and patience as you still have rehabilitation ahead of you. Elena will pull through, she is strong. Everything in her life will be fine. She is getting better and better every day. Be proud of all you have done" I kissed Irina`s cheek and we said goodbye to each other.

Thanks to the excellent treatment, only a month after surgery, we were discharged home. Of course, for now we couldn't fly home to Ireland for a few more months.

"Five months of rehabilitation" the doctor had advised, adding "I will review her progress every few weeks. Then I will give you permission to fly when I am satisfied she has fully recovered".

Five months in Kiev, I was thinking, that will be fine. Soon it will be the first of April and it will be warm again for spring.

That time will pass quickly. For the past month, I hadn't seen my son. He was brought a couple of times to visit us at the hospital, but he was afraid. So we decided not to upset him anymore than necessary, so he didn't visit again. I spoke daily to him by phone. I wanted to make this home coming special for him and Yana so we arranged a party. We bought and hung

Time for a Change

balloons. The children were thrilled! Looking at them, I could feel my peace and happiness returning.

By coincidence, there was only one day left before Tim`s departure to Dublin. Five weeks had passed in a flash.

In the evening, before his departure, Tim, sitting with me in the room started a harmless conversation about Henry, Yana and plans for the summer. Then suddenly he said "Taya, my mother said that I obey you in everything! And that you boss around me! You even banned me from visiting my own daughter in hospital".

The most interesting thing was that he believed what he was saying. I got the impression that he had forgotten the true and real reasons why he was asked to leave the hospital, and not by me but by the doctor and to stay away too. For more than fifteen minutes I was unable to respond, then I uttered "And what are your own thoughts on this?"

"I think, as does my mother, that you plan and organise everything" he said thoughtfully.

I freaked out, in every sense of the word and even got confused saying "Ok then, why don`t you plan and organize everything yourself so? You can`t bear responsibility, even in critical situations when you should stand up for and support your family! The best example of this is our daughter`s stay in hospital. You're a dreamer and you march alone to your own drum! What else do you want from me? Should I be grateful for the fact that I can count on you? Don't make me laugh. You are pure selfish only acting in a way that is comfortable to you, without paying attention to anyone around you".

With his now usual calm distant response he turned over and went to sleep! Frankly, after all my experiences with him, I didn`t want to talk to him anymore. I no longer felt his support not his love, just emptiness. We were divided by indifference and apathy.

The next morning, he bought me a bunch of red roses and placed them in a vase in my bedroom. I think he meant it as a sign of reconciliation. An hour before departure, in the airport, he told me "Taya, don`t worry, everything will be fine. Stay with the children and attend to their daily needs. I'll be waiting for you in Ireland" he kissed me and children on our cheeks, we hugged and parted ways.

"Thank you, have a good flight" I said as he walked away.

Chapter 23

A week had passed since. I had slept enough, slowly coming back to my own rhythm of life. Yana was healthy again. April had come and the weather was mild so we could take a walk outside. Henry was attending the kindergarten. Anya lived with me everything was fine now and in a new fresh routine. Only Ivan was missing from my life. What shall I do? I was thinking about him more and more often. On the one hand, I wanted to meet with him and on the other I wasn't sure. Guilt washed over me, suppose I start to see him again and Yana gets sick as a punishment? I would never forgive myself.

I am not a fanatic about religion, but the events of the last two months had changed my relationship with God. I had started to analyze my behavior, trying to find answers. I clearly, was in a philosophical mood. It was absurd! I have just had a disagreement with my husband again and I think of Ivan. I couldn't understand my thinking. Was I seeking revenge against Tim and using Ivan to get it?

But as you know, the mind doesn't always overcome such feelings. Feelings, both negative and positive, slowly gnaw at a person from the inside. Such was the debate going back and forth inside my head.

Anya, as always was a great support to me in all things. We were, as always talking in the evenings, sharing our news. But inside I was empty. With all my stresses my entire positive mood went away, along with my optimism. I now had time again to deal with this matter and Anya was doing everything she could to bring me back to life. Physically I looked fine. But I was experiencing painful waves of loneliness. I felt abandoned, not loved, forced to stay without work, to live in Kiev a few more months. I also had to socialize with my parents-in-law and to suffer their humiliating comments. With Tim there is a whole uncertainty of our future. On my own one evening, not knowing why I did it, I called Ivan.

"Hello?" I heard his familiar voice.

Hesitating for a moment, I said "Ivan, it's me Taya! I'm in Kiev. Can you come to see me" I felt that I didn't have to go into any lengthy explanation, as he understood me so well.

He asked with a mixture of delight and concern "Taya, are you all right?"

"Yes, Ivan, I am fine, thanks. Can you come tomorrow afternoon after dinner?" I answered.

"Yes of course, at four, at your place. I love you. Everything will be fine. I can't wait to see you again".

When I hung up, I heard Anya's voice from the other room "Taya, did you just call Ivan?"

"Yes I did" I replied happily and I came to sit down beside her. "I don't know why I called him? Anya, I

Time for a Change

blame myself for our relationship. I feel guilty about our affair, for allowing myself to be so weak and allowing him to come into my life. Who knows, maybe that was why Yana got so sick? Maybe to give me a reality check?"

"Don't torture yourself, Yana got sick because she got sick! To me too, because of desperation, sometimes, such thoughts come into my head! What do you know? Where is truth and where is the fiction? I am pleased that you called him. He is as essential for you as air is. He will bring you back to life!" my sister was saying sincerely to me.

"Do you really think so?" I was doubting myself.

"Yes" she simply said "You'll see!"

I was walking in the playground with my daughter when he came. He was wearing a light sports jacket and jeans. He looked tired and worried. In his hands, he was holding a bunch of pale pink roses. "Hello, this is for you, he gave me the bouquet and kissed my cheek. Where's Henry? Why are you only with Yana? What has happened? Why are you so sad?" he said with real concern.

"Henry is in the kindergarten till six. We can go to pick him up together in a while" I smiled.

"What do you mean, in the kindergarten? When did you come? First, tell me what's wrong?" he asked confused.

"Ivan, I will tell you everything later, it's a long story. How are you? You also look tired" we went to sit on a bench.

He lit a cigarette, "well, you know Taya, I changed my job, I thought it would be better. I thought I had found a job, as a cook, in a nice restaurant. However they were a rotten team and I couldn't get along with them so I quit that job. I was two months unemployed after that. The restaurant business is in a recession at the moment so another job was difficult to find" he was smoking and continued telling me "at that moment, I was fed up. I thought of going home. But what is waiting for me there? Unemployment there is even worse. I was going to pop down to my brother to Yalta, if I don't find another job. But I found a new job and I remained. I work now in the city center. It's a crazy place, the owner saves on everything"

I was looking at him, listening and understanding him. Then I realized that I missed him, his voice, his tone of voice, his smile, his eyes, even his manner of smoking.

"I'm so glad you didn`t leave" I said, smiling honestly.

"Yes, what a surprise your visit is! I believe that when you're here, I will succeed. You're my lucky charm" he said and a flame of hope and enthusiasm was lighting up in his eyes.

Having talked about the little things, we went to pick up my son. On the way to the kindergarten, I briefly told him about Yana's surgery and my failing relationship with Tim. I wanted to complain to him and get his support. This is not a normal characteristic for me. Today I wanted to feel sorry for me and to be understood.

Henry recognized Ivan and joyfully hugged him. Ivan was pleased and he didn`t hide it. Returning home then we cooked dinner together. The children were happy playing together. Fanny, as usual, was begging for food. It felt like there had been no eight months of separation between us at all. It felt like it was just yesterday since we parted.

It also seemed to me that Tim was not in my life either.

Our meetings became frequent and April and May passed easily. We felt good together and he was helping me a lot.

Tim called once a week and enquired after daughter's health. He was asking routine questions. I understood from his voice he wasn't missing us in Ireland or lonely because of our absence.

I didn't share with Ivan the details of my failing marriage to Tim. I tried to focus on just one day at a time and enjoying Ivan's company and his presence in my life now.

Four days before Ivan's birthday, I was still thinking about what to get him as a special present. At last I made my decision. I wanted to give him a memorable present. To give him such a gift that he'd remember for all of his life. During our last meeting I saw that he was tired. His new job had him completely exhausted and because he was in a new job he hadn't yet worked up enough time to take a long vacation. He often talked about missing his home place and his parents. I understood how he was feeling. The wild rhythm of city life, monotonous work, living in rented accommodation, constant traffic jams just don't promote a good mood daily. Ivan rarely complained. By nature he is an optimist. My Tin Soldier, but even soldiers need a rest, despite the fact that they are tin, I was telling myself and smiling. I was thinking about buying clothing for him, a shirt or cool jeans or aftershave? But all these ideas were boring and predictable to me.

By accident, I saw an advertisement in a magazine "Fly and relax with local airlines." I'll give him three days, but where? By airplane! I just love flying. But where can we go for just three days? I was thinking and thinking. Then a great idea came to me, of course, to Yalta! To Simferopol! Three days at the seaside. He can meet his brother and perhaps with his mother. He never traveled by planes, I remember, he told me that when we were meeting Oxana. I had asked him then "and would you like to fly? Dreams do come true especially the bright and kind ones".

Three days in Yalta! An excellent idea! I decided to call to the Ukrainian airlines. The ticket prices shocked me, much more expensive than European Airlines, I was thinking. I needed his passport to book his seat. I would have to try to get it somehow but disguising the real reason. So I called him "Hello, Ivan. How are you?"

"I`m working, I can't talk to you at the moment" he said quickly.

"I've got to see you urgently. Please, come tomorrow, and be sure to bring your passport" I requested.

"Why?" he said suddenly paying attention.

"Ivan, don`t be a child, I just need it. Just don`t forget, it's very important. Also do tell me, when you have days off?"

"I have a day off for my birthday and the next day off too. Why is something wrong?"

"No, that's all perfect. Oh, could you swap shifts with a colleague? So you have a three-day weekend?

Time for a Change

This is very important! Try to swap, please" I beseeched Ivan.

"Ok, I'll try" he said distractedly "Taya, but why?" he pressed again.

"Ivan, this is very important! Just, do it for me, please!"

"All right, darling, kisses. I'll call you and we'll arrange for tomorrow. OK? I have to go now" then he was gone.

Great! The main thing is for him to swap with someone. Having made a cup of coffee, I sat down at the balcony and lit a cigarette. Good, that Ivan had forgotten them.

I've was in Yalta nine years ago. Certainly, in those nine years, lots of things have changed there. A lot of water has flowed under the bridge since that time. I had a holiday there nine years ago and I will never forget that, no matter how much time has passed. In Yalta, nine years ago, I was with Tim. It was our coupled vacation, only for a week. During that unfortunate week, we had decided to divorce, a mutual decision. It was to be our last holiday together and then we would divorce, tears and talk.

I remember a heavy storm one night. Waves were coming out over the banks and spluttering foam like champagne and wetting passersby. The sea was so black that night. I was afraid to look at the sea. We stayed eating in a restaurant called the "Laguna". It was built in a shape of lagoon, on high stilts and fifty meters into the sea. I wonder if this restaurant is still there? We had dinner, drank wine and danced until two a.m. We were the last guests to leave.

Well, we were divorced for two years. Trying to realize our mistakes and understand whether we need each other or not? My cigarette went out as I sat thinking. I threw the cigarette away as the memories over take me. During those two years, Tim had a few bad affairs. I had a civil marriage behind me and a whole new experience of life for both of us. I lived in London and he lived in Kiev. We kept in contact with letters, cards, poems, messages and phone calls.

Loneliness, frustration and of course, hope, all contrived in time to work their magic on us. We were talking again. Tim managed to convince me that he didn't need anyone else, it would be me and only me he needed. His love for me was eternal. After our divorce, we lived together again for five years. Tim persuaded me to start from scratch. He wanted children. It seemed to me that he had grown up! He was twenty-seven years old. I decided to believe him and we got married again. I loved him! I loved him since I was seventeen years old! I wanted children for him, to build a family, our family, genuine and friendly. I left England and all that was dear to me. I went back to him and we started all over again.

What has happened in that five years? Tim stays in Ireland. I no longer understand what he thinks or feels. I wonder who he is sharing his bed with? I'm here, in Kiev, plan a trip to Yalta with my lover!

"It's a crazy life and crazy world!" I said out loud and took another cigarette. "Our children, our wonderful children, a common home, perhaps that's all we have! All that's left of our love" I was smoking, trying to understand where we made a mistake and how? After all, we had been together through a lot

Time for a Change

which included the death of our daughter ten years ago. It seemed then that all the worst was behind us. But this was not to be. That grief didn't unite us. I remembered fondly then Dasha, our little girl, who is no longer with us. She would be ten years old this Spring. I threw away the cigarette and stood up. I needed a drink so I poured a shot of brandy. I sighed, tears came on me suddenly. I drunk and the tears ran down my cheeks, every time I thought of Dasha. Probably doesn't matter how many years pass after the death of a child. I love her I will mourn, remember her and cry for her, always. I am her mother.

With these sad thoughts, I went into the children's room. They were sleeping, I stood next to their beds and I prayed for them. I prayed that I would not make any more mistakes in my life. Then I went to the kitchen to cook dinner. I turned on the radio quietly. No matter how hard sometimes in my soul I need to live and love life!

I was peeling potatoes, thinking of my life's purpose. Everything will be fine. The change will come. I believed in it.

The day passed in the usual daily cares and troubles. These sad thoughts vanished replaced by the children's happy faces. Once again, I was happy with them. We were walking outside in the evening. I shall tell Anya about Yalta, in the evening, I thought. She arrived home at the usual time and as always, we were having dinner and talking.

"Anya, I've come up with a great idea for a present for Ivan's birthday. My plan is that for three days, I would fly to Yalta, with Ivan!" I informed her. Anya looked at me questioningly. "His birthday is next week.

I want it to be a surprise! He doesn`t know anything. I asked for his passport and requested him to take three days off" I paused, hoping to hear the comments.

My sister was listening silently waiting to see what I say next. "You know" I said "I`m freaked out. You know, I don`t smoke but today, I smoked two cigarettes in a row. I think I'm going crazy! After Yana`s surgery, I can`t get my life back to normal. I`m crying like crazy and next I'm laughing for no reason. I want to forget everything for three days, as they say "a change is as good as a rest" sighing, I continued "you live with me and you help me lots for which I'm very grateful for. But I think I'm depressed. I don`t know what to do?" I poured my heart out to her.

"To fly to Yalta will do you both good" Anya said sincerely "do not worry I'll look after your children. I think, mum too will agree to help too. We just need to think of a story to tell mum of where you will be gone to for three days! Mum would have a heart attack, if she knew the truth".

"Your right" I sighed.

"All right, this is the plan. You can say to everybody that you are going to a conference on "New Medical Technologies". You have to travel to Lvov by train. It's just two nights by train, there and back. I think everyone would believe that" Anya has offered such version.

"Don`t you think it looks suspicious that for no reason at all, I go to a Conference?" I doubted.

"You know, Taya the more risky your lie is, the faster it`ll be believed" she reassured.

"Maybe you're right" I pondered "ok, let's see first whether Ivan can arrange time off at work. If he can, then I will surely go and hope that my lie holds up" I concluded.

Ivan called me in the morning.

"Taya, I've swapped shifts just as you asked me. Maybe now you can tell me why? Why do you need my passport? What's going on?" his curiosity climbing.

"Ivan, let's meet in the center in an hour. Bring your documents, and then we'll see, maybe I will tell you the secret then?" I intrigued him.

I brought my children to my mother-in-law and rushed to Ivan. He was waiting for me in the café. He had ordered me a fresh juice and coffee for himself.

"Hello" I kissed him and sat down at a table.

"Hello Taya, here is my passport, I'm off from the ninth till the twelfth, just as you requested. What's going on?" he said holding out his passport to me.

"You will find out on the eighth, in the evening" I was laughing. "It's nothing dangerous for your life. Believe me, I'm not going to use your passport with sordid motives" I uttered with a sinister voice and laughed.

"What is your work roster for the next five days?" I enquired.

"Tomorrow I have a day off and then, for the next four days I work. Then, I have my three days off, as you requested. I miss you. How are things at home? How is Yana feeling herself? Does Henry like the toy jeep that I give him?"

"Yes, thanks, everything is fine. Henry really likes his new toy jeep. Yana is fine, thanks and recovering very well. I too miss you. Please come tomorrow for lunch. I'll wait for you" I was finishing my fresh juice. I wanted to stay with Ivan, but time was running out. I still had to go to the store then return to my parents-in-law to collect my children. I kissed him and took his passport "see you tomorrow. I love you, don't be sad. Tomorrow will come very quickly" I said smiling sweetly at him.

We left the cafe and went to the tube. We parted ways on the platform. We were sad but what can be done? This is my life now.

That evening, I called mum and told her about the opportunity to go to the "Conference." She questioned everything and I gave her bright explanations and she believed me. Mum promised to look after my children and to stay at our place for two days. Anya also promised to stay with my children. Can it be true, that all my plans are working. So I can book the tickets? Happy thoughts were throbbing in my head.

Chapter 24

In the morning, I called the air ticket office. I booked our tickets and the courier delivered them. I was as happy as a child. I was cooking food and singing songs. My sister, as always has gone to work in her salon. The children were busy with their own activities.

Ivan called to me at one o`clock p.m. My mood was excellent, and he immediately responded to this. We had lunch and put the children to bed for a nap. When they woke up, we planned on going for a walk with them to the park.

Ivan was washing the dishes, I walked up behind him. He stood with his back to me. Leaning against him, I hugged him, saying "I miss you" I was kissing his shoulder and reaching his neck and whispering sweet words of love to him. He turned his face to me, picked me up and carried me to the living room. Here, he put me down on the carpet and whispered "Snow White, I really missed you. My beauty" he took his clothes off. I was wearing a light gossamer dress, from which he freed me easily. We were making love on the floor, sweetly, slowly and enjoying every move and touch.

He caressed me passionately. I thought he'd kiss me to death. The inexperienced boy was no longer. I was losing my head and my heart to him, my tough, tender, gentle, terrific man who was making me the happiest woman on the planet. Such thoughts were running through my head. I smiled, imagining his shock from my surprise and our three days together, away from all the problems and worries.

In the evening we were walking in the park and riding on a merry-go-round with the children. We all got hungry so we went home. At home we were met by Anya, she was running her own errands, as she had no plans for the evening. She offered to stay with the children so that Ivan and I could go to the nightclub. But on our way, we changed our minds. We decided not to go to the club but to go to play snooker instead. We played for an hour, drank beer and returned home. Ivan stayed with us until morning. Early in the morning, he went to work from our place. Later I was awakened by the doorbell ringing, it was a courier who brought our tickets. "Just four days till our departure" I happily said aloud.

I still had to go to visit my parents-in-law and inform them about my planned trip. I took the children and went to see them. They were in good mood. Yana and Henry were babbling something in their language and running around the flat. I apologized for our unexpected visit, explaining "I need to go away for three days to a conference in Lvov. I was invited there by acquainted doctors. There will be the topic of "new technologies in medicine." I think it's time to blow away the cobwebs and update knowledge.

Time for a Change

I am leaving in four days" I announced from the doorway on my way out.

"Taya, why should you go to some conference and to pay money for that trip and other expenses too?" Mary predictably asked and sat down on a chair.

Pasha also sat down. The children were playing with the phone, picking up the phone and shouting "Hello" and something else in their children's babble.

"I am going to update my knowledge. To find out what's going on in medicine" I said calmly.

"How much will it cost?" Mary persisted in asking.

"Not much. I think about a hundred dollars. I will stay with friends" I confidently lied.

"One hundred dollars!" she exclaimed.

My parents-in-law had a special attitude to money. They are quite wealthy people. But greed and avarice know no bounds in their house.

For an example, at one time I was observing Mary pouring milk into a pot to boil it. After she had poured the milk into the pot, she then rinsed the milk jar with water and added that watery milk into the pot. I didn't understand what she was doing so I asked her. She was shocked as my innocence explaining "Taya! How can you not understand! On the walls of this jar there is milk residue left. I rinse the jar with water to get the maximum milk residue from it. It's more economical!" she said authoritatively. I decided then and there it was best not to respond to her. So I smiled sweetly, as if I had been taught a valuable domestic secret.

Then one day, I found Mary doing another unusual domestic practice. She was collecting torn plastic bags and sewing them or sewing detached handles together. These packages were many years old, faded and sewed up! Insanity! I was thinking. What purpose do they serve? And all this wasted time doing this! I later found out, from Tim, that she has been doing this for as long as he can remember!

"One hundred dollars! Taya, are you out of your mind to pay so much?" my father-in-law was ranting, his attitude to money was the same as hers.

I said aloud in a clear strong voice "I've already paid, so it's too late to cancel. I'm going and I am looking forward to it. Mum and Anya will stay with my children. If you two want to help out too, you are both welcome to".

They sighed heavily. They were about to respond but were distracted as Yana had pulled down a potted plant on top of herself. She was happily playing with the spilt soil and Henry too was all smeared with it. I excused myself, cleaned them both up quickly and went home.

I was very grateful to my daughter for being naughty as she had saved her mother from stress. Three days later I started to prepare my children's things for my absence. I washed their clothes, organized their belongings and cooked their food. I was hugged myself with delight. Ivan was calling me constantly as now he lived at home. This was more convenient for him. Before the trip, I called him, he had just come from work and was tired, but he was glad to hear me.

"Hi, Ivan. It's now four o'clock. Can you come to "Darnitsa" tube station? I need to see you. I will have my children with me.

"Yes, that's fine. I can meet you at 6pm. How about in our café?" he suggested.

Time for a Change

"Great. See you then. Kiss you" I hung down then.

During the time I was getting the children ready for this outing, Anya returned. She offered to keep the children at home with her so that I could meet Ivan alone. I arrived a little earlier so I sat down at a table and ordered a green tea and began to wait for him. He was always on time and arrived with a bunch of white roses. He was wearing white linen trousers and a blue shirt. I was entranced by him, such a handsome relaxed, confident and happy man. He kissed me and sat down. He ordered a "Borjomi". "Is something wrong honey?" he asked as he took my hand and looked at me with care and love.

"Ivan" I started "tomorrow is your birthday. I want to give you a present".

"Honey, we can meet tomorrow. I have three days off and you can wish me happy birthday then" he was puzzled as to why we had to meet now today.

"Ivan" I continued "I have your passport here for you" I held out his passport, my birthday surprise tickets were inside also. He took passport and was surprised that there was documentation inside his passport. He opened it with interest and saw that there were two plane tickets inside. At first he didn`t understand at all what this meant. He was reading the tickets slowly, the names and the destination and dates of departure. Ivan stared with round eyes first at the tickets, then at me.

"Darling, I will wish you happy birthday tomorrow. But today, I give you these tickets as your birthday surprise. In the morning, at nine o'clock, we have a flight to Simferopol" I said with such happiness.

He couldn't believe a word I was saying. He was repeating slowly few words "A flight, tomorrow, just the two of us?"

"Yes, darling, this is my birthday present and surprise for you. We have three days in Yalta" I was saying proudly.

He had no words. Ivan was silent for a moment in total confusion and shock. "Taya, I can't believe it. I've never flown before! You and me! Three days together in Yalta! Taya! You're the most unpredictable fantastic woman ever" he jumped up and putting his arms around my shoulders kissing me madly "Thank you, darling, thank you".

"Ivan, Ivan stop!" Your welcome honey" we were laughing happily together. He still couldn't come to his senses and from time to time he was looking at the tickets. "Taya, that's why you needed my passport! I was wondering why you needed it and I couldn't come up with any reason. This is so amazing".

"Honey, as you mature, you'll understand that women are a mystery. I'm very glad you liked my surprise".

When we finished our drinks, we went for a walk. We were planning our trip, talking about the sea and of course, remembering our time in Koktebel.

Ivan went home, happy and in love. He was still a little shocked with my surprise. I went home happy too, occasionally inhaling the scent of roses and smiling to myself. I am in love and I am loved. Tomorrow we will fly away from everyone for our special time together. For those three days we can forget about our responsibilities and worries. I was in a wonderful mood. On my way home, I bought for

Time for a Change

Anya and myself a cake and champagne. We'll drink and celebrate my three-days of freedom!

When I got home, the children were asleep. Anya was busy creating and making a hair piece for a client at work. She had a bride who has ordered a handmade piece for her wedding of tender lemon chrysanthemums. The wedding will be in the autumn and the bride's bouquet will be made from chrysanthemums. The bride wanted to attach chrysanthemums to her hair, studded with Swarovski crystals. Anya was meticulously working on this order. I sat near her as I didn't want to disturb her.

She had different types of tools for this task such as tweezers of various sizes, needles and a machine like a stapler. Her hands worked carefully. She was always such a creative person.

Her hair accessories were much sought after. Year after year she had more and more orders. My sister was making tiaras, hair clips, hair flowers, flowers for dresses, handbags and belts, headbands and brooches. Things she created were collectable and most important were individual. Anya was closely discussing with the client all the details, drawing sketches and working wonders.

Today, she was making lemon-colored chrysanthemums. Amazing talent, I just didn`t have it and with admiration I sat and watched her. I was smitten with my sister. After a while she finished up for that day. All this time she had worked in silence. Signaling now that her work for this evening was done she enquired "What do you think?" she showed me one of the complex finished flowers. The flower looked alive. It shimmered with Swarovski crystals, emphasizing the silky petals.

"It`s so beautiful and perfect. Well done" I was looking with admiration upon her creation.

"There will be ten of them. This is the largest and the rest will be smaller and smaller. The bride's hair will also be decorated with three flowers. Taya, her hair is gorgeous, brown and long! The other seven flowers will be attached to her handbag. She will hold a small clutch bag. I still have a lot of work to do on these flowers" Anya was explaining.

She loved her job and her customers. She had been in this job since she was sixteen years old. She was giving them her talent and putting her heart into each client's creation. People felt it and were always recommending her.

Now she has her own salon and line of accessories. She is happy with her profession, choosing for clients an image and style that they want. She is a true stylist. This work is not just about appearances, but also about the inner world of person.

"Anya, your flowers are wonderful. The bride will be so impressed, I'm sure of that. You know, I bought us "Muscat champagne" and a delicious cake. Let`s celebrate my freedom from the family for the next three days!" I said cheerfully.

Anya cut the cake. I filled glasses with champagne. Champagne was medium-sweet. "Taya, a toast to you" she said. "To us Anya. It was you who supported my idea of travel" we drank. Next toast is to us again "to the best sisters ever" Anya continued "and to the fact that we have each other! And to our dear mother too"

I added. We were eating cake and discussing the news. We went to bed late that night.

In the morning, when I woke up, my heart was beating like a rabbits. I was so excited, at the thought, that, in two hours, I will be with Ivan for three blissful days. Anya did up my hair. I put on fresh makeup, a light silk suit. On my way to the airport, I noticed men looking at me admiringly. On my feet I had comfortable platforms of soft leather. I was not walking, I was gliding. A sense of freedom and of days of live making was carrying me to the airport. Euphoria knew no bounds!

Ivan was in a great mood too. "Honey, hello, I love you! You're gorgeous! You are great! You look magnificent! You're just a super woman!" he took me in his arms. "I can`t believe, three days with you! You're a miracle!" he was kissing me. We were not ashamed of other passengers seeing us together. We were happy to show off our love.

Recently, I was flying by Boeing and Airbases. Before us now was a small plane. It looked more like a cartoon passenger plane. It had funny propellers, like those on a home fan. I said out loud "God, I hope this is not the last flight in my life!" and then stopped short. Ivan looked anxiously and nervously "don`t be afraid Ivan. I am also afraid to fly on this junky plane. But what should happen, will happen!" We entered the cabin sat in our seats. The plane was full, that is reassuring, I was thinking. I felt that meant we were not the only fools to have booked this airline.

During the flight, the plane had to pass through air pockets. It seems like inside you, everything breaks in a split second. Ivan was all in sweat his forehead was covered with small droplets. Looking at him, I thought, poor Ivan! He has managed to fall in love with me, a person who loves flying. I said to reassure him "Ivan, we`ll arrive soon, don`t be afraid, we're not flying to Australia. Imagine how I fly all the time. You will get used to this feeling".

"Does it shake constantly in the air?" he asked with panic in his voice.

"It's called turbulence. Sometimes it shakes even worse" I tried to cheer him, seeing the panic in his eyes. "But my dear, this is my present, you'll remember for a lifetime. Happy Birthday!" cheerfully I said being happy with adventures.

Chapter 25

Simferopol greeted us with sun and dust. There hadn't been rain for a longtime. The earth was cracked from the heat. We reached the bus station. We decided on the way to drop in to Yalta, to Livadia, to see Livadia Palace.

Livadia Palace, is built in Italian style. It used to be the summer residence of the Russian Tsars, the pearl of Crimea. It was always popular among tourists. Inside the palace there is a museum, but we didn't go inside, but enjoyed the gardens. The white palace is lit by the bright summer sun, from all sides surrounded by greenery and flowered walkways with exotic shrubs and flowers. The Palace, which has kept within its walls many secrets, looks majestic. Today, our secret visit, became another little secret, insignificant to society, but important to us. We were walking through the palace park, sitting in the shade of cypress trees, breathing the fresh air of the Crimea, enjoying our first day away from home, hassle and work.

After relaxing in the park, we went to Yalta. Having had lunch in a small restaurant in the city town, we then went onto Kiev. Here we would be meeting our landlady. The landlady was waiting for us with the keys. The apartment was one bed roomed and was spacious and clean. Having discussed and agreed all the details, the landlady left.

"I'll go and have a shower" I told Ivan as I couldn't wait to take a shower after our dusty trip.

When I came out, Ivan was watching TV. I was all dressed up and fresh and called him out from the bathroom "I'm ready! Let's go to walk through Yalta?" He turned off the TV and said cheerfully, "of course, let's go and get this holiday started".

We were heading towards Gorky Park, walking along the seafront. Ivan asked me to wait for him on the bench for a moment. After a while, he came back and handed me a pendant with moonstone.

"Taya, this is for you" he said looking down in embarrassment.

I was slightly confused "Ivan today is your birthday, not mine!"

"You don't like it?" he stiffened.

"Yes, I like it a lot, thank you" I took the stone in my hand. "Thank you darling" I kissed him "I really, really like it, thank you" I said again to reassure him.

"This is a talisman of love. Moonstone brings harmony to lovers also fidelity and understanding. The lady in the shop told me all this. She has a book about the stones" Ivan happily told me.

After a walk in the local park, we returned to the sea. Here, we liked one small restaurant so we went into it. Since we weren't hungry, we ordered a tasty snack and a bottle of "Crimean Muscat" champagne

Time for a Change

and fruit. In the restaurant the band was playing, the vocalist had a nice, velvety baritone tone to his voice.

"Taya, do you know what my dream is? Even if it`s not our destiny, it's that we get married and live together. I would really like to meet with you here in ten years and to reflect on our lives again then?! We could sit at this same table, listen to music and fill our glasses with champagne and I could admire you, your eyes and your smile. I know I will love you, all my life. Even if you don't stay with me! It`s hard to find a woman in life, like you. You're as free as the wind, cheerful and smart. I would like to listen to you for hours and will always admire you. You are everything to me". He took my hand and silently invited to dance.

We danced and I snuggled into him, feeling his heart beating. We went back to our table. Ivan filled the glasses, I raised a toast "it`s already evening and we haven`t had a drink for your birthday. Thank you that you came into my life. I thank you darling, for your love, for your caring and your kindness. With all my heart, I wish you to be that person for all of your life. To you, my dearest love" I drank all that was in the glass and kissed him.

It was our first evening in Yalta, away from everyone and we were in heaven.

We woke up the next morning cheerful and happy. I went into the shower and Ivan made coffee and had even had time to run off to buy berry cakes and fresh strawberries. I liked his youth, agility and enthusiasm. We had our coffee and cakes, then ate the strawberries and went to the beach.

We were walking slowly, hand in hand, along the seafront. Ivan decided to take a swim. The sea was calm and quiet. The waves were slightly rolling in and we could hear the sound of seagulls crying. Ivan was undressing and I was feasting my eyes on his chest and his muscular physique.

"You're damn hot!" I said out loud as I could see young women looking at him as they passed by.

I was sitting on the pebbles, Ivan sat down next to me and took my hands in his hands, so that our fingers intertwined saying quietly "Snow White, you're my fairy. Thank you for everything! I`m like in a dream, just don`t believe that you are mine night and day. My beauty" he was kissing my hands and having pressed them to his lips, he whispered "I love you. Everything that is happening to me now, with you, is the best I have ever had in my life".

"Thank you my dear Ivan. This is my present to you for your birthday and our present to be enjoyed. We're here and we are together, only for each other. Go to swim! I'll admire you, sitting on the shore" I said, squinting against the sun.

Ivan kissed me and ran to swim, he swum far out. I was glancing over the pebbles at my feet, looking for the ones that were flat, so I could throw into the water to make them hop. I was good at doing this, I was singing a song to myself. This is the life. Ivan got out of the water and dried himself ttoo. Then, suddenly he picked me up in his arms, whirled and yelled "Taya you`re mine! She's mine" he was shouting to a non-existent audience. Some people, in the distance, with looking in our direction, confused at the yelling.

"Stop it, please let me go!" I was embarrassed. "Stop fooling around Ivan, do you hear me?"

"I want to be fooling around and enjoying you all my life!" he hollered back.

Releasing me from his arms, I was splashing water at him. I also wanted to have some fun. We ran away from each other, he caught me and threw me on a pebble, not giving me a chance to escape and kissed me to death. Lying on the beach, I was looking up at the Crimean bright blue cloudless sky. The sun was smiling at me and I, in response, was smiling to the whole world.

We went to a café to have a snack. We had our pizza, drank our beer and continued walking around Yalta. Over the past years, the city had changed a lot. The sea-front had too many fashion boutiques, cafes, restaurants and bars. All you could hear was pop music, coming from everywhere. It seemed as if we weren`t at Yalta at all, but somewhere in Bulgaria. We had a long walk along the sea-front.

Returning back to our apartment, I was so tired from the June sun and the beer which I drank before and I needed to sleep badly. Ivan turned on the TV and settled in the living room. I went to lie down for a nap and I fell asleep like a baby.

Sometime later, Ivan woke me up. He quietly entered the room and placed daisies all around my bed. He broke off flower heads and laid flowers on my pillow. But one he left on the stem and tickled my face with its petals. Having opened my eyes, I was dumb founded. I saw a sea of daisies all around me, it was such a lovely surprise. It was quite unusual to wake up with flowers all around me.

Ivan was naked. He slipped between the sheets and continued caressing me with the flowers, kissing and caressing me. I woke up to a dream like reality, he is my dream and I disappeared into his love.

We were making love for a long time, Ivan was insatiable, restless, this feeling passed on to me too. My luxurious blond hair was covered with daisies. Ivan was laying out flowers on my chest, tummy, hands, not letting me to move. I laid there, so that no flower, could fall as he was driving me crazy, with his lips and tongue. It is such a sweet, wonderful torture to belong to such a man. I could feel his breath and kisses on my neck and back. He confidently went down lower and lower, I was squirming and purring like a cat. I longed for him, now it was not him who was shaking. He made me shutter with desire and I whispered entreatingly "Take me, I want you. I can`t bear it, I'm dying".

"Taya, why are you in such a hurry? Love is an eternity, feel it, enjoy it" he was whispering. I was falling into the ocean of love and tenderness, with closed eyes, I was whispering "oh yes, more, more, more". With all the flowers around me it looked like a flower storm. Ivan was collecting the flowers in his hands and showering me with them. We were losing track of time, being enriched by love and each other. Ivan could no longer hold back, his finale was powerful. I was melting underneath him, I belonged to him, all of me. Daisy fragrance filled the room. This is paradise, I thought and smiled.

Ivan, lying on his back slyly narrowed his eyes and was watching me. He gathered again a handful of daisies and showering me with them, cheerfully said "daisy summer rain, for the most desirable woman in the whole world".

"You`re so romantic, my adorable handsome hero" kissing him, I was saying. Reluctantly then I slowly got up and headed to the shower.

When I came out of the shower, I was rested and tired at the same time.

"Taya, I`ve made you some tea" Ivan shouted from the kitchen.

Wrapped in towel, I went into the kitchen and sat down on a chair. On my face, there was still a wandering smile, remembering the daisy storm and feeling the warmth of our lovemaking spread again over my body. I sat with a blissful expression. I was too lazy even to move, I was sipping tea and looking at Ivan. He was also drinking tea. At this moment, his phone rang, it was his brother Alex.

After talking to him for a while he turned to me and asked "Taya do you mind if Alex calls in on us? He finishes work early and would be here in a couple of minutes?"

"Of course I don`t" I smiled "and besides we can then get acquainted". I got up and went to dress. What a disappointed, I didn't even want to have to get dressed, I was thinking.

Ivan went to meet him and at the same time he bought some food for dinner. He and Ivan arrived together. His brother, Alex, was older than Ivan by several years. He was taller and thinner, more tanned and equally as handsome. They had similar smiles and eyes and a familiar tone in their voice and mannerisms. In a word, for sure they were brothers. They haven`t seen each other for three years.

"Alex" his brother handed me his hand as he introduced himself.

"Taya" I replied as I shook his hand.
"That is an unusual name" with a smile, Alex said.
"She is a rarity, just like her name" Ivan joked.
"Ivan, stop telling our secrets" I said jokingly.

The two brothers went to the kitchen to begin cooking dinner. I took a magazine and settled onto the balcony. I was relaxing and reading in a wide comfortable armchair. Let them talk, they haven`t seen each other for many years. Dinner was cooked, quickly and very tasty. Ivan had brought a bottle of cognac, now it came in handy. The three of us were sitting at the table. Ivan was telling his brother about himself, his job and his accommodation. Alex, not interrupting, was listening to him, enjoying the food.

After a while he turned to me and asked "Taya, where do you work?"

"I work as an interpreter of Russian into English. I am qualified as a Doctor". He nearly choked "A doctor and an interpreter! It is a strange combination!"

"Yes, it`s strange career combination, but I live in Ireland. There everything is different. For now I work full-time as an interpreter" I answered.

"Where in Ireland?" he asked "and how did you meet Ivan?"

"It doesn`t matter how" Ivan joined the conversation "it is important that I met her and I love her more than life!"

They slowly were becoming tipsy. The evening heat was rising and it was getting humid. The conversation flowed in various directions. They were talking about their acquaintances and friends. I was sitting at the table, looking over a magazine. Later, I excused myself, made myself tea and went to watch TV. Unknown to

Time for a Change

me, I had fallen asleep. I woke up sometime later as Ivan was carrying me to bed. His brother had left by then and I hadn't heard him leave.

The next morning was sunny and warm. For breakfast we had coffee with ice cream and candies. He kissed me "Snow White, are you ready to meet my parents?"

I hugged him and answered "yes, it's a part of my present. Your meeting with your mum, you haven`t seen her for two and a half years. What will you say to my mum about who I am to you if she asks about our relationship?"

"Don't worry. The most important thing is that I have you for me. I was telling her a lot about you on the phone" he reassured me.

"Believe me she will notice that I'm older than you".

"That's not a problem. She will feel calm once she meets you and sees that you are smart and such a great person" he was encouraging me.

I put on a dress with shoulder-straps, lemon in color with large white polka-dots. Its length is above the knee and it shows the shape of my figure very well. I pinned up my hair and refreshed my makeup. I looked like I was twenty five years old. Modest, beautiful, parents like such girls. Hugging Ivan I said "well, it`s time to go? I'm ready".

"Well, beauty, let's go!" Alex is ready.

His brother was waiting for us in the minibus. He was in a great mood. He was driving fast. Alex was a good driver and he knew the road well from visiting his parents often. His mum is a teacher and his father is an electrician. On the way the two brothers were telling jokes and funny stories from their childhood.

We arrived quickly. On our way we had stopped by a roadside market. I bought a beautiful wicker basket, a present for his mother. They bought fruits and flowers. We drove on into Ivanovo town.

"The town is small, it has a population of about forty thousand citizens" Ivan was informing me as we were driving. He was showing me sights of the town, his school and kindergarten.

Ivan had a brick house in a big yard. His mum loved flowers. There were flower beds around the house with phlox, dahlias, and begonias. In the courtyard there was a gazebo entwined with vine grape shoots, inside there was a dining table covered with a bright tablecloth. I could feel the caring hand of a housewife in everything. A woman about forty-five years old came out to meet us, in a summer cotton dress. Ivan looks like his mother, I was thinking and his brother does too. Behind her was his stepfather, a forty-eight years old man and very handsome. He was dressed in a family way, wearing a T-shirt and shorts. They were approaching us and smiling. Ivan's mother hugged Ivan and began to weep. They hadn't seen each other for two and a half years. He gently hugged and kissed her.

"Ivan, why didn't you tell us that you were coming? I would have prepared myself better. Ah my Ivan!" she uttered happily. Ivan turned to me and introduced me "Mum, this is Taya. It is all her idea. I didn't know anything about it at all and didn't plan to be here for my birthday" he said, hugging her shoulders.

"I am pleased to meet you, Taya. We are Valentine and Andrew" she smiled as she introduced themselves.

"Nice to meet you both too" I smiled. I was glad I gave Ivan these moments of happiness. Only someone who lives away from home can appreciate that the love we have for our parents, is a holy feeling. Unless, of course, parents have cultivated a negative feeling in their children about them. I liked his friendly parents immediately.

"Come in, don't stand by the gate" happily his mother said. "Taya, how long are you able to stay for?" she asked excitedly.

"We can stay until the evening, around four. Now it's only nine in the morning. We have a full day ahead" I said.

"Why do you leave today? Do you have a train in the evening? How will you get to the station?" she was worrying, fussing and looking with tears of happiness at her son.

"It's because of work, Mum, I was lucky to get these few days off. Taya too has demands on her and could only spare these few days too" Ivan tried to break the news of our short visit to her gently.

His step-father switched on the kettle "Let's have tea after you have travelled such a long way. Then you'll rest and tell us all your news" he said cordially.

I helped Ivan's mother to prepare lunch. We made sandwiches, boiled potatoes and chopped vegetables for a salad. When the lunch was ready, we sat down together. We were sitting outside, in the gazebo. His parents were asking Ivan about his life and other various questions, then his mother asked "Taya do you study?"

"No not now. I work now but not in Kiev, in Ireland".

She was shocked. She was looking at me and her confused by my response.

"Ivan and I know each other for two years now. We meet first when I came home on holidays".

"Taya, will Ivan be going back to Ireland with you now?" she asked with a worried tone.

"It`s not so easy, Valentine. I don`t know yet what our future plans will be" I replied honestly.

"Mum, I'd love to be going with her to Ireland. I love Taya. She has two children, a girl of two years old and a boy of four years old. I love them also!" Ivan suddenly blurted out.

His mother looked at him in confusion. Finally his step-father spoke "don`t worry, Taya, different things happen in life. Children are good to have. When I married Valentine, Ivan was two years old, Alex was five. Every cloud has silver lining!"

I was silent. What could I say? Should I tell them about my husband and my neighboring parents-in-law? I asked him to show me the way to the bathroom. "Ivan! Are you crazy? Why have you told them all this? Now they will worry about you even more" I was saying full of mixed emotions. "Please don`t tell them anything else. You and I don`t know what tomorrow brings us" I sighed. I kissed him on the cheek and promised I would join them soon at the table once I recomposed myself.

When I returned to the table, they were all talking lively about family and friends.

"Do you leave from Simferopol, the train station? Will Alex, take you?" Valentine was asking.

"No, we leave from the airport" Ivan informed her.

Time for a Change

"Do you mean you came by airplane? Well that's expensive" Valentine added.

"Taya gave me the airplane tickets as her birthday present to me. She wanted me to get to see you, dad and my brother" Ivan said with thanks and gratitude in his voice.

"Taya, thank you. We are very happy that you came. You are such a caring, thoughtful person. Thank you again" his mother said with tears in her eyes.

"It was a big surprise. Ivan knew nothing about it at all. I`m also very pleased to be able to visit you too" I answered honestly.

The time was passing quickly. We had to get ready now and say our goodbyes to his parents. It was only four and a half hours until our flight.

With one hour until our departure, we finally entered Simferopol. Alex didn`t know how to get to the airport and we got lost on the way and as a consequence, we had driven down some lane. My patience ran out as I was in panic. Ivan knew that I had to be at home at ten o'clock in the evening. If I don`t get there by ten, my Mum will start to panic.

Somehow we found the road leading to the airport. Having reached the airport terminal, I lost all hope for us to fly away today at all. We were running to the desk with tickets and passports. Our plane was ready for takeoff.

Ivan was persuading some man to return the ladder to the plane so we could board it. He was trying to persuade this man with all sorts of pleading stories. I was standing there, numbed with terror. The man gave two instructions. The first was to Ivan to run to the bar and to buy two bottles of vodka. The second instruction, he gave by transmitter, to the operators to reposition the ladder so we could board.

I was running down the takeoff strip all sweating from the heat and nerves, like a horse. I was running in my high heels and in a sundress. A wicker basket in my hand, it is a present for my mother. My hair is completely disheveled. Probably from the outside, it looked romantic and touching. But really, having reached the plane, I turned around and saw Ivan was running with our bag, all sweating, too. Having entered the plane, we felt all the negative vibes from the other passengers who were waiting for us. Their angry faces, it seemed that everyone followed us with contemptuous looks to our seats. I could feel myself blushing as I walked in silence to our appointed seats. Finally we sat down on the plane.

Thankfully something like this only happens once in a lifetime. It's not every day, people run down a takeoff strip, after the plane. I smiled optimistically and looked out the window. Ivan was sleeping. The flight lasted for forty minutes. Ivan woke up during landing. He looked at me full of guilt, not daring to speak. I was silent too. It was not my brother, who gave us such a stressful event. We silently left the plane. Kiev met us with summer rain. We looked at each other I was waiting for his response.

"Taya" he started, "I am so sorry for all that panic. Forgive me please. I see how you were so nervous. I wouldn't have gone home at all, if I knew that Alex, is such an irresponsible driver. He let us down! I'm sorry".

I saw he felt bad and was awkward to apologize "Ivan" I said, as gently and calmly as possible "I

Time for a Change

will take a taxi and go home. Let`s call each other tomorrow, I'm tired. Bye" I kissed him on the cheek and raised my hand to stop the car.

In the taxi I was still in lost thoughts. I didn`t understand what happened to me. All emotions of our love and holiday fun was now gone. I transformed from a jovial woman into a matron with responsibilities on my shoulders.

"I am at home" I said as I rang the doorbell. My children were so excited. I was hugging them, kissing and caressing them. I took a shower and went to bed with the children so we could chat and hug in the dark. Mum had let me tend to the children. I heard her walking around the apartment, watching TV. But my brain turned off and I sank into my dreams.

Chapter 26

In the morning, we sat down for breakfast. Mum told me that my parents-in-law were still furious over my going to the conference. They consider this as a wild trick, to leave the children for three days. "Mum, do you also think so?" I asked.

"No, baby, you deserve a break. You put so much time into your children and you are alone a lot of the time with them too. It's nice for you to go somewhere different and change your company" mum said.

I was looking at her, my sweet, caring, loving mother. We were having our breakfast. Henry was sitting on my lap and telling us what he had been doing with his nanny, while I was gone. Yana was playing with a spoon. An idyllic family picture, I was thinking proudly. Mum then had to leave to do her own household chores and I needed to start and catch up on mine.

In the afternoon Ivan called "good day. Did you rest well? How are you? How is your mum?" he plied me with questions. I was answering without emotion. "I talked to my brother" he continued "Alex is very

Time for a Change

sorry. He wants to call you, to apologize but I forbade him. I told him I would pass on his apologies to you for him. That was the right thing to do?" he asked not sure of my response.

"Yes, thank you" I said flatly.

"Are you still angry at me? I'm ashamed of him and for the stress that you had to have because of him. I love you and thank you again for my birthday present surprise. I'm very happy, I never expected such a present. When will you be able to get time to see me? I will be working the next three days" he was saying hopefully.

"Ivan, everything is fine, don't worry. You work and in the evenings you have rest. I'll call you later on, in the evening or tomorrow morning. OK? Kisses. Bye" I said and hung up.

The next three days, Ivan went to work. We called each other daily. I was busy spending all my time with my children. We went to the zoo and to visit friends. Strangely, I didn't feel the absence of Ivan in my life. Everything went on as usual. Perhaps he was still feeling guilty. It is good that we don't see each other. I am a very forgiving person. It will take a couple of days and everything will be alright again.

A week later, I started to miss him. We agreed that he would come to me. I was waiting for him, I cooked dinner, wore a bright crimson shirt and white denim shorts. It was an hour before Ivan's arrival and I decided to buy some sweet things for our tea. I asked Mary to stay with the children. She was busy, but she sent Pasha to look after them.

Having bought the Prague cake and berries, I was walking home in the hope that I still have half an hour before Ivan's arrival. Having come out of the elevator, I saw Ivan's terrified face. He was standing and dialing something on his mobile phone. "Ivan?" I gulped in shock.

"I came and called to your doorbell. At least I didn't say "Taya, it's me, open the door quickly!" The door was opened by some old man who asked "who are you and whom do you want here?" Behind him was Henry! Henry immediately recognized me and said "Ivan, hi!" I didn't reply to him directly but said "sorry, wrong floor" and I left before Henry asked me to hold him in my arms". So, here I am in a state of shock and I am just now texting you.

"Oh! Don't worry, I will go up now. Please, wait here for a few minutes. When he leaves, I'll call you" I said trying to calm Ivan down while my own heart was beating too fast.

I opened my door with my key. Thank God, my father-in-law was in a hurry to watch some political program so he went on home quickly. I phoned Ivan that "all was clear now for him" and he came inside. He kissed the children, they were glad to see him. He started to play with them with trains and cars. I made myself a coffee and sat in the chair enjoying watching them playing happily together. Looking at him, I saw in his eyes kindness, caring, love and joy. He's here, he's with us we feel good together. "Taya, don't deny yourself the pleasure. Simply, be with him" I was telling myself.

He felt my eyes on him "I've missed you, it's good that we are together again" he said gently with confidence.

Ivan stayed with me for the night. Lying in his arms, I was completely content and whole. "Soon, I

Time for a Change

will be leaving with the children. We are going for a holiday, for a month. I will miss you" I said to my Ivan.

"I'll come to visit you, it`s just half an hour away from Kiev. Minibuses go there. Taya, my girl, I`ll text and call you. I will bring fresh berries to you and your children. Do you like apricots?" he was saying, gently caressing me.

"Yes, I do love them and I love you too, so very much" I replied in a soft whisper.

"I will love you always. I will bring you apricots" he was kissing me. We were joking and hugging. During the days of separation, we missed each other. We expressed this in our passionate yet gentle touches now that we were reunited. He was no longer that humble Ivan, whom I taught to love a woman's body, a year ago. He was hot and passionate. A great combination! I was smiling at these memories to myself, in the darkness. It`s just sad that everything passes and this love too with its passion will be gone. All that will remain in my mind will be the vivid memories. I felt sad and I sighed. Ivan had fallen asleep, he was tired after work.

I couldn't sleep then so I got up and checked on the children. I then went into the kitchen, picked up a magazine and began to read. But I couldn't concentrate. Thoughts were swirling around in my mind, like a carousel. I felt heavy-hearted, Ivan's parents liked me. His mother might already be planning, in her head, a future for Ivan with me in Ireland. Ivan told me often, that he and his brother were adopted by his stepfather when he was five years old. Since then, he loved them as his own children. Ivan wants to be closer to me, but he didn`t understand that sooner or later, we will separate. And it will hurt. I wouldn`t divorce my husband, with whom I have been with for twelve years. I even miss my husband sometimes. I wouldn`t come back to live in Kiev, not even for Ivan. My life is in Ireland and that suits me one hundred percent.

Let`s assume, if Ivan came to Ireland with me now. What would he do there? He doesn't speak English. What job would he get? Working on a construction site? Or washing cars? Or picking up trash? At first he may be happy. The chance to live abroad is exciting. A new life, with me living near him. Then, in about three months, he would start to miss his friends, Ukrainian bread and suet. In fact everything that he is used to and there are almost no shops selling Ukrainian food and specialties.

A year later his love for me would pass away. He`d become irritable, would drink too much and blame himself for not knowing English. He would torment himself with questions such as "why such a talented cook can't find a good job?" I had made a passing hint about this before to him, but he didn`t believe what I was telling him form experience and he was offended. Ivan was assuring me "Taya, you are the other half of me. I am a strong person. If I was to be in Ireland, I would do everything for you. We`d live happily ever after. He didn`t add "like in a fairy tale", but that's what it sounded like to me. I don`t believe in fairy tales any more or in the eternal love either. It's sad to have to live and not to believe in happy endings. That's it, that's the point. I believe in myself and in my energies and that`s why I don`t change anything in my life. No, I'm not afraid to make mistakes. A mistake can be fixed, I don`t change because I intuitively feel that it`s not time for a change. Ivan is only one of the steps by which I could change my future. I am bound to him now with our two year friendship, added to that our affair, passion and sex. But this is not enough of a reason for me to jump in feet first. There must be something else. Something more! To be his lover is the maximum I can give him in this life. I sighed heavily and looked at the clock, two in the morning. Thinking and thinking eventually I went back to the bedroom. After a while of tossing and turning, I finally fell asleep.

In the morning, we had breakfast and decided to bring Yana to my mother`s and go boating to the Hydropark. Henry was so excited when we get to the boat station. We took a boat for hire. Ivan was in charge of the oars. Henry was trying to help him, clutching his little fingers around the paddle. He was proudly rowing the boat for his mum. The weather was perfect, all was sheer bliss.

The day before, I bought a good pair of sunglasses. I put them on and, after a while I took them off and put them like a band on my head. Having completely forgotten about the glasses, I stretched out my legs and lay in the boat on the bows. Then I felt them slip into the water from my head.

"Oh no, I`ve just lost my new sunglasses in the water" I shouted and a disappointed feeling came over me.

Ivan gave me his paddles and dived in. He was wearing a T-shirt and shorts. He couldn`t see them anywhere "Taya, I'm sorry the water is too muddy and dark. I can`t find them" he said peeping over the edge of the boat from the water.

Henry was clapping his hands. He liked how Ivan goes under the water trying to find the sunglasses

"Ivan is like a fish!" he exclaimed "do it again!" he cheered Ivan on.

"I paid a hundred and fifty dollars for them! I said ruefully. But my mood wasn't changed. I don`t suffer from materialism "you win some, you lose some", I was thinking.

Ivan got upset "your new sunglasses. It's such a pity" he muttered as he rowed further down the river.

When our boat ride was over, we went to a pizzeria. Later Henry went on the carousel and then we went to my mother`s for Yana. I asked Ivan, as always to wait outside. Henry said that he was riding a boat. And that Ivan was swimming like a fish and my mother was laughing. He also chattering about the pizza and the carousel ride. But mum, listening with one ear to her grandson and looking straight at me asked

"Taya, how long will you be keeping Ivan tagging along in your life? You're a mature woman! What do you have in common with him? You're the mother of a family! You're an educated, smart girl! Why do you encourage him?"

"Mum, he's my friend. He helps me in everything that I need" I said, accentuating the word "need".

"Your sister lives with you and I help you. Taya, cut off all ties with him. It's not fair on him" mum said sternly.

"Mum, do you want me to burst into tears here and now in front of the children?" I pleaded with her.

"No, not at all, heaven forbid" mum got scared.

"So, the truth is, I don`t want to divorce. Ivan is my escape. He makes me realize that I'm a woman! I feel that I am loved, sexy, young and beautiful. I don`t want to deny myself this happiness. You know very well that we live with Tim for the children and his parents. Please I don't want to talk about this now. I have to go. I love you very much mum. I blame myself for this situation. I can only promise you that he won't be your son-in-law!" I hugged my mother and, just like when I was a child, firmly kissed her on her cheek.

I felt that the weight of all this weighed heavily upon her. But I couldn't behave differently and hoped that mum would understand me. I took Yana and we came out of her apartment.

The day of our departure to the recreation center was approaching. I said to my children that we were going to a new place. We would live in the forest, collect cones and Anya and nanny would visit us. We gathered a lot of clothes and also a bag with toys. Anya's friend, Lesha, will take us to the recreation center. The day before our journey, in the evening, we were having dinner all together. Anya began to tell us about her friend Lesha.

"Do you know that Lesha is getting married soon?" Anya asked us.

"No, I didn't know that" mum shook her head.

"How do you know?" I asked Anya.

"I saw her friend today and she told me. She told me that she felt for Alex and they go to spend time together and now have decided to get married. He has quit drinking. The girl he is marrying is a simple but pretty girl. She loves Alex so he proposed to her".

"I am glad that he had come to his senses. Maybe, with his second wife, he will be happy!" I said sarcastically. This is my ex brother in law and I was hoping Anya wasn't hiding the fact that she was upset a bit.

"What else did the friend say?" I asked and because of this news my appetite had evaporated.

"He asked how I was? And what job I do? He calmed me and said that he knew that Alexei made a real mess of things, but that he is his friend. He also said that I look amazing and can always count on his help! We didn't have much time as we met at the bus stop" my sister finished up.

"It's good that he will settle down again" my mother said thoughtfully "maybe he'll be able to have a better life than he is now. After all he's a good guy".

"Who knows? If she keeps a tight rein on him, then maybe. But even after all the love I gave him and the work I did on our relationship, nothing worked. He is spineless" my sister sighed.

"Now, let's plan about the recreation center! I'll come to visit you and you won't be bored at all" said Anya.

"Oh yes, come all of you, I'll be happy to see everyone".

That evening my mom went home and the following morning we went to the recreation center. The recreation center is called "Forest" and is located in a cone forest. Not far from there is a river, but it is forbidden to swim there. It was good, that on the territory there were a children's playground and many safe places for them to run about.

On the first day we met with the other guests, who also had children. At least the children will have friends. Our rooms were spacious, two bedrooms, a living room, a bathroom and a small kitchen with a refrigerator, microwave and a kettle. And also there was a large balcony. The children were busy, running

Time for a Change

and helping us unpack. Anya left in the evening. We then ate and went for a walk to have a look around.

"It`s a decent place to rest and a lot of space for the children" I was telling Lily by phone. All was good with her too. She was getting married to Robert! We talked about her upcoming wedding plans.

I bathed my children and I was thinking and feeling lonely. It`s such a pity that Ivan is not here. Thinking about him, I dialed his number "Hi", he said happily. "Well, how is it there? Have you unpacked already? How are children? Are you having fun together?"

"All is good, thanks. The children are great. Can you come to join us?" I asked hopefully.

"I can come to you in two days! Is that Ok my darling? I'll bring magazines and fresh fruit. Now you rest and sleep. If you need anything else before then let me know".

"Ok, I`ll let you know, thanks". We talked for a few more minutes and then said goodbye.

The children were now sleeping so since I was tired I decided to go to bed too.

The days in the recreation center were passing quickly. Mum, Anya and Ivan were visiting me. Everyone liked the forest and where we were staying. The children got tanned and were growing stronger. Here, when alone at night, I missed Ireland, my home and my job. Even though I was on leave from my job, I was looking forward to working again when we returned.

Each day here was like the last one. We had our breakfast and waited for mum. She had promised to come to us early and stay until the evening. The children, having seen her, rushed to hug and kiss her. They were wisely reaching into her bag for candies or some other treat. She always had something in her bag for them. I kissed my mum, she was in good mood.

"Finally I escaped from the city. It is so hot there with the buildings and traffic. Good, here is so cool and fresh. Well, how are you?" she greeted me.

We were walking along the alley. Henry and Yana were showing to her pine cones and sticks. Yana was picking flowers.

"We are fine, mum, thanks. Yana met a girl and they play together. Henry met a boy, who's older than him, but they play well together. They play hide and seek on the playground" I updated her.

"Oh, I almost forgot!" suddenly she said and opened her bag. "You received a letter from Tim, it came yesterday. I didn't want to tell you on the phone. I thought I'd bring it as a surprise" she gave me the envelope.

I took the envelope and sighed "thank you, Mum, I'll read it later".

She looked at me with surprise asking "are you still angry with him? It's already about four months since he left".

I silently kept walking, looking at the forest path, I didn't want to talk about Tim. I wasn't sure if I was still angry with him or not.

"Mum, I don't know. I just don't know whether I will be able to live with him when I go back. He is so irresponsible the final straw was his selfish behavior in the hospital. I feel sick when I think of it all. He gave me a bunch of roses and thinks that is all he has to do to correct everything. He only called us a few times

Time for a Change

over the summer. Mum, I'm confused, I don't know what to do. I feel sorry for myself and my children. I feel sorry for that fool too!" I was about to burst into tears.

"Taya, we were all under stress, when Yana was in the hospital. He was under stress too. You have to understand him. Yes, he acted foolishly, played those computer games and not looking after his child" mum tried to calm me.

"Mum, why didn't I "go crazy"? Why do I always have to remember my responsibilities and duties" I said angrily.

"Well, you can't compare yourself to him. You are you. You're strong, sensible and a responsible mother. You're different! I always believe in you and know that you do everything right. You would never damage the family" Mum was saying with an agitated voice. I saw that she is worrying about me and she is sincerely hoping that everything will be fine.

"Ok, Mum, I'll read the letter and then I'll decide what to do next" I said, looking tenderly into her eyes. "Not far from here, there is a cafe, let's go there with children. We can buy ice cream and relax" I suggested.

"Children, do you want ice cream?" she asked.

"Yes, yes, yes" they jumped about her and were telling her about the pine cones they had found.

"Mum, pine cones in the forest are the most important thing!" I laughed. "We collect cones every day and pile them up for the squirrels".

"Squirrels eat them and say yum yum" Yana answered.

"They are delicious" clarified Henry.

"What? Squirrels are delicious?!" I was joking.

"No, silly mammy, the cones are delicious!" Henry was laughing.

We reached the cafe and bought our ice creams and strolled back to the recreation center. Mum spent the whole day with us and happy with the meeting with her grandchildren, she left.

The envelope was left unopened. A few times I took it up, holding in my hand, but I didn't open it. I don't know why.

After putting my children to bed, I went down to the restaurant on the first floor ordered a "Mojito" and a pack of cigarettes. Having taken my cocktail back to my room, I went to the balcony and started smoking. My thoughts were whirling like a kaleidoscope in my head.

I opened the envelope it held his familiar handwriting, which is easy to read. He wrote that he missed us and realized his foolish behavior. That he is ashamed of himself and is sorry. He found the right words to disturb my soul. Tim knew that I was kind and forgiving. He knew how to use this against me when he needed to. I knew it too, but I couldn't help it. I loved him and even my affair with Ivan and his love for me wasn't able to kill the feeling of love that I have for my husband.

I loved Ivan, but it was a different love. I felt good with him. But he wasn't my soul mate, Tim is. Despite all the quarrels and insults, I felt that Tim is my darling and beloved. I lit a cigarette, my third in a row.

"I'm such a fool" I said putting out the cigarette "for the sake of these men, to ruin my health" and I threw a cigarette from the balcony angrily. My "Mojito" was also finished by now. I went back to the restaurant so I could bring the empty glass to bartender. I ordered a martini with ice and lime. I sat down at a table.

What shall I do? With Ivan, everything is gone too far. My children will soon call him Daddy. Ivan loves me I know that for a fact. All this summer, he has proved this with the time he spent with me and fussing over me with presents and flowers.

Tim, on the other hand is now repentant, and he expressed this in his letter. Maybe he's embarrassed? During this summer, he and I didn't talk much at all. What to do for my children? It hurts so much I could cry forever. I sipped my martini, staring at the lime. A text came from Ivan "Good night. I love you. I miss you. See you soon, kiss". I didn`t reply to his message, let him think that I am asleep.

We have another week in this recreation center. During this week, I have to decide what to do with Ivan. Having finished the last sip, I went to my room. I need to sleep. Tomorrow is another day.

During the last week, what to do still wasn't clear in my head. My mind was saying "You are a wife and a mother and your place is with your husband". My heart's response to this was "I desire to be with Ivan and to be loved by him and him only". Oh what to do?

Chapter 27

We returned to Kiev after our mini holiday and I felt refreshed. I quickly settled back into our usual family routine. Outside it was hot and dry, typical for August. It was time for Yana's hospital review as assess her progress since her surgery. This review was a success and the surgeon was now satisfied that Yana was fit to fly home to Ireland whenever we wished to. My happiness knew no bounds.

The next day I rushed to the Vladimir Cathedral, to light candles for my gratitude. It was dim in the cathedral, lamps and candles were crackling. I like the smell of church candles. I was praying with my whole heart I thanked God and asked forgiveness for my sins. For adultery and fornication and asked to set me on the right path and protect me from my weaknesses.

In the evening Tim called, he was so pleased and relieved about Yana's good health news. He asked me whether I had received his letter?

"Yes, I did. Thanks for your words in it. I think we can come home to Ireland earlier now? I miss you, the

Time for a Change

children miss you. There is nothing else to do her for another month" I suggested to him.

"Taya, stay in Kiev and continue to have rest. There is no rush to come home" he said in a strange voice.

Shocked I replied "what to stay here? I want to go home. I want to feel settled again". Tears pricked in my eyes.

"It`s raining here, there was no summer at all. Continue to rest there. No need to hurry" he repeated, a little softer this time.

Not up to an argument just now I gave in and replied "Ok, I`ll think about it".

"I love you and miss you all. I send you a kiss and to the children too" and then he was gone.

I could feel anger and resentment rising inside me. I have to fly back home. I talked about it with mum and Anya. Henry has to go to school this year, he was five years old. In Ireland, this is the age children start to go to school.

It was two weeks before the end of September. I decided we would leave in five more days. It was an extremely busy few days before we left with all the preparing to be done.

Ivan was very sad. I could feel it in his mood. But what could I do? I decided we needed to sit down and talk and spend some valuable time together. I arranged for an evening where we could be alone at home. Anya was gone to spend the night with friends. Ivan came to see me after work. We were having dinner and drinking wine. In the beginning the conversation was strained. Ivan was nervous and trying to hide his tension by using jokes. But his jokes weren`t funny and neither was he at this moment.

"Ivan, I couldn't stand it stain between us. You knew from our first meeting that I am married. We both knew that sooner or later, we'd have to be apart" I broke into a monologue.

"Taya, don't start all that again" he interrupted me. "Do you love me? Do you want to live with me?" he looked at me with pleading eyes.

"Ivan, I do love you, but love is not enough. I am a mature woman with my own responsibilities and family. I can't just drop everything and live with you. Also, I'm not that easy to live with.

"Taya, I've lived with you for three months. And I have known you for three years. Don't talk badly about yourself. It's easy to live with you, you are wise and real" he was saying with hope.

I got up from my chair and hugged Ivan's shoulders and said "I'm not ready to change anything. I have to go back to Ireland. To my husband and to my home" I said as gently as I could.

He abruptly stood up and walked out on the balcony. He lit a cigarette.

What can I say him? That I want to start everything from the beginning? That I love my husband and miss my husband? I miss talking with Tim and how we talk about everything in the world. He is a mature man and I feel my world interesting with him in it. Well, should I say, "Ivan, the fact is, I got together with you because of my despair, my emptiness and my quarrel with Tim". Thoughts like these were galloping through my mind.

Ivan returned to the kitchen, I was sitting at the table, lost in my thoughts. "Taya, I can't live without you. I've gotten so used to you and to your children being in my life. My mum always asks about you and sends you her greetings. They like you a lot and think highly of you. Tell me what I shall do without you near me?" he grabbed my head in his hands and pressed me to his breast. I could feel him trembling from stress and tension.

"Ivan, you have to live and work! If it`s our destiny to be together, then we definitely will be" I tried to sound reassuring.

"Taya, people make their own destiny and you are flying away from me?"

"My dear, it`s our last evening together, please, don`t spoil it" I said trying to get through to him.

"Taya, you've made your choice! You are flying away! You probably won`t come back? I can see that your eyes are burning with happiness when you talk about Ireland, about your home there now" he sighed and sat down resignedly. "Looking at it all from one point of view" he continued "I am like an unexpected guest who burst into your life. So I'm sorry. I'm sorry".

God, I felt so much pity and love for him. My heart was tearing apart. But there was no way out, I realized that I had to make it final.

We sat in silence, staring at each other. Each of us is having our own thoughts. Ivan filled the glasses with the last of the wine and trying to gather himself, he said "To you my one true love of my life, I wish for you all that's good in your life always" and he emptied his glass in one gulp. He looked at me expecting me to say something too.

Taking my glass, I said "To you, my dear Ivan, let your life be filled with the brightest of colors and much happiness too" and I also emptied my glass in one gulp.

"I'm going home now, it`s getting late" he said sadly.

"I`ll see you out" I got up, clearly realizing that he won't stay here with me for the night. If he did it would make breaking up even more painful.

Standing in the hallway, watching him put his coat on, I was saying goodbye to him silently in my heart. We went out to the lift. Suddenly, he hugged me, so gently and strongly that he almost lifted me off the floor. He whispered "my darling, Snow White, see you later. Maybe it will happen sometime in the future that you will be mine? Who knows?" with these words, he put me on the ground and entered the lift.

"See you soon" was all I could utter. The lift doors closed. "See you soon, my dear Ivan" I repeated again to myself and left my hand on the closed lift doors to feel the last of his energy.

I returned to the kitchen. I sat on the chair where Ivan had been sitting a few minutes ago. My heart was breaking.

"That's it, Taya, that's it" I said and began to cry. I felt sorry for myself, mum, Anya, all my relatives. I am again feeling this infamous separation from the beloved people in my life, my family and friends here. I do have a wonderful family. They always support and help me. And most importantly, they understand and forgive me all my weakness. They love me and I love them. There will never be anyone or anything more precious than my family. I was sitting and crying, thinking and crying, until I completely washed out and drained.

The last day passed by quickly. I was packing, checking everything, I was nervous as I had huge luggage.

Time for a Change

The children were happy they were flying back to their Dad. They missed him all this time. They were constantly asking the same questions "when do we get the plane? Will Dad meet us?"

"Yes, he will, Dad will certainly wait and meet us. He loves us all" I was assuring them and myself.

We ate our last dinner at home. Mum stayed with us for the night. Having talked late into the night, she went to sleep. Anya and I continued to talk almost until dawn. We slept then for a few hours only.

Our flight was in the morning and we woke up with sore heads. Not having had enough sleep and heavy-headed with emotions. I took pain relief and started to get ready for our long journey.

As always, my dear neighboring parents-in-law came to say goodbye. Mary, despite her senile debility, had gotten attached to her grandchildren for these months. She shed tears about how much she will miss them. Pasha, every five minutes was asking me the same questions "Do you have the passports? Do you have the tickets? Do you have money? Do you have something to drink for children?"

"Yes", I was replying patiently "I have everything. Thank you. Don't worry".

A few minutes later, he was again asking the same questions in the same order. He was slowly driving me crazy!

Chapter 28

Arriving in Dublin the weather was mild for it is early autumn. Tim was waiting for us. Our flight was delayed due to some technical reasons. We were not given a clearance for takeoff for a long time in Budapest. My heart was beating quickly, until we received our luggage. I had missed Tim and hurried to him. I wanted to hear his voice and finally realize that I'm home. All this nightmare about Yana`s disease has ended.

We hugged and kissed each other. The children, like little monkeys hung around his neck and were hugging and kissing him.

"At home, at last" Tim said addressing all three of us.

"Yes, we're home" I repeated, adding "and together again".

"Yea, we are in Ireland" Henry screamed and jumped up and down.

We looked at him with surprise and Tim said "he has grown up so much in these past few months".

"Yes indeed he has and his is so bright too" I said proudly.

We drove up to our house. I was full of joy. For the whole journey from the airport, we were telling each other our news and various different stories.

It was the first of September and it was time for Henry to go to school. What a handsome boy he was in a new uniform. He had smart trousers and a tie and his backpack on his shoulders.

Yana, was circling around him all morning. She was singing "Henry goes to school, he's a big boy. Henry is a big boy". This lasted for an hour while we were getting ready. Tim took a day off and we all went together to bring Henry to his new school.

Henry liked his school very much. We collected him at lunchtime and he told us everything that he could remember. We took pictures as a family near the school. Then we took pictures of the children, together and separately.

After, we went to celebrate the first of September to pizzeria. I was happy and at easy. All our family was together. As before, everyone was cheerful and happy. Anxiety and sorrow were left behind. By the end of the day I was filled with light excitement.

The day was full of emotion and the children fell asleep quickly. We also went to bed early. I could feel how much I had missed my husband. I was cuddling into him like a kitten. I wanted to hug and kiss him and talk gentle sweetness. I was myself again. I forgave him his selfish behavior and the emotional pain he had caused me. I was lying there full of desire to start our relationship from scratch. This has to be a new beginning.

But Tim didn't seem to be interested in me. He was kissing me without much passion and the sex turned out, as before, quick and boring.

"That's strange?" I was thinking as I fell asleep "I have been gone for months and that's all he can do to show me how much he missed me?" He hasn't been at work today so he shouldn't be tired. Maybe I've got used to Ivan and his wild energy for me that now I expect this from Tim too. Yes, that must be it and with these thoughts I drifted off to sleep.

I settled back into my usual domestic role of caring for Yana and bringing Henry to school. Arthur visited me a few times. He told me all the local news and gossip. I was very glad to see him.

Outside we were having an Indian summer. Tim left for work in the morning and on his way he brought Henry to school. I planned to go to the park with Yana for a walk. We had breakfast and were almost ready to leave when we heard a knock at the door. "Who could it be this early in the day?" I thought and went to open the door.

"Arthur? Hi. What had happened that you come to us in the morning?" I was surprised.

"Taya, are you in a hurry?" he said hastily, looking around all the time.

"No. I'm not in a hurry. What happened? Come in" I invited him as I was surprised by his visit and strange behavior.

"Are you alone in the house? He asked, with agitated body language.

"Yes, I am alone. What has happened? Tell me please, you have me worried" I was losing my patience.

He came into the house and said, shifting from foot to foot "today at 12:00 in the cafe 'The Irish Star' Tim was there with a woman!"

I was in shock. "What? What are you saying?" I stared at him with my eyes wide. I stammered "Tim and a woman? Are you sure about it? Maybe she is a business contact?"

"Taya, I can no longer hide it. I see you again faithfully in love with him and he is deceiving you". He was covered with sweat and flushed. He continued, "Taya, if you don`t believe me, go there by yourself and see he`ll be there with her, one hundred percent. I don`t want him to cheat and use you" Arthur grabbed his head then he abruptly grabbed me by my shoulders. He was shaking and nervously said "I implore you! Go and see for yourself. You have to know the truth" finishing these words he ran out of the house like a crazy man.

From the open door, the autumn wind blew on me. I don't believe this. I don't want to believe this. It just can't be true! Having gathered myself, I dressed Yana and called a friend to take her. Having left my daughter there, I went frantically to town. "This is some kind of a joke?!" I was thinking.

Time seemed to be passing very slowly. That's always the way it is when you wait for something, time seems to freeze and stop. Today was no exception. I was at the café before I know it. It was a large two-story bistro and during a lunch time it was always full of customers.

There were a few free tables. I looked around the room and froze in horror. At a small table for two, down the back, sat Tim and a woman. She was dressed in a black sweater and her shoulders were covered with a wide scarlet scarf. Stendhal "The Red and the Black" flashed through my head, my husband's favorite style.

Not far from them, a lonely old man was sitting at a table for four. I ordered a coffee and asked him for permission to sit down. I smiled sweetly at him and sat down. Tim was sitting with his back to me I had the honor to view his new woman.

The woman was about twenty five years old. So she's younger than me, the thought flashed through my mind. She was neither Irish, nor European. Asian blood flowed in her veins. Maybe she's from Brazil? To identify her nationality was proving to be difficult. I was looking straight at her.

Large build, short stature with massive, like a wrestler, shoulders and arms. Black-haired, eyes are slightly slanted, thin lips. By chance, my eyes fell on her feet. Lord! She must be a size 10. Well, definitely not a Cinderella! She looked like a short, square-shouldered troll. Where did he find her? Or maybe she found him? All these thoughts were whirling like a carousel in my head. She was grinning at Tim from ear to ear. They were eating, he was occasionally touching her hand and because of this she was smiling even more. I was watching all this as if I was at a movie. I couldn`t believe what I am seeing but its true!

"Are you ok?" asked the old man.

"Yes, thanks" I nodded and smiled automatically it was all I was capable of.

Their lunch was coming to an end.

"Ok Rose" Tim said loudly, leaning over and kissing her gently, she laughed. He asked for the bill, it was clear that they were going to leave.

Time for a Change

I left the money on the table for my coffee, I nodded to the old man and I headed to the exit.

Coming out of the cafe, I somehow made my way to the car and sat down. I was shaking like a leaf. I couldn't believe my own eyes. For him to be having an affair right under my nose! This thought was making me sick. How could he do this? My ideal, the person I loved and trusted. He betrayed me and our children. And who is she? This woman who looks like a troll! This fact was hardest of all to take. My hands were shaking, my whole body was shaking and my teeth were chattering.

What do I do now? Why has he done this? If I ask him straight out what will he tell me? More lies? What a mess!

I opened the car window. I feel that I am going to be sick. I need more air to breath. My underarms and back are wet with sweat and fear. I must calm down and control my breathing as it's so difficult to breathe right now. I clutched my heart, feeling its fast beating, I am scared. "Breath, deep breathe Taya, calm down, it's not time to have a heart attack. You have children, you have to live" I keep telling myself. It was getting dark in front of my eyes. I frantically opened the door of my car. I felt very sick. I vomited right on the pavement. God, this is so embarrassing. I closed my eyes. Clammy, cold sweat covered my whole body. I can't drive my car. I'll have an accident driving in this condition. I will have to walk. Not thinking of where I was going, I wandered down the street. Unfamiliar faces were looking at me, I kept on walking.

It's over. It's over. I can't forgive him. He was sleeping with me after I returned. He was kissing me after coming from her. I remembered his lips and spit. I winced. It's too disgusting. Hatred consumed my soul. "Taya, you're strong, you'll survive, don`t cry" I was saying to myself trying to calm myself, tears were pouring down my face.

I sat down on a bench. I was in the park now and I hadn't noticed where I was. I looked around, there was no one around. Only swans were swimming in the lake, beautiful, majestic, proud birds. The water was calm. The sun was bright, the grass was green and autumn hasn`t yet painted its golden tones. I was looking through a veil of tears.

"Your life has never been easy Taya. Move on Taya, move on" I was repeating in my head. Life goes on and you have to think about your children. Everything passes in time, even pain. Such thoughts were tumbling in my brain, confusedly jumping from one to another.

I had recomposed myself and I was driving slowly. I was trying to unscramble everything in my head. "So he is having an affair" I said aloud to myself. "I wasn`t at home for the past seven months, our relationship is not in a good condition for almost two years! So where do I look for clues, at his work place or among our friends?" I sighed heavily and the tears started to flow again.

The day was sunny, thank God, I was thinking, so I can wear sunglasses and hide my red swollen eyes. I have to collect the children. They are excitedly telling me all their news of their day. They then noticed my tear stained face and Henry asked "Mummy, were you crying? Why are you upset?"

"Oh, it's nothing my dear little man. I slipped and fell down" I answered with the first thing that came into my head.

Time for a Change

"Are you hurt?" asked sweet little Yana clinging to me.

"No, dear, I had pain, but it`s gone now. Let`s go home. I'll make you a pizza. Would you like that?" I replied cheerfully.

"Pizza, pizza" they were happily jumping and ran to the car.

At home they were playing with their toys and watching cartoons. I was waiting for Tim. He returned home from work at the usual time for his dinner.

"Hello" he said cheerily as he entered the house.

The children rushed to hug him. I could hear the sounds of their kissing him from the hallway. They chattered to him about their own news. I remained speechless, riveted to the kitchen sink.

The children then ran back to their own activities. I could feel him looking at me intensely as he entered the kitchen. Continuing to wash the salad, I didn`t pay any attention to him.

"What's for dinner?" he enquired as if nothing had happened.

"Did you not have enough to eat at the café earlier?" I quipped, without looking up. I wanted to push his calm arrogance to its limit.

"In what cafe?" he replied calmly.

"In the café where you were eating today, with Rose! I can see, you were so fascinated by her, that you didn`t notice me at the next table!" I tried to speak without tears but they were pouring down my face. I gasped again and I trembled in hysterics. "Get out! Get out! Get out of my life! Get out!" I was shouting at him and in anger I broke the salad bowl. "Get out! You betrayed us! You're a monster! And to whom do you barter us away? You were bored with me in bed? I'm not going to compare myself to your troll like lover! You were using me for all the time we are together, like a landing place. I provided you with a comfortable home life, where I cherished you. You're a vegetarian for twenty years and for the last ten years I cooked your vegetables and salads separately. All for Tim, all for my beloved! All your suits, for your work, were bought in boutiques. Your shoes are only the best of fine leather. I am like a donkey in your life, shouldering all the housework, the children and my job in addition. And what did you do?" I was spitting fire now.

He was looking at me with his stupid, confused eyes and didn't even try to make excuses.

I continued. From anger and resentment, my tears had dried up. "You were coming from work, attending your Kung Fu classes, relaxing watching TV, reading your newspapers and eating all the delicious food I prepared especially for you. Not to mention you're sitting at that bloody computer playing your games day and night. Of course you have a very comfortable life. How very convenient for you to cheat on me as well. Have you anything to say in your defense?

"Taya, I have being having this affair for two years now. She is twenty five years old. We met at a Doctor's conference. She was there as one of the organizers" he flatly replied.

"Two years? Two years!" I screamed. My head was throbbing by now. "You are scum. No wonder you were happy when I was in Kiev and you weren't anxious for my return. You pretended you wanted me to take more rest! I can see the whole picture clearly now. Oh God, you were having this affair as I carried Yana!"

Time for a Change

He nodded it seemed he had no courage or need to answer.

"So, all these years, you were instilling in me hang-ups that I'm no longer attractive or good in bed! Making me feel that there is something is wrong with me. Of course, your woman is beyond competition!" he shocked me so much now his calm attitude, that there was no longer tears. I looked at him, my once beloved man and knew in my heart that it is over! There is no future. "Collect your things and get out" I said clearly with a hoarse voice, realizing that I have no energy to speak. I realized that there was no point either.

I went upstairs to the children. They were watching "Tom and Jerry" on full volume. Because of this they hadn't heard me yelling at Tim. He didn't leave, instead he had his dinner and sat down at the computer as usual.

I went to bed early, with Yana, in the children's room. I was exhausted but I still couldn't sleep. Tim and I didn't talk for a week. He was in no hurry to leave. I could see that he was happy at home as if nothing had changed. This maddened and upset me even more.

It was like I was in a dream. I was doing everything automatically. The hatred I had for Tim was rising higher and higher. Once I asked him "Tim, when will you go to her?"

"I'm not going to go anywhere. I'm comfortable here at home. I have all my things around me and it's an easy drive from here to work. I can live with this arrangement and see her as I please at her house. I also get see my children here as often as I want to and feel like a family man" he replied calmly.

"King of his own castle and his life, I will show him" I reassured myself silently. "Ok, I've got that. Thank you for clarifying it all for me" I answered full of disgust and contempt.

A man, such as him, who betrays his family, his children, his love and his friends, will betray for again for sure. It`s a pity I realized it all too late! Like a fool, I believed in his words in that letter. He thinks that I have no way out of this foul situation. That phrase he told me stayed in my mind "who would want you with two children?" I will show him!

Firstly, I am proud of myself and my achievements in life and especially my two children. Secondly, little does Tim know that someone else very special has found me and loved me deeply. So someone else even with my two children is interested in me and wants to spend his whole life with me. Of course, to be honest to myself, I broke up with Ivan because he is much younger than I. I didn`t want to add to his life pressure with the care of my two children. I broke up him because I am not selfish. I love Ivan in my own way and I wish him well for all of his life. I wish with all my heart, that he meets and falls in love, with a special girl and they live happily ever after. But it is not necessary for Tim to know any of this.

Chapter 29

Having gathered my courage, I went to an internet café. After a few hours there I had found a nice house in for the children and I elsewhere. This will be our new home. In my new home a traitor such as Tim will never set foot. I left my children with a friend and went to view the house that I had booked to see through the agency.

My life taught me always to have emergency money kept, so I had the deposit for this house to rent. That same evening, once the rent and details were agreed, I signed the contract to rent this new home.

In the morning, when the children were at school and kindergarten, I collected their necessary things and toys. Arthur had a minibus and he helped me to move in.

That day once school and kindergarten were over, we moved to our new home in another city. A new life awaited us. Arthur was driving onwards in his minibus and we were driving after him in my car. The children were sleeping and I was contentedly listening to Lyric FM on the car radio.

I was aware of all the burdens of the current situation I was in. All the red tape with documents, child care arrangements, a new school and kindergarten to view and I needed to find a job. Not to mention our divorce. I would have to explain everything to my mother and Anya and to Tim's parents too! I will take each of these problems one by one and solve them. The most important thing is that I am free and happy.

I tried to imagine the look on Tim's face when he returned that evening to an empty house! To the house where there is now nothing but the memories of his lost life. No more laughter from his children. In the kitchen, he'd see the letter where I wrote a few sentences. "Tim, we've left you. Don't worry, we are starting our new life without you. You are left without me and without your children. You can no longer take me for granted. My lawyer will send you a letter. You had time to leave and find accommodation, but you are comfortable in our house, but I'm not. I can't live with you and know that you're not mine. It is too painful. Take care of yourself. I wish you to find yourself. Goodbye".

When the car had stopped, the children woke up. They were surprised and carefully looked around them, unsure of where they were.

"This is our new home" I proudly told them. "We will live here" I said joyfully, as I unfastened Yana's car seat.

Arthur was unloading our belongings and the children were inspecting the house. I stayed near them, I could see they were confused and didn't understand what was happening.

Time for a Change

"Where's our house and Daddy?" Henry asked.

"Today other people have moved into our house and from now we will live here. You'll have your own rooms and you'll go to a new school and Yana to a new kindergarten" I was trying to answer their questions simply.

"When will Daddy come to be with us?" Henry asked again.

"He has a lot of work to do and in the meantime we will live alone without him. He will see you sometime. Now, what room do you want to have Henry?" I injected excitement into my voice.

"I want to stay with you in your room" Henry replied with sadness in his small voice "and me too, mummy" Yana said squeezing my hand in hers.

"Great! We can all live in my room" and I bent down and kissed them.

Arthur was bringing all the boxes and loose bits and pieces. I felt like I was in a dream. I was like a robot giving him instructions "put that there, move that there" and he was doing what I was asking obediently. We had a take away dinner together that evening. The children were tired so once the beds were sorted, I put them to bed. They slept immediately. Arthur continued to unseal our boxes and place items around to their correct place.

I came downstairs from the children and thanked him for his help and friendship. I began to cry again. I was exhausted and it's hard to be strong all the time. My heart and life were broken.

Arthur was silently patting me on my head and I was crying on his chest. "Shall I stay with you until you settle in?" he asked caringly.

"No, thanks. I will be fine. You can leave, I want to be alone. Don't worry, I just need to get my head around things" I was saying weeping "everything will be fine. I'm strong, I just need time".

"If you need anything call me, ok?" he kissed me on my cheek and left.

I was sitting among all my boxes and black bags filled with my things and looking around in a daze. I have to sleep, tomorrow is a new day, and I went to sleep beside my children.

Five days passed, Tim didn't call or text. That's the proof I needed, the price of his love for me and the children is nothing. "If there is no man then there is no problem" I remembered that phrase from some movie and smiled to myself.

During this time, I settled into our new life and routine. I sent Henry to school, but I didn't bring Yana to a kindergarten just yet. I had no job, so I didn't have the need to bring her to a kindergarten. I sent out a few CV's through the internet in search of a suitable job for myself. I busied myself with the normal routine of life at home with two young children.

Arthur called me a few times to check in on me. Everyone thought it was their duty to support me and I appreciated them. "A friend in need is a friend indeed" that's how that saying goes and it's so true.

Tim texted me a week later. It was a short, curt text "I hope you're fine, if you need help call me".

"That's it, that's how my family life ended" I sadly told myself. "This is how he sees everything, I left so this is my problem as far as he is concerned" I said out loud adding "I'm not afraid to solve this and move on with my life and I will solve it. In time my children will

Time for a Change

understand all but in the meantime I will protect them from trauma and grief" I resolved to myself.

Several weeks passed, at last I had an interview to attend. The job was as an interpreter in a company dealing with the import of medical equipment to Russia. I was successful and got the job. My joy and self-pride knew no limits. I enrolled Yana in a kindergarden. Now it's my turn to settle into my new job and life.

Every evening I hurry to take them from school and kinder-garden. We come home and light the fire making it a cozy homely place to be. I cook dinner for the three of us. I am so glad that I have these two little people in my life. They are my most important, most precious and most beloved in all the world, my two children, Henry and Yana. They will be my helpmates and best friends. For their sake, I have had to overcome my sadness and grief and face our future with hope and joy. For their sake I will strive to be better mother and person. I will be someone in whom they will be proud of, just as I am always proud of them.